In praise of *The Kennedy Chronicles: Losing Rylie*

Through heartwarming and heartbreaking moments, Kennedy's struggle in being a minority, a Christian, and a teenage girl were not only relatable, but real life issues. *Losing Rylie*, put me through a myriad of emotions. I laughed, blushed, cried, and got angry right along with Kennedy. I felt what she felt and her experiences turned into mine as well. As a Christian teenager in modern America, I understand how easy it can be to slip away from God and into the world. *Losing Rylie* presented Kennedy to me as not only a role model, but also as an example of how to come to God with all of my issues and struggles, especially when times get tough.

Madison K. – age 17; James Wood High School

The Kennedy Chronicles: Losing Rylie is a riveting, inspirational, and most of all, relatable novel. As a biracial young adult, the main character of the book, Kennedy, reminds me of myself. It is modern and refreshing to read, especially as a Christian. The author did a great job of tying together all of the elements of being a young teenager going through life. Young women of all cultures will definitely not only enjoy and relate to this book, but will learn how to depend on God in the toughest of situations.

Dariona Lewis, 18; student at Lord Fairfax Community College

Kennerly takes us through the ups and downs in the life of Kennedy, a student trying to find herself after experiencing a double tragedy that tests her entire being. *Losing Rylie* is a modern coming of age tale of loss and discovery, a story for those seeking hope, faith, family, and self.

Val Muller, author of The Scarred Letter and the Corgi Capers mystery series

Losing Rylie helps teenagers navigate the complex and emotional challenges of living life after the death of a loved one. The loss of

i

Rylie changes her family, but faith, grace and new beginnings revitalize their broken and wounded hearts. My 17 year old daughter could not put this book down, she was moved, encouraged and her faith in Jesus Christ was strengthened. She has already recommended it to my 14 year old daughter and I approve!

Mark David, Pastor, Impact Christian Church, 134 N. Loudoun Street, Winchester, VA 22601

In one fell swoop author Clarissa Lee-Kennerly in her young adult novel, *Losing Rylie,* has managed to blend sensitivity, spirituality and realism into a well told tale to which teenagers will relate and understand. Life for young, 14 year old Kennedy will never be the same after a car crash kills her younger sister, Rylie, and causes her mother to withdraw from life. Kennedy and her twin, KJ along with their Dad, must learn to cope with the upheaval of their lives.

Clarissa Kennerly paints a poignant picture of a family trying to understand and digest tragedy. Teenagers in our world today face many challenges that question their faith, love of their family and the unpredictability of the world in which they live. Mrs. Kennerly has taken a tragedy and woven it into the thoughts and dreams of her young protagonist trying to find a way out of the abyss that has been created. Through Kennedy's trials and tribulations, young readers will be able to explore their own feelings and questions about love, faith and endurance.

Kudos to Clarissa Kennerly for a job well done, and her next book in the trilogy can't come soon enough!

Tara M. Johnson; Assistant Principal of English (retired), August Martin High School, New York City Department of Education

The Kennedy Chronicles

Losing Rylie

(2nd Edition)

CLARISSA LEE-KENNERLY

Published by KHARIS PUBLISHING, an imprint of

KHARIS MEDIA LLC

Copyright © 2021 Clarissa Lee-Kennerly

ISBN-13: 978-1-63746-103-7

ISBN: 10: 1-63746-103-8

Library of Congress Control Number: 2015959677

All KHARIS PUBLISHING products are available at special quantity discounts for bulk purchase for sales promotions, premiums, fund-raising, and educational needs. For details, write:

Kharis Media LLC

Tel: 1-479-599-8657

support@kharispublishing.com

www.kharispublishing.com

Dedicated to every teen who is still trying to figure out how to navigate through the ups and downs of life...this one is for you.

CONTENTS

CHAPTER 1

August 8th was the worst day of my life. That is when we lost Rylie. She was nine years old. I was fourteen.

It was a sticky oppressive day in Southern California, the kind in which people sit out on their stoops because somehow it seems hotter inside than it does outside. Air conditioners are broken and people fan themselves as if waving the hot air in their faces somehow makes it cool. Toddlers are playing in their baby pools and girls like me are laying out in the sun, trying to get a tan.

Football season had just begun. KJ was really excited. It was his freshman year in high school and he just knew he was going to make the team. He's cocky like that. The girls swoon when he walks by…his caramel bi-racial skin freshly kissed by the sun, his green eyes, long eyelashes, sandy brown curly hair, and dimples are all that's needed to make his head swell. My twin wasn't always full of himself, conceited, arrogant, and anything else you want to call it. He used to be the most caring person I knew. He always had my back. The girls would make fun of me, telling me I wasn't all that beautiful just because I had "good hair" and was a zebra. I wasn't white enough for the white girls with my black swag that my mama had passed down to me. But I wasn't black enough for the black girls either. Hazel eyes, light skin, and long curly hair didn't meet their approval, or so they told me. But KJ would tell them to shut up and to leave me alone. He held my hand when I cried and ate lunch with me if I was alone.

My brother was my best friend until that thing happened that happens to boys in right about the seventh grade. Those same girls that he told to shut up before looked different to him now. They

1

were not the girls who tortured his sister anymore. These girls had the beginnings of hips and boobs and legs, and he noticed. They noticed him noticing, and that's all it took. His charisma, his looks, his cockiness, and his athleticism shot him right up to the top of the popularity score board, leaving me to deal with all of the "haters" on my own. But mother, she wasn't having it. She taught me that I was who I was made to be. I couldn't be anyone else, so I needed to wear it and be proud. I miss her voice, her smile, her wisdom. We lost her the same day we lost Rylie. Her shell is still here, but her soul is gone.

"It Never Rains (In Southern California)" is a 1990's song by Tony! Toni! Toné! My mom used to sing it all the time when she was cleaning the house or driving in the car. She said she loved California because she was not a big fan of the cold, snow, and rain she endured growing up in the back hills of Virginia. She said she would take a little shaking up any day over a snowstorm. And then she would shake her curvaceous black booty and we would laugh. Dad would always say that he liked that in a semi-creepy way. The laughter would turn to a sick feeling for us kids - even Rylie, although she didn't know what he was talking about. The lyrics go, "Now it may be cold on the east coast but on the other side of town it never rains...it never rains in Southern California." The song is wrong.

This is the way I imagine it. Because when it all went down I was in my room singing Beyoncé's "Halo" getting ready for my next talent show. That's what I do. I sing...or, as my mama used to say, "that girl can *sang.*" Dad was downstairs doing what dads do and I was listening to the song on my iPod. I just couldn't get that part right that says *"I can feel your halo, halo, halo, I can see your halo, halo, halo, I can feel your halo, halo, halo I can see your halo, halo, halo"* and Beyoncé's voice goes up at the end; kind of like the beginnings of a yodel. I heard the thunder over my music, over my voice. It startled me and the lights flickered on and off. Then I heard the rain. It was one of those rains that comes down so hard that you feel like you are looking outside of your window right into a waterfall, one of those freak storms that seem to come out of nowhere. Just as I lifted the earphones out of my ears and took a deep breath of the freshness sauntering across the room from my open window, the phone screamed. At that very moment my heart skipped.

~

Approximately an hour earlier, Mom had left to pick up KJ from football practice. Rylie wanted to come into my room but I was trying to get ready for the talent show. She would be a distraction. She would make unwelcomed comments and ask unwelcomed questions and make unwelcomed touches on my desk, on my bed, on me…so mom made a suggestion that would make everyone happy.

"Rylie," she said. "Why don't you just ride with me?"

That way, I would get some peace for a little while…but I didn't want Rylie's absence to last forever.

~

The phone screamed.

I can't explain how I knew something was wrong, I don't fully understand it myself. I found myself running down the steps to ease my anxious mind, only to find my father already on the phone. My heart was beating fast when KJ told Dad on the other end of the phone that they hadn't arrived. Dad didn't even get the chance to process KJ's information because call waiting chimed in.

"Hold on KJ," Dad said. "That is probably them."

Dad picked up the waiting phone call and listened quietly for a few moments. The rain and thunder couldn't drown out the pain in my father's voice when he said, "I see."

The phone call ended, and Dad walked slowly toward me. He winced as if every part of his body hurt as he handed me my jacket.

"We gotta go," he said in a breathless whisper that I barely heard.

"Is everything ok?" I asked. He didn't answer. He never answered, and somehow I knew. We never talked about it in detail. Not in the car ride home from the hospital. Not through the wails and screams when we got home. Not at her funeral… never. I have replayed the incident over and over in my head, trying to forget but not being able to bring closure to it in my heart. All I knew at the time was that Rylie was gone forever and I couldn't breathe.

~

It was a combination of rain and speed that caused the crash. My grandma always said when she came to visit that Californians couldn't drive in the rain.

3

"Who in their right mind," she would say, "would stop my program with breaking news 'Storm Watch 3000' over some freaking rain."

The man who hit my mother and sister obviously didn't pay attention to the news that day. He was arrested and sentenced to twenty-two months in jail for involuntary manslaughter in taking the life of my sister. He didn't even say he was sorry.

It was also the day that life left my mother. She wouldn't eat and barely spoke. The only thing she could do was sleep. My father became a single parent overnight. He did the best he could, but he was out of his element—trying to take care of us, take care of her, and take care of himself. Eventually it was like we were all strangers living in the same house. Dad threw himself into his work, KJ threw himself into sports, and I drowned myself in my music.

I remember nights playing the piano until my fingers ached, trying to drown out the pain, drown out my mother's sobs, drown out my father's sighs. I was sick of eating fast food every night and started resenting Dad for not coming to my shows and not taking care of us the way Mom had. I started resenting Mom for leaving us altogether. Why was she so weak? Why couldn't she get it together? We were her kids too. Did she forget about us?

Of course Mom didn't go back to work, so things were tight. When Dad forgot to pay the bills, we came home to a dark house with no running water. KJ and I were basically taking care of ourselves. Our lives were falling apart.

Dad knew he had to do something when KJ's demeanor starting changing and his grades started dropping. KJ's silence was deafening, and his anger surreal. Dad received emails and calls from school every other day about his son's attitude problem and how he wasn't doing his work.

Dad called Grandma, and before I knew it, we were packing— leaving for Virginia to live with my grandparents. Grandma and Grandpa could help take care of Mom and us, and Dad would find a job there to help us get on our feet.

"I don't know what else to do," Dad told us, his eyes filled with tears. "I need help, and I need your help. I need you to understand." I did, but KJ slammed the door so hard that the whole living room shook as he stormed out of the house. I wasn't surprised. Dad was determined to get our lives back and I respected him for that, even though I didn't tell him at the time.

Days ran on while Dad made preparations. We would wait until the end of the school year. That's how much time he would need to sell the house or at least find renters for the price that he needed. Mom showed no signs of change, continuing to exist without really living.

When Grandma and Grandpa came out for Christmas, it was the happiest I had been since the *Event*. Even Dad and KJ laughed and smiled. I saw a sense of relief in both of them. Grandma bathed and fed Mom to take the weight off of Dad. Grandpa tossed the football with KJ and talked to him about the good ol' days. At first I thought KJ was just humoring him and showing Grandpa respect by pretending to be interested, but the look in his eyes showed that he was hungry for more.

For the first time in months, my family came to one of my shows. That first concert after the *Event* proved to be as difficult as forcing myself to get dressed for Rylie's funeral. I did not want to go, likewise, I didn't want to go to the concert either but I had the lead. Of course, my choir teacher Mrs. Wiley would have excused me from it. She said everything that a teacher is supposed to say. "You take as much time as you need. Your position will be here when you feel like you are ready to return. I am so sorry for your loss." And of course I retorted with the typical, "I am fine. I will be there. Rylie would have wanted me there."

I dedicated my performance to Mom and Rylie. Their usual seats were empty when I pulled back the curtains to see the crowd. Grandma and Grandpa were sitting there, though, and their presence strengthened me. I belted out "All I want for Christmas is you," a song that had never been so true for me. As I sang the words I realized what I wanted and what I needed. I wanted Rylie and I needed mom and our lives back. In the moment the crowd rose to their feet and screamed and hollered, I had done it, managing to sing without my cheerleaders. I realized I was stronger than I had thought, and that's when I recognized that if I wanted our lives back, I was going to have to fight for them.

That Sunday at church, the pastor preached about not giving up. It was exactly what we needed to hear. We hadn't been to church since August, but Grandma was adamant about us going, so we left mom in the care of an in-home nurse and attended the service.

Pastor said that we were overcomers through Christ Jesus, that no weapon formed against us shall prosper, and if the Lord was for us, who could be against us.

During the service I looked over and saw KJ fighting back tears. I hadn't seen him cry since he was ten-years-old, when he sprained his ankle after doing a wheelie and falling off of his bicycle. Since we lost Rylie, KJ had become so hardened, so private, so mean. As far as I knew, he hadn't cried at all. But that day in church he was preparing to fight. Before he could, he had to let go of all the pain, hurt, and anguish that he had felt.

KJ grabbed my hand. He didn't look at me, but I knew. He grabbed Dad's hand and two single tears streamed down his face. The pastor shouted out that we had the victory.

"By His stripes we were healed." God had a plan for all of us and we could not allow the enemy to steal our joy, even if we were in pain. We were to cast our cares upon God because he cared for us.

KJ looked at Dad and said he understood what he was doing and why he was doing it—the move and all. He said he promised to stop being so selfish and that he was sorry. Dad hugged him like a dying man holding onto his last bit of life. In some respects, I think he was.

A week later, Grandma and Grandpa left. Dad hired the in-home nurse and things got better. I think that was the moment when we started to heal, at least a little bit.

Mom still couldn't find her way back, though. Either we were not doing the right things to help her, or she didn't want to be helped. It continued to take a toll on us, but we were a unit this time. Instead of three individuals trying to make it, we were a family determined to survive. The hardest battle was packing up Rylie's room. Dad couldn't even go in there without breaking down. So one day after school, KJ and I took care of it. Surprisingly enough it was KJ's suggestion. Maybe he wasn't as bad as I thought. We hadn't talked so much since he'd changed. But we laughed as each item that we placed in the box brought up a memory. We sat in silence as each item brought up a memory. We cried as each item brought up a memory. It was a tough day but Dad's sigh of relief was worth it all. "You are great kids" he managed to squeak out while trying to hide the anguish in his eyes. We shook our heads while trying to hide ours.

The week after the realtor closed on our house, we were prepared to leave. The new owners would be arriving in three weeks so we needed to be gone. Grandma was going to fly in to take Mom back with her. KJ was going to help. I was going to drive to Virginia with dad in the U-Haul. It was going to take us three days.

"I didn't make as much money as I hoped on the sale of the house," he said. "I need to spend as little as possible so that we will be ok until I find a job. How does my princess feel about sleeping in the U-Haul, instead of staying in hotels?"

I laughed and told him not to hold his breath. He laughed and said, "That's my princess." I felt like I had my old dad back.

The day before the move brought with it a boatload of mixed emotions. KJ was on the phone trying to convince his latest honey to give him a going away present that neither of them would ever forget, while Dad and Grandma were downstairs discussing Mom.

Mom. I really missed her. It is hard to miss someone who is there, but really not there. The reality was that she was living, I could see and touch her whenever I wanted, but she was dead on the inside. I was grateful that she was still alive but seeing her was a torture that I could not comprehend. Every now and then I would go into her room and talk to her about my day, brush her hair, and sing to her. She never reacted, though, and it was as if we were suffering two losses rather than one; it didn't seem fair. In those moments I couldn't tell which would be worse: her actually dying, or her continuing to live on in this state.

As I walked through the empty halls of what used to be my home, I ran my hands across the walls, not wanting to forget this special place. I remembered the first day my parents brought Rylie home. Her cries filled up the whole house. I was five. I remember asking dad how we could turn that loud "thing" off. He laughed and explained to me that she was not a toy. At that time all I had ever known was KJ and I. It is strange to think that we are here again. Why did God give her to us if she was going to be taken away in such a short time? I shook my head at the thought. Grandma warned us against asking such questions.

"The Lord giveth, and the Lord taketh away," she said. It wasn't up to us to understand Rylie's death, but we were called to accept it as a part of God's plan. When we meet God one day, we could ask Him.

I thought about living in Virginia and all the things that I would miss being here. I wondered what my new school will be like. Could I try out for the choir, and if so, would I make it? What would the people be like there? Would I be accepted?

I wandered around the house, searching for answers that I knew were not there, and I found myself in front of KJ's room. His door was shut but not locked. I slowly pushed my way in. He was lying on his bed while talking on the phone. I wondered if he was nervous too. KJ saw me, sat up on his bed and gestured for me to come in. Much to my surprise he told Asia he would call her back. He then looked at me curiously, waiting for me to say the first word. I didn't speak, but my expression said it all. He sighed and motioned for me to come over to his bed. I sat. If I ever needed us to have that twin ESP nonsense that people always talk about, it was now. KJ put his arm around me and we sat in silence. As the tears began to stream down my face he hugged me closer and told me it was going to be ok.

"Just wait," he said. "Things will get better. They have to."

We drove Grandma, KJ, and Mom to the airport the next day. They were concerned about her flying, but everyone agreed that a three-day journey in a truck was probably not the best idea for her in her condition. A four-and-a-half hour flight would be best.

As I looked at my grandma waving good bye I noticed what a strong woman she was. She was so wise. I envied and admired her at the same time. She was sixty-five, but she looked like she was fifty. She had the smile of an angel. I thought about the way she handled Rylie's death. She was strong for the rest of us. She took care of Mom, just as she took care of us. She was like a machine.

"One day I will take care of her," I told myself. I would work hard so that she no longer needs to. I would pay her back for her strength, her encouragement, her knowledge, and her love. I would make her proud.

"Well Princess," Dad said—the pain in his eyes, the worry in his skin relaxing. "You ready to go?" I nod my head.

"I am ready to leave this life behind," he said. "I am ready to start all over." I smile but say nothing. I don't know what to expect, and that scares me more than anything else. Of course we had visited Virginia before, but Grandpa and Grandma were always so excited to have us and took us all over the place. We never had a moment's rest.

"Rest?" Grandma would say. "I am getting too old to rest. I need to live every second like it's my last because it very well could be."

I laughed to myself and took my dad's hand as we walked toward the truck.

"This is it," I told myself. The beginning of something new.

I will never forget that day.

CHAPTER 2

We were in Utah when KJ called to say they had landed safely and were waiting for Grandpa to pick them up. I was hoping that the trip would somehow spark something in her to cause her to snap out of it. I mean, my goodness, she hadn't been out of the house since Rylie's funeral. When I said it out loud it sounded dumb, but in my mind it made perfect sense. Maybe it is too early, I told myself as I settled down in the seat. Maybe it would just take some more time. But on the other end of the phone Dad sounded more hopeful. He even chuckled a bit and said, "Alright, sounds good…no, that's great." Then he turned to me and gave me a thumbs up. The anxiousness that filled my body made me nervous and excited at the same time. I wanted him to get off of the phone. After what seemed to be the longest part of trip, he finally did.

"Well?" I asked in keen anticipation. Dad turned to me, seemingly holding out as long as he could to deliver the news.

"When she saw her room she smiled, Kennedy. She smiled."

It was hot in Utah. The U-Haul did not have an air conditioner so we sprayed water in our faces to keep cool. I made it a game. Every time he said something corny, which was often, I sprayed him in the face. Every time Dad sang a lyric to a song or tried to do an old school dance he was sprayed. Every time he told a not funny joke or did something gross like fart, burp, pick his nose, he was sprayed. Before we knew it, he was soaked and we laughed. It was a great feeling to know that Mom had showed some kind of emotion. We had been through so much, and this smile was a welcome revelation that there was still hope that she would get better. I needed it, but it appeared as though Dad needed it more. It seemed like the farther we left California behind, the younger he had become. Since Rylie died and Mom left he had gotten so old. Lines in his face, more white hair than normal, and he was slower. It seemed like everything he did was in slow motion. Grandma said it was the grief. That he wore it like an item of clothing. She warned me not to let the sorrow get me. She said that the only way she was surviving was because she gave her angst to the Lord. Left it right as his feet and walked away from it. And I must do that too if I wanted to survive. And I wanted to survive but I knew I hadn't let go…not completely yet.

It was late when we got to Denver. Dad went in to the hotel to get our room key. I was tired. It had been a long day. I couldn't help but wonder what life would be like ahead in the days to come. What would my new school look like? Would the people there be nice? Would there be any cute boys? What about singing? Would I be good enough to join the school choir, would they even have a school choir? Grandma and Grandpa kept us so busy in the past when we came to visit that we really didn't get to meet anyone. It hadn't mattered before, but now I wished we had gotten to know some of the other kids. Dad interrupted the questions scrolling across my brain.

"Room 215," he said as he got in to drive us around to the back of the hotel. "I got us two twin beds. It was the cheapest."

The room was old. It had dingy yellow bedding that matched dingy yellow curtains with big burgundy flowers surrounded by forest green greenery. It smelled of old moth balls and cigarettes even though it was a nonsmoking room. While Dad was in the shower, I locked all three locks on the door. He wasn't lying when he said he didn't have a lot of money. Mom would have never allowed us to stay in a room like this. My resentment of her leaving us returned. I felt it rise up in my chest like smoke and lava erupting out of a volcano. I was angry and I couldn't let it go.

Despite the room's repulsive smell and obnoxious appearance, the bed was astoundingly comfortable. I didn't want to get up when the alarm went off. His bed didn't want to let him go either, or maybe it was him that didn't want to let go of the bed. Either way it was a skirmish that Dad eventually won. He came over to my bed and helped me win too…although he did most of the fighting.

Dad's sunglasses made him look like a cop. There he was, at a rest stop in Kansas City looking at the map.

"We need to make it to St. Louis. That is another eight hours. We should arrive by midnight." I nodded my head as I made my way from the restroom back into the truck. Today was an easier day. It wasn't as hot and time seemed to go by fairly quickly. Dad and I reminisced about old family vacations, holidays, and funny situations. We played the license plate game to see how many states we could spot. We even saw Alaska. No luck on Hawaii, Washington State, or Delaware, though. We played the ABC game three or four times and enjoyed the scenery. It was a good day - a great day.

Grandma called to check on us and let us know that Mom was fine. Disappointment slapped me in the face when I heard her response to my question about there being a change. It had been such a great day. I thought that just maybe she would come back. She hadn't, though.

It was right about 12 a.m. when we pulled into a hotel. Our room was baseball themed. The trim at the top had men at bat in their red, white, and blue baseball uniforms, men pitching and men trying to steal base. The curtains were blue linen, the walls were white, and the comforters were red.

"We got the patriotic suite," Dad said. "It's a heck of a lot nicer than the other one. And it smells fresh, too," he added. "This has been a good day."

"Do you miss her," I asked Dad as we pulled out of the hotel the next day.

"Rylie?" He asked.

"No," I said as I looked down at my hands. "Mom."

He grimaced. And then we sat in silence for a long time. He finally spoke when an old country song came on the radio.

"Sweet Home Alabama," he said. "I love this song." He turned up the radio and started singing. He fumbled through most of the verses but sang the chorus loud and proud. I had to laugh when he started tapping on the steering wheel with his thumbs. No rhythm. He knew what I was laughing at and at the same time we said "the disease." That's what we called it in better days. Mom, KJ, and I all had rhythm, but Rylie and Dad - not so much. Mom would say, "Well looks like Rylie has your dad's disease!" It was always on a Saturday that Mom would turn the TV to the cable music channels and we would have a dance party. That was when the "disease" would show its hilarious face. I never envisioned those times would end.

It was a quarter to ten when we pulled up to Grandma and Grandpa's house. The house's porch light was on and the reflection made the red brick look dull. The house seemed aloof and very quiet. There was no welcoming committee or any signs of life. It was just kind of, there. I breathed hard as I felt Dad's hand rest on my shoulder. I knew this day was coming, but somehow I just couldn't believe that it was actually here and that my life was actually changing.

For the first time ever I felt afraid and unsure about what the next day would bring. Yes, I had travelled all that way, and yes, and I'd had months to prepare, but somehow it all still felt like a dream. Was Rylie really gone? Was Mom really sick? Was this really my new home and my new life? Of course I knew the answer, and I think that was what scared me the most.

KJ opened the door and yelled to let Grandma and Grandpa know we were here. We would only take in our shoulder bags tonight. We would unpack the U-Haul in the morning. Grandma praised God that we arrived safely and showed me to my new room. It had been Mom's when she was my age, twenty-five years ago and it looked like it. I had some work to do, but I didn't mind. Grandma gave me carte blanche to do whatever I wanted with it - anything to make me more comfortable.

I sat on the bed, and thought of Mom when she was 14. What were her dreams and goals as she sat on this bed? Did she dream about the man who would eventually become her husband, and did that imagined person look anything like my dad? Did she dream of the children that she would one day have and how many of them did she want and what names did she want to name them? Did she ever think that one of them would be taken from her so violently and change the course of her life? Did she ever imagine herself so sick with grief that she would not be able to eat, sleep, or think?

At that moment, I needed to see her. I prayed before I did, as always. I prayed with faith that when I saw her she would recognize me. After all, being here did make her smile. And even though she hadn't smiled since that first time, I still believed that something about this house would bring her back from this place she had run to and sought refuge so that she didn't have to deal with the aftermath of Rylie's death. The Bible says that you only need the faith of a mustard seed, and I did, so it had to work this time, right?

I crept over to the guest bedroom where Mom and Dad would be staying. Dad wasn't around. I saw the back of her head. I spoke, but there was no reply. I walked in front of her to see that same blank stare I had seen over and over since the *Event*. No smile that the rest of the family had witnessed, just the pain in her eyes and that despondent deposition on her face.

I had been let down again. I wouldn't pray anymore, I told myself. I wouldn't waste anymore of God's time.

~

Grandma's house looks like a museum. The shelves are lined with fragile knickknacks organized by themes. The phrases, "Home is where the heart is" and, "And the greatest of these are Love" are sprawled across the walls in cursive. Even her wallpaper is black and white with little red hearts in the center. On the shelves, figurines hold hearts with the word love written on them. It wasn't hard to see that cooking was Grandma's favorite pastime.

The dining room is filled with Bible verses and prayers. They range from the 23rd Psalm to something as simple as the saying, "As for me and my house, we will serve the Lord." There are crosses and pictures of "Jesus," a black one and a white one. I remember at a young age asking her which one was the real Jesus. She said neither, quickly making the point that it didn't matter what He looked like, but it was all about what He represented and what He did for us.

Her living room is filled with family heirlooms. Her father's white Bible is the centerpiece in this room. There are pictures on every space on the wall dating back to the early 1900's. You really get a sense of family history here. There's nothing modern. All of the pictures are in their original frames and there are several treasures enclosed in glass. An old baseball from my great, great grandfather's days in the United Negro league. A hat, feather boa, white gloves, and pearls from my grandfather's grandmother's days at the Savoy. I picked up a jewelry box. I inhaled a little of the dust that brought on a coughing fit and made my eyes water. I opened it up, and a beautiful dark skinned girl twirled in a rusty white tutu and leotard to "Amazing Grace." I wondered how old she was, how long it had been sitting here, and who she belonged to. I almost dropped it when Grandma put her arms around me and started to hum to the music. Her voice had a deep sense of hope in it. I rubbed her hand and

14

hummed along too. I hoped that some of her hope would rub off of me.

"Why don't you get out of this house?" she said. "Go meet some people. Go do what young people do." This was a concept that was foreign to me. I had forgotten what it was like to have fun and to be carefree.

I went outside and sat on the porch and watched the rain. The flowers straining at their root to have their thirst quenched. Dad was at a job interview, and KJ had walked down to the school to see if anyone was there playing ball. I sat on the porch and just rested. It was nice. I breathed. I didn't have to worry about Dad and KJ anymore. I didn't have to rely on the microwave for dinner. I didn't have to worry about the electricity or water being turned off, or about not having the internet for homework. I could just breathe. Of course I would still worry about Mom, but Grandma was taking care of her so that I could just be my fourteen-year-old self.

With all of that worry removed from my brain, my thoughts settled on my little sister. She would have loved it here. Her whimsical spirit would have danced to the music of the jewelry box. Her imaginative eyes would have lit up upon seeing the ballerina. Her restless hands would have tried to touch everything that her hands were not supposed to touch, and her precious smile would have been at the heart of it all.

For the first time since the *Event*, her memory was not accompanied with pain. No, not this time. It was accompanied by love. My 15th birthday was in one month and I could finally look forward to it. I could look at my new life with a sense of purpose that I hadn't felt in so long. It felt so good that I laughed to myself. I became excited about the endless possibilities that this new life held for me. And as tears ran down my face, I was both surprised and elated. This was the release that I had been waiting for. I hadn't forgotten Rylie, but somewhere along the way I had forgotten myself by thinking about everyone else. This was my chance for me to find me again. I breathed, stuck my headphones in my ears, and found #7 on my iPod. It was Halo. I sang:

"Remember those walls I built?
Well, baby, they're tumbling down
And they didn't even put up a fight

15

They didn't even make a sound
I found a way to let you in
But I never really had a doubt
Standing in the light of your halo
I got my angel now..."

And though I couldn't admit it to myself at the time, I knew this song was about Rylie. As I sang the words, I felt a release. It was as if I had been holding onto her, but now I had set her free. She could be an angel, always watching over me, which gave me the freedom to move on.

CHAPTER 3

Summer moved by fairly quickly with a few pauses. The first one was July 4th when I finally met some kids that would be going to my school. Most days since we arrived I spent with Grandma shopping, cooking, cleaning, going to church, and laughing. There never seemed to be a dull moment. She always had something for me to do and something to teach me. I learned how to make banana nut bread, no-bake cherry cheesecake, sushi, and hot wings. You can tell by that menu that Grandma had eclectic taste. I dusted, scrubbed floors, and even painted while singing hits ranging from Morris Day and the Time to Kirk Franklin. Grandma also enjoyed taking me to Bible study and bragging about her granddaughter. I could tell by the look of her fellow church member's faces that if they heard her say "Ohh child, and she can *sang*" just one more time, they were likely to vote her out. But Grandma didn't care, and one day, she warned, the sound of my voice would have them all in tears.

Other days I spent with Grandpa. We would fish, clean the car, play cards, and go for long walks. I looked forward to spending time with him. He didn't talk much, but when he did speak, he would say things like, "Looks like today is going to be a good one, let's listen to what God has to say," and that would be it. We would look at all the beauty that was not in California. The mountains, the trees, the silence; it was beautiful. And every day I would check on Mom. Nothing changed. But I decided that I wouldn't be sad for her. The place she was in, wherever she was, must be where she found her peace, just as I was finding mine. I just hoped that, one of these days, she would come back.

KJ was invited to a 4th of July party. He had met a few football players at the school one day when he went to shoot hoops. Trey was a big husky guy, a linebacker, about 6'2 and 250 solid pounds, while Isaiah was tall and slender with a square head. He had to be at least 6'4. Struck me more as a basketball player but KJ said he was a running back that had all of the moves. They had been over the house a few times and seemed nice enough. They listened to Grandpa's stories, helped KJ mow the lawn. She enjoyed having young people around. She often said that we brought life back into her home.

One evening when I was sitting on the porch with Dad, the boys were leaving. They said goodnight to Dad and before they walked off of the porch, Trey told KJ that I was invited to his 4th of July party too. Everyone would be there. KJ glanced at me, back at Isaiah, and then back at me again. "Her?" he managed to croak out. That's when Dad chimed in. He told KJ that of course I should go. As a matter of fact he couldn't go without me. I had no say in the matter. KJ slumped his shoulders slightly and with a long sigh muttered, "fine." It was a done deal and I didn't even get to read the fine print or sign the contract.

When the night of the party arrived, I was very nervous. I didn't know what to wear.

"It's a cook-out." KJ said. "Wear whatever."

I chose a pair of dark jean Capri pants with a fold at the ends and strategic holes with strings lined across them and a simple fitted hot pink *Baby Phat* shirt with *Baby Phat* spelled out in gold writing. I wore my pink *Toms* and flat ironed my hair, topping it off with a pair of medium gold hoops, a light raspberry lip gloss, and my favorite mascara. As I sprayed on a little perfume Grandma came to door.

"You should wear your hair up in a ponytail." She said. "That way they can see your beautiful face and earrings better." I smiled and took her advice. An unexpected pain welled up in me when she walked out. I missed Mom. She used to give me advice like that. But before I allowed the pain to dredge up those feelings, KJ appeared and said he was ready to go. He asked me to keep some gum in my purse in case he needed it and instructed me to stay close but not too close. He didn't want anyone to think we were together. Little did he know that stay close was exactly what I intended to do. I only knew Trey and Isaiah and I certainly did not want to hang out with them all night. If KJ didn't know the meaning of a clingy sister, he was about to figure it out tonight, whether he liked it or not.

When dad pulled up to house he intended to go in with us. He wanted to know who these parents were and at whose house he was leaving his children. KJ convinced him to stay in the car, though. We would be fifteen in twenty days, he pleaded, asking Dad when he was finally going to trust us. We had our cellphones and Dad had forced Miss Responsible to come with him, so what trouble could he possibly get into, KJ questioned. Besides: this was our first real party in Virginia. Dad certainly didn't want to embarrass us.

Dad conceded but warned us that he would be there at 11 p.m. sharp to pick us up. KJ sighed reluctantly and was getting ready to argue when Trey tapped on the window and motioned for us to get out. KJ jumped out of the car while Dad gave me a kiss and reiterated that he would be there at 11 sharp. I let him know I understood and slid out of the back. As Dad pulled away I looked for KJ and noticed he was gone. He had already gone to the backyard for the party. My plan was not working out.

The "Wobble" was playing in the background. I slid through the lines of dancing girls who were trying to keep a beat by watching the girls next to them. There were Christmas lights hung connecting the huge trees and an old gentleman was manning the grill. There had to have been at least 100 people there already. And since KJ had insisted that we arrive fashionably late, people had already formed into their cliques and they were spread out along the fence that enclosed the huge yard. I jumped as I heard the popping and booming of the fireworks that were being lit nearby.

I could feel eyes on me as I tried to find my brother. No one knew me, and I had been a victim of the mean girl syndrome too many times to not recognize what this was all about. I had already been through the worst of it, so at this point, I didn't care. What could they do to me?

I finally made my way over to the fence where I figured I would spend the rest of the night looking at my phone, people-watching, and being bored. So I settled in. The DJ was really good. I found myself humming and singing a lot of my favorites. I even lost myself a few times in the music but was able to catch myself before anyone saw. While people-watching, I realized that there were not a lot of girls that looked like me. In fact, there wasn't very much diversity at all. There were a few African Americans here and there, less Latinos, and even less Asians, Middle Easterners, and Indians. This was nothing like what I was used to. It made me wonder how I would be received. It was Trey's party, however, and he was black, so it must be okay.

Just as I was contemplating getting some food, I heard my name. I turned and saw Isaiah. I waved nervously and he motioned for me to come over to meet somebody. Reluctantly, I pushed my way through the myriad of grinding that was now occurring on the makeshift dance floor until I reached the food table.

"This is Brevin," Isaiah said. And with that he smiled and walked away.

"Hi… Brevin," I said as I stuck my hand out to shake his. "I'm Kennedy."

Brevin looked up, and I froze. I froze! His deep blue eyes, sandy blond hair, and perfect smile stuck me in a space that I never even knew existed. I was uncomfortable and pleasantly surprised at the same time. He smiled.

"Brevin," He said. I smiled. "So Kennedy," he started. "Nice name, I really like that."

"Thanks," I said.

"Isaiah told me you and your brother are from California. What part?"

"Woodland Hills," I respond. "It's a suburb of L.A."

"How long have you been here?"

"About a month," I said. "We moved here… we moved here to be closer to our grandparents." It was the first time that I had to confront the real reason that we moved, but I couldn't bring myself to say it. I realized that I wasn't ready.

"How do you like it so far?" he asked.

"It's cool," I said. "Not much to do, but it's alright."

"Yeah," he said. "Imagine living here your whole life." I giggled, and then regretted it immediately.

"Isaiah said you guys are twins? Uh, you and your brother?"

"Yep," I answered as I prepared myself for the typical twin questions such as, "who is older?" and, "do you guys really have twin telepathy?" But he didn't say any of that. He just said cool. And then we just stood awkwardly for a few moments as I watched a few guys walk by and dap him up.

"Do you like to dance?" he finally asked.

"Sometimes," I lied. I only danced in the comfort of my room. I was hoping he wouldn't ask me to, and he didn't. How did this guy know all of the right things to do? Finally he confessed that he had wanted to meet me and had asked Isaiah who I was, and Isaiah had taken it upon himself to call me over. At first he was embarrassed but now he was glad that he did. Brevin said he enjoyed talking to me and had just come to the party to support Trey. Then he asked me the question that caused me to question if this guy was for real. I mean, he was beautiful, knew what to say, and then this:

"Are you hungry?" It was like he could read my mind.

"I could eat a little something," I said. Brevin proceeded to get a large plate and put a little bit of everything on it. Cheese, crackers, vegetables, dip, fruit, meatballs, and wings. He grabbed two forks and napkins. I smiled.

"I'll get the drinks," I said. There were only a few tables with chairs, and of course they were all occupied. Brevin suggested that we pull up some grass and cop a squat. I agreed.

We nibbled on the food and made small talk. We laughed and sat in times of silence. We smiled the uncomfortable smiles and looked at each other and then quickly looked away. We did all of the clichéd things that you see people do in movies and in books. It was incredible and awkward at the same time, and I loved every second of it. It was getting close to 10 and he had to go. There was church in the morning. He didn't even look at my face when he said that. Most kids that I knew would want to see the reaction someone has when they mention church. Brevin didn't. That means he didn't care what I thought. I liked that. It was confident and secure and real. He was being real with me and true to himself. No games. So I decided to do the same. Something about the church comment gave me the unbridled confidence to ask if he wanted my number.

"Maybe we could talk again sometime," I said.

He smiled, looked down at the ground and then back into my eyes, and uttered a perfect, "Of course." My hands were shaking as I shook his hand good night.

~

I stared up at the ceiling, lying in my bed. The yelling had finally stopped. The door slammed, so I assumed that KJ went to bed. I sighed. It didn't bother me so much that they fought. It was the manner in which they did it. I looked at the pattern on the ceiling, how it shifts and changes. I wondered how the artists did it. How they made the paint come out in a 3D fashion with little points at the end. How did it dry like that without dripping to the floor? I looked at how not one pattern is the same yet it somehow comes together to make the ceiling beautiful and unique.

I check my phone. It's 1:10 a.m. The fight was a lot shorter than I expected considering that we only got home an hour ago.

I replayed the night in my mind: The moment we pulled up and Dad clearly stated that he would pick us up at 11 p.m. sharp. The tapping of the window by Trey, dad pulling off, and me realizing that KJ had left me alone. The music, the dancing. *Brevin...* my mind stayed there for a minute and a smile crept across my face. I didn't recognize it was there at first, but my smile must have been big because the creases of my lips began to hurt and I realized I was grinning. I replayed our conversation, mouthing every word, trying to remember every expression, and rethinking everything I did.

Was I too forward by offering him my number? Did he even say he would call? I replayed the handshake before he left. Was I cheesing as hard then as I was now?

I recalled the hour I spent looking for KJ when he was nowhere to be found. I met a pretty Latina girl named Julia who said she saw him leave with someone named Mia. She even volunteered to help me look for him. We engaged in small talk and discovered we had a lot in common. She was going to be a sophomore at County like me, and we seemed to like the same things. She said she would look for me when school began. It was nice to know would I recognize at least one other person.

At 11 dad pulled up like he said he would and I was sitting on the front porch of the house praying that KJ would make an appearance soon. He didn't.

"Where's your brother?" Dad asked.

"I don't know" I said reluctantly. I had played out this scenario in my head and rehearsed how the conversation would go.

I was right. Dad was furious. He asked me why I hadn't stayed with him, so I explained that I hadn't seen him all night. We sat, we waited, we walked around, we asked around... no KJ.

It was around midnight when Dad was about to blow a fuse. He couldn't believe how immature, selfish, and disrespectful his son was.

He hadn't raised him like that.

I knew that KJ was all of those things and more. I couldn't understand why Dad hadn't seen it. This wasn't the first time KJ had played a stunt like this, and I didn't think it would be the last.

Dad began to blame himself and said that maybe he hadn't been there for KJ like he should have. Then he started to blame Mom but backed it up with, "she just can't help it." Dad questioned what he was going to do with KJ and muttered on about how he was never going to trust his son again.

Suddenly KJ came out of nowhere and got into the car without a word. He knew he was wrong. In a few moments the silence turned in war of words. He hadn't heard Dad say 11. He thought he had said 12. And even though he hadn't heard Dad, had he heard him, he would have said that Dad was being overprotective.

"We were fine," KJ said. "An hour waiting on him hadn't hurt us."

Dad said he was sick of KJ's lies and that he wouldn't stand them or his selfishness. He called KJ's actions despicable and demanded to know where he had been. KJ maintained that he was at the party and that it wasn't his fault that I couldn't find him. There were a lot of people there. Maybe I had just missed him.

This continued the whole way home and long after I was in bed. I was glad it was over so I could finally sleep. I was looking forward to going to church with Grandma and Grandpa tomorrow. There I could get some peace.

~

I didn't expect to get a text so quickly. I was sure he would follow the "three day rule." Not that I would know. I'd never had a boyfriend, or even a guy besides Dad, KJ, or Grandpa text me

It was after church. I was sitting at the table waiting for Grandma to finish lunch. Dad was next to me looking at the classifieds and KJ was helping Grandpa with the yard. I was scrolling through my list of songs when the phone beeped and vibrated at the same time. I went to my messages only to find:

Brevin

Hey

I froze, just as I had the previous night at the party. I glanced to the left to see Dad circling what he thought was a job opportunity in the paper. I glanced to my right to see Grandma putting the finishing touches on dessert. And I glanced in front of me to make sure the text was real. It was.

I slid quietly out of my seat and ran to my room, hoping the text wouldn't disappear on my way there. It didn't.

I wondered what I should write back. I knew that I shouldn't take too long because I didn't want him to think I wasn't interested, but I didn't want to text right away because I didn't want to look desperate. Plus, what would I say?

"Get yourself together girl. It is only a text," I told myself. Grandma called my name to tell me that lunch was ready. At that moment I felt ready. I mustered up my courage and sent him a text back that read:

Kennedy

Hey

I didn't know if I should add an exclamation point because that would make me sound way too excited. A period wouldn't do either because then I would sound boring and not enthusiastic. A question mark would make me sound like I didn't know what "Hey" meant. So I settled for the "hey" without any punctuation at all. Keep it simple.

I knew what I had to do next. There was no way that I could sit here and await his response. I left the phone on my bed and ran down the stairs to eat lunch. Surely, that would occupy my time and give him plenty of time to respond if he wanted. It also distracted me.

The table was very quiet. Dad and KJ hadn't said a word to each other since last night's blow out. I was eating intensely trying to get back upstairs to see if Brevin had responded. Grandma was humming like she always did and Grandpa never spoke when he ate. He would always say it was because he was concentrating.

"You got somewhere to go?" Dad asked. I was so engaged in my food that I didn't even know he was talking to me. Upon his repeating the question twice, and clearing his throat, I asked him why he would ask me that. He said I was eating like the food was not going to be there tomorrow.

"I'm just hungry," I replied, counting that one in the win category because hey, I was, after all, actually hungry.

I finished before everyone else and started up the stairs when I heard Grandma yell that the kitchen would be ready in 30 minutes. That meant she would be ready for me to clean it. I would. After my conversation.

I ran to my bed and picked up my phone. There it was!

Brevin
How are you?

Kennedy
I am fine, how are you?

I couldn't help but think that was corny, but he'd asked me first. We had to start somewhere. Normally I hated small talk, but right then, in that moment, it made me smile.

Brevin
I can't complain. What are you doing today?

What am I doing today? What am I doing today? Nothing. Not a doggone thing. Or at least, just the same thing I do every day. Play checkers with my grandma. Hang out with my dad. Walk with Grandpa. Read. Sing. Pray for mom. Do the dishes. Get annoyed with KJ…

I didn't know how to answer without sounding like a loser. But there was something different about this guy. Something that made me feel… brave. I was going to go for it. What did I have to lose?

Kennedy
Why, did you want to hang out?

I couldn't believe I sent that! One day I am going to be rich by inventing a retract button. I sure wished I had one then…

Brevin
Sure. What did you have in mind?

I fell on the bed, laughing uncontrollably. I couldn't believe it. He'd said sure! He wanted to hang out with me!

Oh no! He wanted to hang out with me! I had never been on a date before let alone hang out with a guy that was not family. What would I do? What would I say? What would Dad say? Would he let me go? What about Grandma, Grandpa and KJ? And how lame would I look if I had to tell him that I couldn't go now. I was the one who offered it! Think Kennedy, think!

Mutual ground. There was no way he could pick me up. We would have to meet somewhere. Just then I heard KJ's door swing open. He must have been talking to Grandma when he said he was going to the school to play ball. I jumped up and ran into the hallway.

"KJ wait," I said. "I want to go with you." He bent his head back in disgust without moving the rest of his body.

"Really?" he said.

"Yes, really," I responded. "And I need to talk to you now."

I pulled him into my room and shut the door. I took my time explaining to him what was going on. He listened impatiently and asked me to skip all the details.

"Basically," I said, "I want to meet him at the school, without anyone else knowing. All of the times I had your back, it's your turn to have mine."

First he stared, then he laughed.

"Alright," he said. "I'm meeting Mia there. You keep my secret, and I'll keep yours."

I ran to get ready, almost forgetting to text Brevin back.

Kennedy
You wanna play ball at the school in an hour?

Brevin
LOL. You play ball?

Kennedy
Sort of…

I lied. I enjoyed watching it, it was kind of a family pastime, even though I didn't know what was going on half of the time. But me playing it? Never.

Brevin
See you in hour.

I screamed. KJ was texting Mia to tell her he would be there soon but he had to wait for me. I ran into my closet. I had to look like I could play ball, but be cute at the same time. After about 20 minutes of trying on different outfits and KJ rushing me, I finally settled on putting my hair up in a ponytail again, slipping little silver hoops into my ears, and wearing a purple, gray, and white Nike shirt with a gray athletic skort and white on white Nike tennis shoes.

"How do I look?" I asked KJ.

"Who cares," he muttered while rolling his eyes. "Let's go".

Grandma caught me on the way out the door. She reminded me that the kitchen was still waiting. I asked her if she could let it slide just this one time, telling her I wanted to go with KJ. She smiled, and let me know that they would be waiting on me when I returned. I sighed but said okay. Brevin was worth it.

~

The whole walk there I felt like a defendant in a court of law who was on the stand. KJ was grilling me. He wanted to know who this guy was, and how I had met him. When I tried to turn the tables on him about this Mia chick, he told me to mind my business and that this conversation was not about him. It was about me and he wanted answers. I told him. What did I have to hide? He reminded me that we weren't allowed to date until we were fifteen. And the last time he checked, we still had nineteen days left. It wasn't a date, I contended. We were just hanging out. He said he would see about that. I really didn't think he cared, and as much as it annoyed me that he was acting this way, I was kind of relieved that he did. I knew that KJ loved me. Things had been tough and we kind of went our separate ways, but I was still his sister and nothing could change that. The twin thing was real.

KJ hung around at first, staring at Brevin out of the corner of his eye. I guess he was content because when Mia came, he again was nowhere to be found. Before he left, however, he told me to text him if I needed him and made it a point to look at Brevin right in his eyes when he said it. I know it made Brevin a little uncomfortable, but I could tell he understood.

Mia looked exactly how I expected. She was tall, slender but not skinny. She had long brown hair, freckles, and the appearance that she'd just stepped out of a tanning bed. She didn't really speak to me other than a slight smile. Her tattered jean shorts were short enough to show "all of the business." Her bright yellow shirt actually looked good against her newly tanned skin, but you wouldn't hear me say that. She gave me stank attitude, and that's exactly what I gave her in return. I wondered if Brevin noticed her, or if he even cared. She was a simple pretty, KJ's type. I felt dull next to her and couldn't wait for her to leave. It wasn't long before they did, and Brevin and I were left alone.

"Do you know her?" I asked.

"Who? Mia? Who doesn't?" His tone didn't sound very favorable. I smiled.

"Did you bring a ball?" he asked.

"No," I said with a giggle. "You?"

"Remember, you asked me." I laughed.

"I did, didn't I?"

"Yes, yes you did." With that, he walked over to his car. It was a dark gray Volkswagen Jetta. Four doors. He popped the truck and took out a light blue and white basketball. As he dribbled it over to the court I could tell he had skills.

"Tarheels?" I asked. He looked surprised.

"You play?" he asked.

"No," I answered. "But I like to watch. Especially March Madness." Now I was speaking his language.

We shot around a bit, him taking a shot and then passing it to me so I could shoot as well. We played horse several times and I got beat several times. It was almost like he was trying to lose. He couldn't. Either he was that good, or I was that bad.

We talked the whole time. He told me he played on the high school team and shocked me when he said he was going to be a senior. I think I shocked him when I said I was going to be a sophomore. I was relieved to find that he was only sixteen.

"I just made the cut," he told me. "My birthday is October 12th, so

28

they allowed me to go to kindergarten as a four-year-old."

I think he was relieved to find out that I would be fifteen in nineteen days. He asked me what I wanted for my birthday. I couldn't tell him what I really wanted… not yet. I confided in him that I hoped my dad would take me shopping. Shopping with Grandma wasn't exactly what I had in mind. I wanted to go to the mall and shop for new clothes. I loved shopping with mom. I hadn't gone with her in so long.

The more we talked, the more I laughed. He was funny and cute and he knew it. He had that swag and smile that make a girl knees buckle. We were there for what seemed like hours. When KJ came back I discovered it had been.

"Come on," he said rudely as he grabbed my arm. "We have to go. The last thing I need is to hear more crap from Dad." Brevin looked at his cell and realized he had to leave too. It was already seven; each of us had missed dinner. He offered us a ride which KJ declined for the both of us.

"We'll walk," he said.

"Text me later?" I asked.

"Sure thing," he said, as we walked away.

"Why are you in such a rush?" I asked KJ. "And where's Mia?"

"I walked her home," he said. "And I told Dad we would be back by 6. We're late."

"Duh," I said to myself and started walking more quickly than he was. I certainly did not want to worry Dad. That's the last thing he needed. I also didn't want to get into trouble, either. That was a feeling that KJ was used to. Me: not so much.

When we got home we discovered our Grandparents and our father were all sitting at the kitchen table engaged in conversation. They were eating and laughing, much to our surprise. Dad told us to fix our plates and pull chairs up to the table. It was fried chicken, greens, mashed potatoes with gravy, and dinner rolls. I keep telling Grandma she was going to make me fat with all of this cooking, but I sure didn't mind eating it.

"I was wondering when you guys would be coming back," Dad said. "I have good news." He must not have remembered KJ telling him we would be home at six. Since Rylie passed away, he had become more protective. Who could blame him? It seemed like he was in a good mood tonight, but I didn't want to get my hopes up.

In the moments that we waited for him to tell us his news I dreamt up a scenario in which in he would say that Mom was better, followed by her coming into the kitchen, hugging us, and sitting to eat with us. She would ask us to forgive her but say that she had just needed a break. She was back now and looking forward to living in Virginia with us. Just as I pictured her saying that she would never leave us like that again no matter what happened, Dad broke my concentration by blurting out that he had found a job. A good one, too. He would be working in a prominent relator's office doing what he did best: selling houses and managing property. KJ congratulated him and grandma and grandpa questioned him about his houses and his pay. I played with my food.

"Kennedy," Grandma said. "Don't you have something to say to your dad?"

"Oh," I said, absentminded. "Congrats Dad. I know you will be great!"

He said he had orientation on Monday, Tuesday, and Wednesday of this week and that he would get paid just in time for our birthday. That put a smile on my face and Dad noticed it. He smiled back and put his hand on mine. I could tell that he felt good about himself, and that made me feel good too.

I had just finished the last dish. Grandma made sure she left me the lunch dishes as well as the dinner ones. She had told me she would and she kept her word, so it took me a little longer than usual. I was tired. It had been a long day. I was getting ready to stretch out on my bed and watch a little TV when I decided to check my phone. There was a message from Brevin. Evidently he kept his word as well.

Brevin
Hey

Kennedy
Hey, what are you doing?

Brevin
Nothing, u?

Kennedy

Nothing...

Brevin

So, when can we hang out again?

Kennedy

Mr. Johnson, are you asking me out?

I waited. Nothing. Was I too forward? Was he not asking me out on a date? I started to panic. I thought we'd had a good time today. Did I just make a fool of myself? Okay, calm down Kennedy. Maybe he had to use the restroom. Maybe he had to do something for his parents. Maybe his phone died. Or maybe I had just messed up royally. I tried not to look at my phone for his response. I turned on the TV to distract myself but there was nothing on. I didn't want to seem desperate by texting another response. I needed to wait. I couldn't go out on a date with him anyway. I still had nineteen days. I sighed. I picked up my phone and tried to distract myself by playing "Words with Friends." I was playing against Grandma. I swear she cheats. Who says the word "mytacism"? What does that even mean? I decided to look it up to kill time and not think about the fact that Brevin still hadn't responded. "The excessive use of the letter "M." I knew she was cheating now. And just when I decided to test her word out by making a list of words that use the letter "M," I heard the sound I had been longing to hear for the last twenty-five minutes. All of my worries were all wrapped up in two little words:

Brevin

Sort of...

Sort of? Sort of? Well at least he didn't say no. I didn't want to sound like a gump and tell him that he had to wait until I was fifteen, but I didn't know how to respond. So I took a page out of his book so I could figure out what to do next.

Kennedy

What did you have in mind?

31

Brevin

Bowling…with my youth group.

Well that wasn't exactly what I had in mind. But I would take it. Dad would be more apt to say yes if I said I was going to a youth group meeting. I could tell him that it was with a friend I'd met at the party. I mean it was the truth. My grandma would like it too and it sounded like fun. I wasn't doing anything and I would get to spend more time with him. I was in.

Kennedy

When?

Brevin

Wednesday evening. I could pick you up. Let's say around 6:30?

Kennedy

Sounds good. See you Wednesday.

Brevin

Alright. TTYL

And that was it.

~

Sixteen days till our 15th birthday and things had pretty much stayed the same except for Dad was working. It was good for him. He had only been in the office for three days and I could already tell a difference. He seemed more jovial, more alive. He whistled and hummed as he walked through the door, dominated the conversation at dinner, and started taking more pride in his appearance. He seemed to be making some sort of a recovery like the rest of us…well, most of us. Things with mom didn't change and sometimes, way in the back of my mind, I didn't think they would. I couldn't let those thoughts take over although I dreaded what was next. The anniversary of Rylie's death was right around the corner. Every time I thought about it, I felt a pang in the pit of my stomach so I tried not to think about it although I knew it was coming. We all did. But no one said anything, I guess hoping that no one else would notice. But I did.

When Brevin picked me up, I rushed out the door. My family was all excited that I had met a friend. And even though I never said who the friend was, I think KJ knew. He just looked at me out his translucent green eyes. We had an unspoken arrangement and he snickered in agreement. I told them my new friend was picking me up. I think they assumed that the friend's parents were driving. I didn't say any different, and they didn't ask.

Brevin's car smelled of new leather. He started to get out of the car to open the door but I got in so quickly that I didn't let him. I didn't want them to see him. I wanted to go. I inadvertently smiled as he pulled off. I didn't even notice until he asked me what was so funny.

"Nothing," I answered, embarrassed as he pulled up to the first red light. We sat in the awkward silence for about five minutes before he asked me if I had ever bowled before.

"Of course!" I said proudly. We bowled all the time as a family, or at least we used to, and I was pretty good. I looked forward to wiping the floor with him as he had me when we played basketball. He didn't believe that would happen. He was a natural, he said. I was a winner, I said. And we laughed and chatted as we drove to the bowling alley. This was the first time that I had been nervous. I felt comfortable around Brevin. Being around him felt natural. The thought of having to meet other people made my nerves kick in. Especially after Brevin grabbed my hand before we walked in. I couldn't help but wonder what that was all about, him grabbing my hand. Did he want people to think we were a couple, was he just leading the way, or did he sense my nervousness and hold my hand to help me relax? Either way it worked. It lessened my fears, at least by a little bit.

We made our way through a crowd and walked towards a group of rowdy teenagers. I wasn't used to a youth group being that "hype". They were yelling, laughing, pushing one another, and genuinely looked like they enjoyed one another's company. There was no youth group at Grandma's church. Everyone went into the sanctuary to hear the Word. Grandma said in her day there was no youth group and she didn't see a reason for it now. Everyone needed the Word. They needed to learn how to sit down and be quiet. It would seep in.

After all, it had for her.

We had a youth group in California. It was boring though. We never went anywhere or did anything like bowling. We went to a room, listened to Youth Minister Stevens speak, and that was it. She told us stories from the Bible, but not in a way that applied to our young lives. It was better than sitting in the sanctuary and not understanding anything but it was *nothing* like this.

A tall tanned man rose out of the chaos and motioned for us to come over. He had dark hair and bright green eyes with a few tattoos on his left arm and medium gauges in his ears. Something told me he was the youth leader, but I didn't believe it. It couldn't be. I'd never seen a youth leader look like that before. All the ones I had met were so normal. So straight-laced. So predictable.

"Brevin," he started. "What's up?"

"*What's up,*" I thought. He must be the oldest member of the group.

"This is my youth minister, Chad," Brevin said. If what I felt on the inside was shown on my face I would have looked like the picture "The Scream" by Edvard Munch, but I was able to keep it together. "This is Kennedy," Brevin continued.

"Glad you could join us," said youth pastor *Emo Shocker*. But before I could say two words, I felt like I was being mobbed by the rest of the group. My security was broken as I was herded off to play on the girls' team and Brevin was whisked away with the boys. What then followed was a barrage of questions and comments that made me feel like I was in a whirlwind. Where was I from? How old was I? How did I meet Brevin, and why did I move? I was told how pretty I was and how nice Brevin was. They said they couldn't wait to get to know me and they were glad that I came. I smiled and tried to keep up the best I could. I tried to associate names with faces so that I wouldn't forget them and seem rude. Sammie had blond hair and freckles. Sammie Sunshine; got it. Nikki was easy. She was the only black girl in the group…Nikki Minaj. Got it.

The list went on. There were at least ten of them. All very nice, all very excited, all very talkative. Shocker gathered us all around and prayed that we would all have a good time and be safe. He thanked God for the opportunity to work with all of the kids that were there. He also thanked God for me, thanking Him for compelling me to come tonight, prayed that I would have a great time and see God's and feel God's love through everyone there. He prayed that I would come back. That made me feel good. I felt wanted.

As we pulled up to the house that night, I wanted to get out quickly because I didn't want Brevin to be seen, but I also felt like I could sit in the car with him forever. After being asked for the 300th time if I'd had a good time, I turned to him and smiled.

"I had a great time," I said, hoping that saying more than "yes" would get the point across. Just then Grandma's porch light turned on. "I think that's my cue," I said, half hoping that no one came out and half not caring if they did.

Brevin took my hand and kissed the top of it. Shivers that I had never felt before ran down my spine. Butterflies started to take off in my stomach and I knew I had to go.

"I'll text you," he said. I knew he would. I smiled, told him goodnight, walked up the stairs, and watched him drive off.

For the next two weeks Brevin and I spoke to each other every day. Each Wednesday I told Dad and Grandma that I was going to youth group with my friend. Brevin always picked me up and I went to hang out with Youth Pastor Awesome and the crew. It was good for me. I was accepted for who I was. I also got to spend time with Brevin.

~

"Happy Birthday to you, Happy Birthday to you, Happy Birthday dear KJ and Kennedy! Happy Birthday to you! Make a wish!" I knew what I wanted to wish. I wanted Mom to come back to us. In eighteen days it would have been a year since the *Event* took place—the day that she and Rylie left.

Grandma, Grandpa, and Dad tried to make it up to us. They made us breakfast and put candles in our pancakes like old times. It was bittersweet. It was our first birthday without them, and the first birthday of our new lives.

All of my praying had given no results, and I'd started believing she would never come back. Maybe this was God's will for our lives. I was learning in youth group to leave everything in God's hands. So, that's exactly what I was going to do. I would use this wish for something else, for someone else. I was fifteen, it was time, and I had the perfect person in mind.

I had made up my mind that today would be the day I introduced my family to Brevin. They were getting suspicious and asking too many questions. Brevin started to question me, too. He didn't understand why I always ran out of the house and told him to leave when we were on our way to church. There was no way I could tell him that it was because I didn't want my family to see or meet him. Then I would have to explain why. If I told him I wasn't allowed to date until I was fifteen, it would be awkward because we were, after all, just friends. That is what he introduced me as, and we had never discussed anything different, although I was hoping all of that was about to change.

Grandma had started questioning me about this "friend" that I was always texting and running out the door to meet. Why hadn't I invited "her" to dinner? Why didn't they know "her"? Why was I being so secretive? She had even brought it up to Dad a few times. He was never home when I left, only when I came home.

"I think it's nice she has a friend," he said. "She will introduce her when she is ready." But after three weeks of not seeing "her," I saw Dad looking out the window, trying to get a glimpse of this mystery person. The jig was up. It was time to come clean.

We didn't have anything particularly exciting planned for our birthday. I wasn't bummed though. Dad had only been working a few weeks and had to catch up on old bills so that, in his words, we "could break even and have a fresh start." Grandma and Grandpa had been taking care of all of us. There was no way that I would ask them for anything. KJ surprised me by not asking for anything either. He had plans at Mia's house and even though we were not allowed to date until today, everyone already knew about her. KJ didn't even attempt to hide her, and no one said anything.

Shortly after noon I receive a text from Brevin.

Brevin
Happy Birthday young lady!

Kennedy
Why thank you sir! What r u doing today?

Brevin
Better question, What r u doing?

36

Kennedy

Not much. My grandmother is fixing me a birthday dinner with all of my favorites. You should come…

I regretted the invitation immediately after sending the text. I wasn't thinking. Well, I was. I thought it was a way to come clean, and then I would get to spend time with him. What I wasn't thinking about was how my family would react when they saw him. Would they question our relationship? Would they be upset that "she" was a "he" and embarrass me in front of him? And how would he respond? This could ruin everything. How could I get out of the situation? Tell him that we don't have enough food? Don't be silly Kennedy, think! Tell him the dinner was cancelled?

A minute passed. Maybe he couldn't come. I didn't want to lie, but I didn't want to ruin everything either.

BING!

Brevin

You're right, I should come. What time?

Kennedy

Around 6

Brevin

Great! See you then.

Yeah… great.

CHAPTER 4

I cleared my throat to prepare to address the gazing eyes of my audience. My father was staring right through me; I could tell he was preoccupied. My grandma had a look of intense interest on her face. I could tell she was trying to figure out what my announcement was all about. And my grandpa looked like he could care less.

In my head I played a recording of how this conversation could proceed. It will either go really well, indifferent, or terribly wrong. In any case, I was prepared to handle all three scenarios. I'd practiced for 30 minutes in my room before gathering everyone together.

I hoped this would work. As I began my script KJ walked in.

"What's going on?" he asked.

"Sit down baby," Grandma said. "Kennedy has something that she wants to tell us."

KJ grabbed an apple and hopped up on the counter. He took a big bite and chewed with a smug smile on his face as if to say, 'I've got to hear this.' "

I breathed. Here goes nothing.

"I've gathered all of you together today to tell you—"

"Where are we, a wedding?" KJ interrupted.

"Shut up son," Dad said. "Continue sweetheart," he said while glaring in KJ's direction. KJ shifted uneasily and then put the smug smile back on his face.

"Well, as I was saying, I invited someone to dinner."

KJ spit pieces of his apple across the room and almost choked on his laughter. He knew. Dad turned around and told KJ he was dismissed. Grandma chimed in that he was not leaving until he'd cleaned up his mess. And Grandpa, well, he seemed to just be waking up.

"No Dad, I swear, I'll behave. Just let me stay. And Grandma I am going to clean it up just as soon as Kennedy finishes."

The eyes of disapproval left him and focused on me.

"I don't know why KJ is being so silly. I think it's nice that you have invited your friend over for your birthday dinner. Is it the girl you've been going to youth group with?" Grandma asked.

KJ snickered again, but this time he was able to reel it in before anyone said anything.

"Well, yes and no," I started. Yes, it is the friend that I was going to youth group with. But she is a he." There. I'd said it.

"She is a what?" Grandpa had woken up. "A She He?" He asked.

Grandma and Dad stared at me as though Grandpa's question was legitimate. They wanted to know the answer as well. KJ was red by now. He had been trying to hold back his laughter for at least a minute.

"She is a He." I repeated more boldly. I was shrinking rapidly. Dad's look of disapproval made my heart sink. He shifted in his chair, pushed his glasses up on his nose, and glared. He wanted an explanation and he deserved one. Grandma's countenance spoke for her as well, her eyebrows up and mouth open. Grandpa, well, he just stared.

"His name is Brevin," I started. "He's just a friend." No response from anyone. Not even KJ wanted to touch this one. "Well, aren't you going to say anything?" I pleaded. "You are not going to say anything?"

"Nothing that you don't already know yourself," Grandma said. "You lied."

"I didn't lie," I defended. "He *is* a friend." They just stared. I knew I was wrong but something in me told me to fight this. "Are you guys really mad?" I asked. "This is so unfair. The rule is that we are not allowed to date until we were fifteen. KJ has been dating Mia and everyone knows about it, yet you say nothing. But I go to youth group, to church with a boy, and I am in trouble?" Still silence.

Dad slowly slid his chair away from the table, got up, and walked out of the front door. KJ hopped down from the counter and announced to everyone that he was "out." Grandma got up after a moment and noticed that KJ did not clean up his mess.

"Well," she said. "I guess, since we are having company that I should clean up and set another plate." She moved just as slowly as Dad did and made her way over to the sink.

I slumped down in my chair. It was unfair. I was the good girl. I always did the right thing. And the things that I did which were considered wrong weren't even that bad. Shouldn't my family be praising me? I didn't drink alcohol, I didn't do drugs, I wasn't having sex, I made good grades, I went to church... I mean, what else did they expect from me? I breathed hard, placing my head in my hands.

"You're right." I looked up. It was Grandpa. "You didn't lie. Not outright, anyway." "Finally," I thought. Someone was on my side.

"You see," he said, smacking his lips together and pausing in thought. "It's not what you said. It's what you didn't say that is causing your problem. See, what you did was leave out vital information. Leaving out vital information isn't lying. It's worse." I crinkled up my nose in disbelief. Where exactly was he going with this? I'd thought he was on my side.

"It's worse," he paused again, "because you were being manipulative. You knew that we trusted you, which is why we didn't ask you many questions. You used that trust to your advantage so that you could continue doing wrong. It takes more energy to be manipulative than it does to flat out lie because you have to be more creative with it, more calculated. The difference between you and KJ," he started in his Bill Cosby voice, "is that he didn't lie about Mia. There is something to be said about someone who knows they are wrong, and admits they wrong. At least they are okay with it and are not sneaky about it. But someone who knows they are wrong, keeps it secret and can live with it, well," he smacked his lips together again. "Go on in the living room and get me my cane."

I felt sick inside. Grandpa was right. I knew what I was doing and I was okay with it. It made me feel like a horrible person. Everyone was mad at me and I wasn't used to that. This was KJ's role. Not mine.

When I got back from getting Grandpa's cane, Grandma was cooking and humming to herself. Grandpa had laid his head on the table and was asleep. I owed them an apology. Placing the cane next to a table, I went to find Dad. I had hurt him the most, and I knew it.

I found him sitting outside on the porch swing. I had no idea what I was going to say. I sat next to him and watched him stare out into nothingness. I was hopeful that he would speak. I mean, it was killing me inside. I just wanted him to say something.

Finally I blurted out, "I'm sorry!"

The floodgates opened. I wasn't sure if it was because I was in trouble or that I was honestly sorry for what I had done. I think it was a combination of both. I just wanted everything to be better. Dad put his arm around me and held me close. When I tried to explain he interrupted me and said he knew why I'd kept Brevin a secret. And that while it didn't make it any better that he understood, at least he did. He said the thing that hurt him the most was that I had kept it a secret and used his trust against him. There would be consequences for that. Our relationship had changed and he wasn't sure when he would be able to trust me again. He told me there were rules for a reason, not to punish me, but to protect me. By lying I had not given him the opportunity to protect me, and that wasn't fair. All I could say was to repeat that I was sorry.

Dad said he forgave me and kissed me on the forehead. He wiped the tears from my eyes and told me go get cleaned up. After all, I was having a guest over for dinner. He said he'd better clean up too since he didn't want to embarrass me in front of my "friend." I planted a big wet one on his cheek. He smiled and said that he loved me too.

~

The nerves didn't kick in until about a quarter to six. What was I so nervous for? KJ wasn't going to be home, and I'd made it clear to my family that Brevin and I were just friends. The problem was that it wasn't clear to me. I mean we never talked about it. Not even once. And I didn't even know how to approach it. I'd never had a *real* boyfriend before. I'd had the little "I like you, do you like me" elementary school relationships. But any time a boy looked at me sideways in middle school the mean girls made sure to make a big deal about it so that the boys wouldn't so much as say a word to me or else they would commit social suicide. KJ was the worst, though. In the eighth grade, Bernie Hobbs didn't care what the mean girls thought. He thought I was very pretty and felt it very apropos to tell me every so often. I would smile shyly and tell him thanks and we often smiled at each other across the room, in class, in the hallways, and even at lunch. It really made me feel good about myself. And just when I found the courage to have a real conversation with him, KJ intervened. We were at my locker. Bernie asked me if he could carry my books to my next class. Right before I answered, I saw KJ walking down the hall. His eyes met mine and then he started to jog. I know my disposition changed because Bernie turned just in time for his face to meet KJ's fist, and that was the end of it. KJ got suspended for three days for what he told my parents was "protecting his little sister's honor." Bernie got a busted lip, and I got a reputation for being known as a girl you did not want to mess with if you were a guy. No guy wanted to look at me, let alone talk to me; KJ made sure of that.

But all of that had changed now. I was older and technically allowed to date. I had never even really wanted to before I met Brevin. I guess I'd changed too. I didn't just like Brevin. I *really* liked Brevin. I anticipated his calls, and his texts made me smile - even if he was just his normal salutation of, "What's up?" I watched for him on Wednesdays to come get me for youth group and had butterflies in my stomach every time our eyes met. He was easy to talk to, and not bad to look at… not at all. As a matter of fact, he was *fine*. He was spiritual, funny, athletic, and as I started to go through all the reasons that I liked him in my mind, my nervousness turned to dread. I liked him. I really liked him, but what I realized in that split second was that he could not possibly like me. Nope, not him. I was a skinny, curly haired, bi-racial, silly chick. Being the butt of so many jokes, I knew that some of it had to be true. He could only like me as a friend. Maybe he saw me as a charity case. He probably took one look at me and knew that I was going to have problems and he needed to "save me."

I sighed heavily and looked down at the floor. What was I doing? Setting myself up for heartbreak? I stared at the mirror. Cute coral dress, fresh flat ironed hair, gold sandals, lip gloss, and mascara. I was all dressed up to have my heart broken. And just when I felt like I couldn't sink any lower, the doorbell rang. He was here.

By the time Dad finally came to my room to see what was taking me so long I had thought of every single scenario in which people had said hurtful things to me and put it all on Brevin. In my mind he had committed those crimes in his mind and was just too nice of a guy to actually say them. He thought he was better than me and that I was high yellow, a zebra, a half breed, and that I didn't fit in anywhere. He thought I was weird, lucky to be KJ's little sister, and -

my personal favorite - that KJ must have gotten all of the looks because I was born with none.

Dad walked through the door and said, "You didn't tell me that he drives? How old is this kid and what is taking you so long?"

I turned to look at him with tears streaming down my face. I didn't know how I was going to face Brevin and what I was feeling. I couldn't tell Dad. I needed Mom, the old mom. Without her I felt helplessly, hopelessly lost. Dad tried to pull it out of me, but all I could do was cry, so he went to get Grandma.

"Kennedy!" Grandma admonished me. "Kennedy, now you have got to pull yourself together. You have a guest. He has been downstairs waiting on you for the better part of 30 minutes. What is wrong with you child?"

"Oh Grandma," I whined. "I am afraid that I have made a terrible mistake by inviting Brevin here. I just want him to go home."

Grandma put her hands on her hips and gave me a look like "Aint' nobody got time for that."

"Well, you should have thought of that earlier," she said. "You was not raised to be rude. We are not a rude people. Now cut this mess out." She handed me a tissue, told me to get my butt downstairs ASAP, and slammed the door behind her. After a few seconds she shouted, "Don't make me come back up here!"

"Yes ma'am," I whispered to myself. If there was one thing I knew about my grandmother it was that she means business. So I did my best to make myself look presentable, said a prayer, and went downstairs.

I found Brevin in the living room with Grandpa looking at The Negro American League Baseball cards. They were his prized possessions and Brevin seemed genuinely interested. It made me smile.

"Oh there you are," Grandpa said. "Your gentleman caller was just sharing with me his knowledge of sports so you know I had to show him the cards," He said with a smoky laugh. "Happy Birthday," Brevin said softly. "You look lovely."

"Thanks," I said, trying to keep the butterflies away. "Shall we eat?"

The dinner table was alive with conversation, most of which was the family questioning Brevin and him answering, his answers sparking several topics of conversations. One of them would ask him a question, he would answer, and then Dad, Grandma, or Grandpa would agree and bring up a story that placed them in the same place, same predicament, or same topic. This happened several times. It went sort of like this:

Dad: So, Brevin, since you are going to be a senior this year (Dad side-eyed me and I gulped) what are your plans for after graduation?

Brevin: I am definitely going to college, sir (I loved the fact that he called Dad sir, and I knew that secretly, Dad did too)

Grandpa: Where abouts?

Brevin: Well, I am definitely applying to Virginia Tech and George Mason. I will be staying in state. It's much cheaper that way. I am not opposed to going to NOVA for two years and transferring to a university after that either. It all depends on what financial aid I get. But my dream would be to go to Tech and get into social politics, social work, or even civil law.

Grandma: Now what would you do with that baby? (Everyone was her baby. I was embarrassed the first time she said it but Brevin didn't seem to mind. I think he even liked it because he smiled every time she said it.)

Brevin: To tell you the truth Mrs. Lee, I'm not sure. All I know is that people need help. We shouldn't live in a country that has such poverty with so many opportunities. I believe that God always gives us a way out. The problem is that people don't know that there is a way out, and if they do know, they don't know how to get there. I intend on informing them and helping them the best that I can. If the avenue is politically, socially, or civilly, I plan to make it happen.

"Wow," I thought to myself. It sounded like he was running for office right then.

Grandpa: I remember when I graduated from high school. The best thing for a young African-American male like myself was to go into the service. You ever thought of going into the service? They always need help. Well I bet a young intelligent Caucasian male like yourself would become a five-star general.

My mouth dropped.

Grandma shouted: Monroe Willis Lee! (You know she is angry when she calls him by his full name. Most folks just call him Willie.)

I looked to Dad for some relief. He causally took a bite of salad as though nothing even happened. But Brevin, he did the best thing of it all. He laughed. And so went the rest of the night. A question, an answer, them embarrassing me, and Brevin acting like none of it ever happened. By the end of the night, I knew what I really wanted for my birthday. And after Grandma brought out the cake and everyone sang, I closed my eyes and made a wish. I wished for courage.

I walked Brevin out as everyone told him goodnight and said how much they enjoyed meeting him. Even Dad gave him a firm handshake and looked him straight in the eyes and said, "Until next time."

I stopped on the porch but he motioned for me to come to his car. He had something to give me. He handed me a small pink gift bag with purple tissue paper coming out. He said he wanted me to open the gift first and the card last. He promised that it would all make sense.

I said the clichéd, "Aww, you shouldn't have," while feeling the clichéd, "I'm glad you did," although I didn't say it. As I started to dig in the bag, he grabbed my hand and asked me to open it after he left, in my room all alone, and to text him after I did. I agreed. I wanted to tell him how I felt inside and what I wanted from our "friendship," but my lips wouldn't allow me to speak. So much for the birthday wish.

Then Brevin did something that he had never done before, something that I didn't expect. After telling me what a great time he'd had and how my family was awesome, he reached out to give me a hug. And to my surprise, I hugged him back. Maybe the wish had worked after all. It was a little awkward because I didn't know when to let go. I felt like in our minds we were going back and forth saying, "you let go," "no you let go," "no you let go." But finally we both let go and he got in his car and left. I stood for a second to watch his car go down the street and then thanked God that KJ hadn't seen our hug. But as I turned to walk back in the house, I realized that while I was right, KJ hadn't see it, everyone else had. There they all were. Dad and Grandma sitting on the porch swing pretending to have a conversation about the weather, and Grandpa standing in front of the door and looking out of the screen. There was no shame in his game; there never was.

"Well," I thought. Two of us can play this game. So I walked right pass Grandma and Dad, completely ignoring them, and then told Grandpa to excuse me as I made my way back into the house. I went right up to my bedroom, locked the door and sat on my bed and stared at the gift. I was almost afraid to open it but the suspense was killing me. What kind of gift do you open before reading the card? What did the card say? If it was a good thing then why would he want me to open it after he left? Why did he give it to me at the end of the night and away from my family? And then these thoughts led to the hug. He'd never done that before. Was that his way of telling me goodbye, indefinitely?

"Okay," I thought to myself. I was not going to sit here and drive myself crazy with this. If he liked me, great. If he didn't, oh well. It wouldn't be the first time I was disappointed and it wouldn't be the last. I was a strong girl. I could take it.

I took out the purple paper and fished out a little black box with a red ribbon tied on it. As I pulled the ribbon I heard a knock on my door followed by, "It's KJ, open up."

I set the box down, unlocked the door and opened it slightly.

"What do you want?" I asked.

"Open the door!" He demanded.

"It is opened," I retorted. "Now what do you want?" KJ leaned on the door with all of his might until I couldn't hold it anymore and walked right passed me. "What do you want KJ?" I asked.

"Why are you being so mean to me?" he asked sarcastically. "All I want is to wish my twin a Happy Birthday."

"You could have done that on the other side of the door. Now what do you want?" "Nothing really," said KJ. "Why are you stuck up here in your room? Did you get in trouble?"

"Not really," I answered. "They basically told me how disappointed they were in me and Dad said he didn't know if he could continue to trust me."

"Hmm…" KJ answered. I could tell he was distracted but I continued anyway.

"The thing that really struck me was when Dad said I didn't give him a chance to protect me, and then Grandpa—"

"Today was hard for me," KJ interrupted. I knew where this was going. "Did you even think of them today?" He looked up. I could tell he was hurting. I wanted to hug him but instead I sat on my bed.

"Yes," I answered. KJ took another breath.

"I miss them," he said.

"I do too," I said.

"Do you ever think things will be the same?"

"No," I answered. "But do you want to know what I do think? I think we will be a family again. I think Mom will get better and we will be a family again."

KJ smiled. He got up and walked toward the door. He turned and said, "Love you sis." "Love you too," I responded. With that he was gone.

I almost forgot about the present until I fell in my bed and felt something hit me in the back. It was the box. I sat up and stared at it for .4 seconds before pulling the ribbon and ripping off the lid. It was a charm bracelet with a faux diamond cross charm hanging from it. I immediately put it on. It was beautiful. The way the light hit the diamonds made it sparkle and I loved it. I went to text him to tell him how much I loved it when it dawned on me: present first, card second.

As beautiful as the charm bracelet was, it gave me no clues as to what could be written in the card. He took me to church. The cross could be a representative of that. I got out of my head and carefully removed the card from the envelope. When I opened the card another charm fell out. It was a heart, and my heart, well, it stopped. The front of the card was purple with stars and black swirls in the background. The front of the card read, "For Someone Special."

I opened the card and briefly looked at what Hallmark wrote which was something about having a blessed birthday and wishing that all of my dreams come true. I wanted to get to his writing on the other side of the card. This is what it said:

Dear Kennedy,

First of all I want to say happy birthday! I have really had a great time getting to know you. I believe that God puts people in our lives for a reason. I am really glad he chose you to be in mine. You are funny, sassy, intelligent, and not to mention beautiful. You have been a great friend, but I was hoping that we could be something more... give me a call or send me a text to let me know what you think. Happy Birthday again.

Brevin

I screamed and put the card to my chest, fell back on my bed and kicked my legs up and down like a mad woman. I pranced around my room and danced in delight. I had a boyfriend. A real live boyfriend, and he liked me for me. Evidently after KJ left I forgot to shut and lock the door because as I did a Michael Jackson spin into a "Hee Hee" on my tiptoes move I saw Dad standing in the doorway. He clapped as I took my embarrassment like a champ. I was ecstatic. I was entitled to a little Michael Jackson celebration! Dad asked if I had time out of my busy dance schedule to talk. I said sure. I knew what it was about, but I thought I'd better ask to be sure.

"Brevin?" I asked. He nodded his head. I was kind of relieved. If Brevin was going to be my boyfriend, I was going to do this right. Dad sat down on the bed and tapped the spot where he wanted me to sit. I felt like Daddy's little girl. It was nice.

"Well," he started. "Let me start off by saying that from what I have seen tonight, I think Brevin is a nice kid. He seems to have his head on straight. I think I could like him."

"But…" I said, intentionally dragging out the "but."

"But," Dad said as he shifted on the bed and pushed his glasses back on his face. "He is too old for you. Seriously Ken, he is a senior, you are a sophomore, and don't let me start on the fact that he drives. He drives!" he emphasized. "He has been driving you to youth group, correct?"

I sucked in my lips, let out a breath and reluctantly said yes.

"Is he your boyfriend?" He asked and searched my eyes to see if I would tell the truth. I did.

"No, at least not yet."

"Now what does that mean?" he crossed his arms and his legs.

"It means not yet. I wasn't even allowed to date until today. I didn't even find out that he really liked me until today."

Dad cleared his throat and asked me if I liked him. I pulled my hair back behind my ear and stated the obvious. He uncrossed his legs and put his face in his hands.

"Dad," I reassured him. "Brevin is sixteen. He is a young senior. He is a Christian and he loves God and apparently likes me."

"But he is a senior, Kennedy. He will be leaving after this year to go to college. Don't you think that if you become invested in this relationship that you will get hurt?"

I had, but I didn't tell him this.

"Dad," I started. "I understand why you would be concerned, but I'm a big girl, I can handle this. I know that this is an ironic statement based on the events that happened today but give me a chance. Trust me. I promise I won't disappoint you."

Dad looked at me and pulled me close.

"I love you Ken," he said. "Don't' forget that." And with that he left. I was glad that I had his approval and now it was time to tell Brevin that he had mine.

Kennedy
Hey

Brevin
Hey, I was starting to think that you lost my number

Kennedy
Of course not. You know I had to deal with the fam and then KJ came home and I finally got a chance to open your gift which I love…

Brevin
I'm glad you like it

Kennedy
I do. I am wearing it now. The cross and the heart…

Brevin

Kennedy
I also liked the card…

I really didn't know how to approach the topic of the "something more." I didn't want to sound corny by asking if he was my boyfriend. I was hoping that dropping subtle hints would make him say something.

Brevin
Great

Fail. Was he really going to play this game?

Kennedy
Well, I've had a really long day. I think I am going to go to bed, unless there

was something else that you wanted to talk to me about…

Brevin
No, I'm good. You have a great night.

Was he really this stubborn? It was like we are having an unspoken fight and we weren't even dating yet! There was no way I was losing our first fight. He had no clue how stubborn I could be. I would not break first.

Kennedy
Ok. I will talk to you tomorrow.

Brevin
Good night.

Crap. Why does everything have to be so difficult? All I wanted was to go to bed with a smile on my face knowing that this beautiful boy was more than just a friend. Was that too much to ask? Let's not forget that he started this with his dang card saying that he wanted…

My phone rang. I picked it up, and the caller i.d. said "Brevin." I let it ring a couple more times because I didn't want to seem desperate. Right before it went to voice mail I answered.

"Hello?"

"Hey, you weren't asleep were you?"

"No, not even close. What's up?"

"I just kind of wanted to talk to you if you are not too tired."

"I'm never too tired to talk to you."

"Well I'm glad to hear that."

I giggled a bit. Not sure why, but I did.

"Kennedy," he started. "You have to forgive me, I'm a bit nervous. It's just that, I really like you and I was wondering how you felt about me, and how you felt about not just being my friend but about being my girl. No pressure. And if you don't, it's fine. I would still like to be friends."

Wow that was a mouth full. Now it was my turn.

"Yes."

"Uhh, yes what?"

"Yes, I would like for our friendship to be something more, yes I really like you, and yes, I would love to be your girl."

Silence on the other end.

"Was that too much?" I asked, a little nervous that I had ruined everything.

"That (pause) was (pause) perfect," he said.

The sound of his voice was warm and it made me blush. That night we talked until dawn and I couldn't have asked for a better birthday.

~

I had spent so much time with Brevin over the last two weeks that I almost forgot about the anniversary of the *Event* but August 8th came just like it does every year. It was just a regular day in the calendar, until it wasn't. It will never be the same. It's funny how we could go for days without hearing a peep out of Mom, even a day or so without seeing her. I didn't even know that she was aware of time, let alone what month or day it was. But early that morning I was woken by a scream. It was Mom. She knew.

She screamed and cried all day. She fought the nurse, fought Dad, and said she was going to commit suicide. The only person she didn't fight was Grandma. When she saw her mother, Mom broke down, said she missed her little girl, and fell into Grandma's arms.

I didn't go see her. I couldn't. KJ left without a word. I knew he wouldn't be able to handle it. He ran to Mia's just like he always did when times got tough. I had no one to run to, I had nowhere to go. And I felt bad about leaving Dad alone. He didn't go to work that day. He had that lost look in his eyes that he had right after Rylie's funeral when Mom left. Today all of her screams were like little knives stabbing all over my body. She did it at such random times that my heart dropped so often that I felt like I was going to die. I couldn't even grieve the loss of Rylie because I was too worried about Mom, Dad, and even KJ. I couldn't think about anything else and the more I thought about it, the angrier I became. Mom was so selfish. No one else could grieve because everyone was *so worried* about her. So what if she killed herself, would it really be that different around here? Maybe we would finally have some peace. Eventually my anger turned to sadness. I didn't want her to die. I just wanted her to get better. I needed her to get better. We all did. She just wasn't strong enough and I felt sorry for her. She was missing out on life.

I hadn't told Brevin anything and he never asked. I wondered when the day would come that he would ask me about my mother, where she was, what happened to her, why he never met her, and why I never mentioned her, but he didn't. He was too much of a gentleman. Even if I did want to tell him, lean on him, or cry to him, I couldn't. He was away at UVA for basketball camp for the next three days. He might call, he might text, he wasn't sure if he would have time or even be allowed to. Either way this was not something that you tell someone over the phone and it was certainly not something to be discussed after two weeks and one day of dating. I didn't want to scare him away… at least not yet. He wouldn't be back until Saturday morning anyways and at the risk of sounding insensitive, I really hoped that all of this blew over by then.

~

As the day went on, Mom's screams and sobs lessened, but they still came. I hadn't seen Grandma all day. The nurse left yelling that they didn't pay her enough to deal with all of this so Grandma took over. I put on my earphones and set the station to Pandora to try to drown out the sounds. Alicia Keys radio. I tried to encourage myself by singing, but the lyrics brought me back to where I really was. As I sang, *"She's living in a world and it's on fire"* I felt the tears start to come in my eyes. I didn't realize how real it was. Next I sang *"Feeling with catastrophe but she knows she can fly away."* The tears started to stream. I wish I could fly away, but where would I go? I sighed as Mom's piercing scream overshadowed the encouraging part of the song. I wanted to scream that I looked like a girl but that I was a flame, so bright I could burn your eyes, to make you look the other way… I wanted to be on top of the world, I wanted to have my feet on my ground and have my head in the clouds and not come down.

~

When my music could no longer drown out the noise I knew I had to get out of the house. I had been dealing with this all day. I went to find Dad and found him where he always was when he was thinking. On the front porch on the swing. I could tell he had been crying. His eyes were red-rimmed and there were white tear stains on his pale face. I sat down next to him. He said he didn't know how much more he could take. I understood. I didn't know how much I could either. I asked him if he wanted to get out of here. Go somewhere to clear our minds, to give us hope, to give us faith and to give us peace. It was Wednesday night. This would have been the first youth group meeting that I would have missed since I started going. I not only wanted Dad to take me, but I wanted him to stay. He hadn't been to church since our first Sunday in Virginia around two months ago. He didn't like Grandma's church. No one did, I'm not even sure that she did. A part of me thinks she went because that's where she always went. She was used it, her friends were there, she was a significant staple in that church because she had been going there for years. She felt special there, important, like she belonged. Everyone there was black and kind of old. They sang old spirituals and played their music on an organ. I was always concerned about Dad when we were in those situations. I wanted him to feel like he belonged. We weren't used to that kind of church. Mom grew up in this church but she and Dad chose to attend a church that worked for everyone. It was diverse in every aspect: the people, the worship, the sermons. It was a place where we all fit in - where we all felt like we belonged.

Brevin's church wasn't as diverse in terms in people, but everyone there made me feel loved. Dad could use an environment like that, especially then, and to be honest, I really could too.

I asked Dad if he wanted to go to church with me.

"The youth group?" he said, confused and kind of sarcastically.

"Adults are there too," I said. "We go to the youth room and the adults go to the sanctuary."

"And you want me to go alone?" He quipped.

"Ahh, you won't be alone Dad," I said. He knew what I meant.

"I can go with you," I said. "I don't have to go to youth group."

"What time is it?" he asked.

"7."

"We'll see."

So I spent the day counting the hours until this day was over. It seemed like time was literally taking its time. There is only so many times you can be stuck on level 91 on Candy Crush without frustration taking over and you wanting to throw your phone through the window. I looked at the clock. It was only 1 p.m. What do I do now?

Going into the house was not an option for me. I was actually looking forward to Grandpa going on a walk today so I could go with him, but who knew what time that was going to take place and I still hadn't heard from Dad about whether or not he was going to church with me. I knew he would take me, but I wanted him to *go*, I needed him to go, even if we were not in the same room. Somehow having him there made me feel safe. Not just for myself, but for him also. I had to watch that man, especially on a day like today. As far as my parental unit goes, he was all I had left. We needed each other. KJ was like Mom. Things get tough, and they retreat. Dad and I were the warriors. We stood and we fought, but neither one of us could fight this battle alone and the more I thought about it, we couldn't fight it together either, we needed a higher power. We needed God.

So I sat on the porch and put my phone down. I bowed my head and I prayed. I asked God to touch my Dad's heart, to touch his spirit, and to compel him to go to church with me tonight. I prayed for strength - not just for myself but for Grandma, Grandpa, Mom, Dad, and my twin. And then I pleaded with God to release my Mom from this hell that she was trapped in. I reminded Him that everything that I had ever been taught said that He could do all things and that all I needed was faith. Over the past year, my faith had wavered but I was back on track now. I needed to see results. I needed God to show me, just to give me a glimpse of something to confirm that He was with me, that He heard me and that He would help mom.

I'd always heard "church folk" say things like, "God may not come when you want Him, but He was right on time," or "Not in your time but in God's time, and His time is perfect." When Mom first went away, I wanted results right away and I expected them right away. Now, all I needed was a sign that help was on the way and I would be okay.

About 30 seconds after I said "Amen," my phone rang. To my surprise, it was Brevin. Despite my excitement I let it ring three times before I answered to quell any indication that I had been waiting for him to call and then answered in a relaxed way.

"Hello?"

"Hey Kennedy."

"Hey Brevin, I didn't expect to hear from you. How's camp?"

"It's cool. We had practice all morning and we just finished lunch.

I have an hour before the next session so I'm sitting in my room and decided to call my girl. How's your day going?"

"It's been ok." I said reluctantly. I really wanted to get the conversation off of me and back on him. I didn't want him to know that anything was wrong. That would be selfish. He was at camp and needed to focus on that, not on me. "So what are the dorms like?"

For the next 45 minutes I listened to Brevin tell me about the UVA campus, about the morning's practice, his roommates, and his lunch. He expressed how much he missed me, which was a pleasant surprise because I missed him too despite the fact that I had hung out with him all day on Monday and today was only Wednesday. He was happy to hear that Dad was taking me to church tonight and that Dad would possibly go too. Before long there was a knock on Brevin's dorm door and I heard a guy's voice telling him that it was time. He told me that he would call or text me later on tonight and that he had to go. I wished him luck and he said thanks and that was it. It was nice to have a break from what was going on in my reality. I looked at my watch, it was close to 2:00. I sighed. Tomorrow was still a long ways away.

Avoidance today was my friend, until my other friend, hunger, began to rumble. I did not want to go in the house. 7-11 was almost a mile away. I would walk. That would kill time. I knew that Dad kept plenty of change in his car for a rainy day. Today was a monsoon.

I was thankful to find that his car door was open. I grabbed a handful of silver bliss and was on my way. I sent Dad a text so he wouldn't look for me and took my time. I knew the slower I walked, the longer it would take, and the more time would pass that would cause this dreadful day to come to an end.

Was this the way it was going to be for the rest of my life? Would I sit around day by day, knowing that the reminder was coming, dreading every second that passed until I relived it, waiting for it to end, breathing a sigh of relief when it did, and then waiting as the cycle wound up again? I couldn't and I wouldn't.

It was heartbreaking to live with the knowledge that I would never see Rylie again but I could not just lay down and die. I had to live for the both of us, and deep down I knew that the only way that I would make it through would be if God's power worked through me. I knew that it would, I just had to let it.

7-11 felt further away than what I'd thought. I would be lying if I said I wasn't relieved to hear the bells jingle as I stepped foot in the air-conditioned store. Two hot dogs with chili, nacho cheese, onions, relish, mustard, and ketchup and a large cherry Coca-Cola Slurpee mix for the road and I was gone. About twenty steps and fifteen napkins later, so was the food, Slurpee and all. So, it came as no surprise when I found myself looking for a bush. I could no longer walk. I had to squeeze my legs together and slide. I was not walking back to 7-11 for fear that I would not make it. Plus, I was closer to the school. They had summer hours. Surely they were open.

The first bathroom I saw as I slid through those huge double doors of my new Virginia high school was staff only, but I didn't care. I had to go.

It was strange to me how all of the classrooms were in the same building. At my school in California we had a main building and several surrounding bungalows. We always went outside to change classes and our cafeteria was outside under some umbrellas because it never rained in Southern California, except for when it did. But here it rained often. That was a good thing. Maybe it would make drivers more prepared.

As I walked out into the vast hallway I almost ran into a familiar face. I said "excuse" and looked her straight in her eyes. I didn't know where or when, but I knew her and I guess she felt the same way about me because she was staring at me too. Just when things started to get creepy I remembered where I'd met her. Like clockwork we both said "Trey's party."

She reintroduced herself as Julia and told me that she came to get her schedule changed. She had gone to a summer program to help encourage minorities to take Honors classes. She was going to try her best subject. It was English. I told her that I was taking Honors English as well. It was unspoken but I could feel the yearning on her part for us to be in it together, not because she didn't know anyone at school but I could tell that none of her other friends would even think of taking Honors. She needed a familiar face, and I didn't blame her, because I needed one too. Brevin was a senior. There was no way in my mind that we could possibly have a class together. KJ wasn't going to be there for me, so knowing someone at the new school would certainly make me happy.

Julia's sister came out and they started a conversation in Spanish. I caught bits and pieces of it but I could not make out the meaning. I started to leave when Julia stopped me. She said we should hang out sometime before school started and that she would introduce me to her friends. We exchanged numbers and I left to face the inevitable, only I wasn't ready. Not again. So I dragged my feet.

The rest of the day went by rather uneventfully. I came home. Sat on the porch, rocked, played more Candy Crush, and rocked. I only went in to use the bathroom. Grandpa went for his walk. I tagged along. We didn't say much but we didn't need to. We both were hurting. Somehow this walk was our therapy. Words would have ruined the moment, ruined the healing. It seemed that with every step we walked further away from the turmoil, and when it was time to come back, it felt like we had gotten stronger.

The walk was longer today. I guess Grandpa needed more healing than usual… we both did. We returned to see Dad sitting on the porch swing. He had had enough. The rims of his eyes were red, his lips were pursed, his jaw line was hard. He swallowed and looked our way. After a beat, he cleared his throat and tried to speak. Silence. He tried again and uttered the words that I was not sure that I would hear.

"I'll take you to church tonight," he said. "And I think I will stay."

Youth Pastor Jason was waiting at the door when we arrived. I introduced Dad and let him know that I would be staying in the sanctuary with him. He understood. I'm not sure how he understood. He just did. I'd never been in the sanctuary before. Usually we went straight into the youth room.

The sanctuary was downstairs. We walked into a bright, crisp, white-walled room with black chairs and a stage. On the stage were four microphones, a clear pulpit, and a set of drums. There were groups of people talking to one another, laughing with one another, and genuinely showing love to one another.

Dad and I found two seats near the back and waited for the service to begin. A short, thick chested man with salt and pepper hair began with opening prayer. I had so much hope for this night, I had so much hope for my family, I had so much hope for Dad.

As prayer went forth I couldn't stop thinking of all of the scenarios that could take place after tonight. Could our prayers be answered? Could today be a blessing, a miracle of sorts on such a horrible day? Could our pain and sorrow really be taken away? Could we be happy again? As I continued on my barrage of questions I heard the man say "Amen." The music began and everyone started clapping. Even Dad managed to put his hands together, even if it was off-beat. This was no ordinary church music. It wasn't the hymns that I was used to singing. This music had some swag to it. If it weren't for the words I would have forgotten that we were even at church. And I liked it. I didn't want to forget that this was a house of God. That was really what I came here for. The music was just an unexpected added bonus. After the second song I even noticed Dad tapping his foot. I knew that he was enjoying it and that gave me a sense of purpose. He was meant to be here, and God used me to get him there.

The welcome was something they called the "lovefest." They had all the new visitors stand and then the members came to great us. I had never hugged and shook so many hands in all my life. I was glad Dad didn't have to stand by himself. My Dad was not a bad looking man. He was tall with small manly features. His glasses made him look distinguished but his pain made him look old. Some of the women seemed a little too eager to shake his hand or give him a hug. Maybe I was overreacting. Maybe they were just being nice. He sure didn't seem to mind though. That made me a little uneasy. It felt strange and brought up some questions that I didn't like. I couldn't even think about it without me feeling queasy so I chased them out of my head and tried to move on.

After offering the choir came up. The choir director said they were singing a song by Kirk Franklin called "Help Me Believe." He started off by saying that he wanted to write God a letter, that he really didn't know how to say it but he had to be honest with Him. Then he began to sing.

I wanna believe
But I'm having a hard time seeing past what I see right now, I see right now

Dad looked up.

I wanna be free
But when I try to fly I realize I don't know how, no one showed me how.
Wish I could see that this mess I'm in will really work out for my good, you said it would.
So, if you can hear me, can you give me a sign cause I don't feel you like I should,

58

please if you could,
My faith is almost gone, I can't hold on much longer, take this cup from me.

Dad took his glasses off. I knew what that meant.

Help me believe
Can I believe
Let Me believe
I wanna believe
I'm no good on my own, please give me another chance
It's hard to believe in what I can't see
To give you my will cause you're what's better for me
You can look in my eyes and see I wanna believe, believe, believe, believe.
(I want you to know)

He wiped his eyes. The singer continued

I wanna believe

If I never hear I'm sorry I can let it go, gotta let you go
Cause, it's killing me. Jesus you know how it feels cause you've been hurt before,
don't wanna hurt no more.

I saw the pain in his eyes. He was thinking of Mom. That is when I
realized that in all of her hurting, she had inadvertently hurt him. He felt as
abandoned as I did. My heart hurt.

I'm trying to hear you speak, but my heart is growing weaker, take this cup from
me.

Dad was searching for his faith again. I could tell because he stood and started singing the song with the soloist. He was crying out…

Help me believe
Can I believe
Let me believe
I wanna believe
I've been here before and can't take that hurt again

It's hard to believe in what I can't see
To give you my will cause you're what's better for me
You can look in my eyes and see I wanna believe, believe, believe, believe

The last line was so true for my dad. I could look in his eyes and see that he wanted to believe. When the singer sang, *"I'm no good on my own please give me another chanc*e" he completely broke down. He was hunched over. He couldn't even lift his head. All of a sudden, neither could I.

I had only met Brevin's parents once. It was at church one night, about one week into us dating. They didn't usually come on Wednesdays, and I went to my grandma's church on Sundays. It's not that he didn't invite me over. I just really wasn't ready to go. What would they think of me, this little bi-racial girl, dating their beautiful snowflake of a son? Not to mention the question. The one that Brevin had avoided. "Tell us about your parents." "What do your parents do for a living?" "When can we meet them?" I had no clue what I would say. I didn't want to lie, but I hadn't even confided in Brevin yet. What would I tell them? But as I poured out all of my emotions, hunched over in the back of the sanctuary at church, letting out all of my hurt and all of my shame, I smelled a sweet perfume and then a warmth around my body and an arm rubbing my back. As I lifted my head, a soft hand lifted my chin and deep blue eyes with a face surrounded by golden blond curly hair looked deep into my eyes. It Brevin's mom.

She wiped my eyes and held me tight. It felt good. It felt right. It was like I could feel the presence of God all around me. It felt sweet and light. As I lifted my head above her shoulder I saw Brevin's dad hugging mine. And my Dad was holding on tight. After the service Brevin's dad and mine talked for a long time. I was glad he had someone to talk to but was afraid of what he would say. I didn't want Brevin to find out from his parents. It was time for me to tell him. I didn't know how, but I would find a way. I had to.

~

It was 10:30 p.m. when I called. I didn't expect him to answer. I hadn't even practiced what I was going to say. I felt afraid and relieved at the same time, with a strange kind of peace. I somehow knew it would be ok. I would have waited, but he had to hear it from me. I owed him that much.

When he whispered "Hello," my heart jumped, but my mouth said nothing.

"Hello?" he whispered again. "Kennedy, are there?"

"I'm here," I said. "I'm sorry I…"

"It's fine," he whispered again. "Lights out is at 10, but we are all awake in here." "Should I text?" I asked.

"No," he said. "I like the sound of your voice. But, it sounds sad. Are you okay?"

"No," I answered. And then I cried. I cried like I hadn't just cried my eyes out at church. I cried like I had been holding it in for years. I cried so hard and for so long that I forgot that Brevin was on the other end of the phone.

When I finally stopped sniffling and whimpering, I realized that he was still there. After a moment of silence, a clearly shaken voice asked me what was wrong. I let it all out. I told him about church first, and worked my way back. Before I knew it I was reliving the *Event* and I believe that he was living it too. I could hear it in his voice when he asked me questions, felt his sniffles in his silence, and understood the sadness in his words. It was 12:30 a.m. when we said goodnight. He had to sneak back in the dorm and said he would text me when he made it back. He'd snuck out and gone to his car when I'd started to cry.

"My roommates have my back," he told me. "They will let me back in." It was 12:37 when he texted me and said he had made it back in and was in bed. I send him a smiley face emoticon and got in bed and settled in under my covers. I thanked God that a day that I was not looking forward to turned into a day of release, not only for myself, but also for my Dad.

My eyes were heavy from all of the crying. It was the first time that I was happy that Brevin was away. I knew that I looked like a hot mess and that tomorrow would be even worse, puffy eyes and all.

I closed my sore eyes and finally began to relax. It was at that moment that I realized how tense I'd been all day. As I started to drift off to sleep, my phone vibrated and lit up the room. I slowly opened my eyes and glanced at my phone. It was Brevin.

Brevin:
Kennedy, I love you.

61

And just like that, I was suddenly awake.

CHAPTER 5

Saturday afternoon couldn't come fast enough. Brevin was coming back and we had A LOT to talk about - especially since I never replied to his text. Why? I didn't know. I'd never had a boyfriend before and, as usual, I froze. I didn't know what to do. I didn't know what to say. And, more importantly, I didn't know how I felt, but I knew I didn't want to lose him. I was hoping he thought I had fallen asleep before receiving his text. He may have because for the next two days we were texting as though nothing happened, although I knew we would have to discuss his text soon. I didn't care. I was just happy to see him. School would be starting soon and I wanted to spend as much time with him as possible before it began.

I went down to kitchen to find KJ sitting at the table eating a bowl of cereal. He hadn't been around much lately. Between Mia and pre-season football practice starting, he was hardly ever home. I poured myself a bowl and sat across from him. I guessed that I would later regret this question, but I didn't have anyone else to talk to, so I went for it.

"KJ," I started. He looked up and slurped his milk off the spoon. I shuttered. "How's football?" He continued to stare and slurped again. "Okay." I said. "How do you know if you are in love?" KJ never missed a beat. He finished his cereal with precision, almost in a rhythm, not taking his eyes off of me once. He got up, put his bowl in the sink and came over to my side of the table.

He put his lips close to my ear and said, "You're not." Then he walked out.

My forehead hit the table and I just let it lay there. Who would I talk to about this now? Dad and Grandma were out! I could never talk to them about this. Grandpa was out as well for that matter. He would just tell me a long story that I didn't have time for, which would ultimately end in great advice, but then he would go on to brag about his advice and tell Dad and Grandma! No thank you. I guessed I'd have to figure this one out on my own.

This was the type of thing I would have discussed with Mom. She wasn't worse since the anniversary of the *Event* passed but she certainly wasn't better. I missed her, but I was learning to adjust. After a year of this, it had become commonplace. The scary thing about it was that I didn't want to be so comfortable with it that I forgot her, forgot to pray for her, or forgot to love her. I made a pact with myself that I would talk to her every day. I knew she wouldn't talk back, at least not yet, but that was ok. At this point it was more for me than for her. I would start today.

It was a little a weird, I'll admit, walking up to her room. I felt like I was in a sci-fi movie or, better yet, a thriller, and that I was the girl walking into the unknown. I could feel a movie theater full of people watching me with bated breath, licking their buttered popcorn covered fingers. Some would want to yell, "Don't do it!" but wouldn't for fear of other movie goers becoming angry...so they'd sit in silence as the inner conflict continued. I could almost hear a sinister theme song playing in the background as fear tried to creep into me. I didn't understand what I was so afraid of. It was Mom. I know oftentimes I felt as though she was just a shell of what she used to be, but it was still her. She was still in there somewhere, I knew it. She had to be.

As I put my hand on the door knob, I heard a voice behind me. I jumped. It was KJ.

"What are you doing?" he inquired. I didn't even turn around.

"I'm going to see Mom," I said flippantly.

"Why? She not in there." I turned to face him.

"What do you mean?" I asked, half afraid of the answer.

"Well, her body is there, but she is long gone." I breathed a sigh of relief and rolled my eyes.

"Well, I'm going to see her anyway." I went on with my mission as though KJ didn't even exist.

"Suit yourself," He said, his tone a mixture of nonchalance and sarcasm. I rolled my eyes again and continued to push my way in.

The nerve of KJ. What business of it was his? Why did he care? As far as I was concerned, he only cared about himself. It was all about KJ, Mia, and football. That's all. He didn't care about Mom, me, Dad, or anyone else. He was a selfish, arrogant butthole and I didn't care what he thought. This was for me.

I hadn't been in Mom's room for a while. It looked the same. Normally the home-health nurse was in there, or Grandma, or Dad, but no one was in there now. Just her and me. I made my way to the side of the bed where she lay. To my surprise, she was awake. I sat down next to her and spoke.

"Hey Mom," I said. I don't know what I expected. I don't even know if I expected anything. But I got nothing. I cleared my throat and continued. "I'm glad you feel better. I know that Wednesday was hard. It was hard for us too." I paused, thought hard, regrouped, and continued. "I met someone and you would love him. He is so special, and thoughtful and sweet. He is cuter than I thought a boyfriend of mine would ever be. And Mom, he is a Christian. He's two years older than me. Dad thinks that will be a problem in the future, but I don't." I paused again, and let out an almost embarrassing giggle. "He thinks he loves me." I smiled. "And the more I think about it, I think I may love him too." I continued. "I think it's too early to tell though. I don't even know what it would feel like and I have only known him for a month! I am trying to be cautious. Trying to heed to all of the advice about boys that you have ever given me. I have kept my guard up like you said as long as I could. And I didn't say I love you back to him because I was not sure. And I have no intentions of ...well, you know... I mean we haven't even kissed yet." I found myself stroking her hair. "He comes back from basketball camp today. We have a lot to talk about, but I am going to relax and be myself just like you told me to be. I won't say anything that I don't really mean. I will be honest with my feelings and not allow myself to be pressured into anything. I have reminded myself that if he really likes me, that he will accept me for who I am and if he can't do that, then I can do better. I can even hear you saying now that I owe that to myself." I smiled. I felt at peace. "Good talk Mom. I'll be back." I kissed her on the forehead and felt at ease as I left her room. I was no longer nervous about seeing Brevin today. As a matter of fact, I couldn't wait.

My grandmother's house is not a mansion. It is a nice size,

though; it's just old. The outside of the house is red brick. It has been aged and at some angles gives off a grayish tint, but this just gives it character. There is a wrap-around porch fenced in with a white banister with a porch swing that Dad and I love. When you walk in, you have to walk up a step that has been tripped over many times by all of us newbies living there. There is a hall that leads straight to the back of the house, but if you turn to the left, there is a living room that we only go in when there is company and to the right is the kitchen. If you follow the hallway it goes back into the family room where Grandpa has all of his historical pieces and off of that room is a bedroom and bathroom. That's where Grandma and Grandpa stay. The steps are in the family room and lead up to the second floor. If you go up the steps and stay straight you will run right into my room. KJ's room is next to mine, with Mom and Dad's room across the hall from his. They have their own bathroom in their room. And between their room and KJ's room is the bathroom that he and I share. And that is where he stood, just outside of that bathroom, brushing his teeth when I exited the room after my conversation with Mom. He was being weird today. I could not figure out what in the world he wanted.

"So?" he said as I turned to close the door.

"So what?" I asked as I turned to look at him.

"Any luck?"

"We had a good talk," I answered.

"She spoke back?" He inquired and the space between his eyebrows crinkled up.

"I talked," I said, "and she listened.

"That's what I thought," he retorted. "A freaking waste of time."

"It's not a waste of time," I said back. "It's therapeutic. For her, for me. I know she's in there somewhere. She has to be. If she wasn't, then how did she know that it was the one year anniversary of Rylie's death? How could she had possibly been keeping time if she wasn't there? She's there alright. She's just lost and she doesn't know how to get back!" As I spoke I realized that if I hadn't believed that my mother was somewhere in the shell lost, broken, and just not able to find her way back to us, I did now. My words solidified it for me. The Bible says in Matthew 12:34 that "out of the abundance of the heart the mouth speaketh" (KJV). That scripture was never so true for me as it was now.

KJ just stared.

"What?" I said.

"Nothing," He responded in that nonchalant way that he always does when he is finished with the conversation. He slid himself back in the bathroom to finish up. But I wasn't done. And I let him know it. This wave of anger and bitterness swept over me in a way that I had never felt before. I was sick of his selfishness. I was sick of his self-righteous, judgmental attitude. I was sick of him escaping from a world that we were all trapped into, yet he played the victim. There must have been a lot more in my heart that I was not aware of, because all of a sudden, it all came out.

"I'm sick of you KJ," I started. "Always walking around here like you are the only one hurting. I am sick of walking on eggshells around you. Listening to Dad, Grandma, and Grandpa saying that you need time, and that this is the way you grieve and that you will snap out of it. I am sick of you walking over everybody thinking you can say what you want and do whatever you want and no one can say anything to you. You are not the only one here living in this hell. We are all suffering and are doing the best we can to survive. You are not better than anyone else. You should be here dealing with all of this too. Helping out instead of making things worse. Having everyone worried about you. You are selfish, and personally, I am sick of it." He stuck his head out of the bathroom door.

"Are you finished?" he asked.

"No!" I answered, my voice had reached full elevation. "YOU ARE A BUTTHOLE! THE WHOLE WORLD DOES NOT REVOLVE AROUND YOU! YOU DO NOTHING BUT CAUSE EXTRA PROBLEMS IN THIS HOUSE! INSTEAD OF HELPING OUT, YOU MAKE EVERYTHING WORSE! INSTEAD OF TAKING SOME OF THE LOAD OFF OF ME BY HELPING OUT AROUND HERE, YOU RUN AWAY AND DISAPPEAR AND I HAVE TO DO EVERYTHING! AND THEN YOU HAVE THE NERVE TO SIT THERE ON YOUR HIGH HORSE AND JUDGE ME? TRY TO TELL ME WHAT WILL WORK WITH MOM AND WHAT WILL NOT? YOU HAVE NO SAY IN ANYTHING! YOU HAVE SELFISHLY REMOVED YOURSELF FROM A SITUATION THAT YOU NEEDED TO STEP UP IN! YOU ARE NOT A MAN. YOU ARE A SCARED LITTLE BOY, A COWARD WHO RUNS AWAY

EVERY TIME SOMETHING GETS TOUGH AND WHO HAS TO PICK THE PIECES? ME! AND I AM SICK OF IT! GROW UP!"

He pretended he hadn't heard me, but I knew he had. KJ finished washing his face and walked right past me. But I still was not done. He was not getting out of this easy, not this time. I grabbed his arm and said, "Where are you running to now? Going to Mia's and let her stroke your ego? Let her make you feel like something you're not?" He pulled his arm away and went down the stairs. Just when I started to feel bad about my outburst he came back up with venom in his eyes and I knew that this was not going to be good.

"DO YOU KNOW WHAT YOUR PROBLEM IS? YOU THINK YOU KNOW EVERYTHING! YOU DON'T KNOW SH..." He paused. "YOU ARE THE ONE WHO WALKS AROUND HERE LIKE YOU ARE MISS PERFECT. WELL I AM SORRY, NOT ALL OF US CAN BE AS PERFECT AS YOU. DO YOU KNOW WHY I RUN? DO YOU KNOW WHY I LEAVE? BECAUSE IT IS TOO PAINFUL BEING HERE FOR ME! EVERYTIME I LOOK AT YOU I SEE HER! SHE WAS MY LITTLE SISTER TOO!" His voice cracked. "EVERY TIME I SEE GRANDMA, I SEE AN OLDER VERSION OF MOM AND I CAN'T HANDLE IT. I CAN'T LIVE MY LIFE LIKE THIS. I WON'T. YOU CAN BE TRAPPED IN THIS HELL IF YOU WANT TO BUT I'M NOT. YOU CAN CALL IT SELFISH; YOU CAN CALL IT WHATEVER YOU WANT... BUT I AM CHOOSING TO LIVE IN THE REAL WORLD. AND I FEEL SORRY FOR YOU... BECAUSE YOU ARE JUST AS TRAPPED AS SHE IS," he said as he pointed to Mom's door.

His voice quieter now.

"You were right about a lot things," he said as a tear tried to make its way down his face. "But there was one thing that you were wrong about," he continued, voice shaking. "I'm not the one who is the coward. I'm brave because I'm choosing to live. The rest of you guys are cowards. You, Grandma, Grandpa, Dad, and especially Mom. Because you guys have chosen to die right along with Rylie ...and I refuse to do that."

He stood there for a second like he expected me to say something, but I couldn't. All I could do was stare. He looked so different to me in that moment, the moment that seemed to last forever. He wasn't a scared little boy. He was a hurt young man. It was Dad who broke the silence. I don't even know where he came from. He touched my shoulder and I jumped.

"You guys alright?" he asked. Neither one of us spoke immediately. I don't know about KJ, but I couldn't find the words.

"We are now," I finally said after I felt like the smoke had cleared. Call it twin intuition, call it woman's intuition, call it what you like but I knew that we would be ok after this, KJ and I. As a matter of fact, I knew that we would be better, closer, and stronger. We understood each other now, and we didn't even have to say a word to confirm it.

"I'm out," KJ announced as he turned and made his way down the stairs.

"See you later, big brother," I said. It was something I used to say when we were kids…he was three and a half minutes older than me. When we were young, I took it very seriously. I used to follow him around and do whatever he did. I was very possessive and I would tell everyone that he was MY big brother. I don't know when it changed and in my mind we became the same age, but MY big brother was back. Maybe he'd never left. I heard him half laugh and then he said, "see you later little sister." That made me smile.

I decided to make Brevin lunch. He would be home around noon but we made plans for him to come over at 2. I knew it was late but I made him promise that he would not eat. He said he wouldn't.

I have never claimed to be the world's greatest cook. I can make things like grilled cheese sandwiches, oodles of noodles, and scrambled eggs. I am one heck of a sandwich maker as well, and can microwave the heck out of anything. I know how to read directions and follow directions (mainly box stuff) and I know my way around the kitchen. Today's lunch: BLT's, potato chips, and sliced fruit. I would top it off with some of Grandma's freshly squeezed lemonade and sweet potato pie. I wouldn't tell Brevin that I hadn't made those unless he asked.

As I worked on my mission Grandma walked in and asked if there was anything that she could do to help. I told her that I had it but thanked her for asking. She sat down and breathed heavy. I knew that was code for, "We need to talk." That's what she always did before a "talk." She would breathe heavily and wait for you to approach her. It's not that the talks were always bad, it's just that they were never good, or about a topic that I didn't necessarily want to discuss, at least not with her. If you tried to avoid it or acted like you didn't hear her she would do it louder and continue to do it until you asked her what was wrong. And to add insult to injury, the longer you made her wait, the longer she made you wait. If you asked her what was wrong she would say nothing, and just when you thought you were in the clear, she'd speak. I learned the game fairly quickly and asked her right away to avoid all the rest of her shenanigans. I wasn't quite sure why she did it. I guess she wanted to be noticed and heard.

"What's up Grandma?" I asked as I finished slicing up the tomatoes for our sandwiches.

"Ahh nothing," she said as she sighed again, tapped her fingers on the table and looked down.

"Ok," I answered as I began on the lettuce. "Well," I said, well-intentioned yet impatiently waiting to get this whole ordeal over with. "After I finish up, I am going to go get ready for my lunch. Brevin's coming over. Remember?"

"Oh," she said with a bit of an exaggeration. "Is that today?"

"Yup," I responded jovially.

"Well before you go…" Bingo! Right on cue. I could have said her next statement right along with her but I did not want to seem disrespectful. I repeated it in my head.

"I'd like to talk to you about something, if you have time."

"Of course," I responded as I put the last pieces of bacon on the sandwiches. "This will be quick," I thought to myself. It had to be about the fight between KJ and me. I'd just explain how we understood each other better now and it was a good thing. Imagine my surprise when she hit me with this.

"Now I don't make assumptions about anyone anymore. I'm far too old and I've been fooled far too many times. So please excuse me if you think I'm being rude but there has been something on my mind. Now your mother should be having this conversation with you but since she is taking a break and you are in the situation that you are in, I reckon it is my responsibility to talk to you about such things."

What situation was I in? What in the world could she be talking about? A conversation I should be having with my mother? This didn't sound like this was about the KJ fight. She couldn't be referring to, no, no, no, please no. She couldn't be referring to…What would she know about that? Surely, she and Grandpa didn't still...

She interrupted my thought life with the word "sex," and there it was. I was so stunned by the notion of her saying that word that I couldn't even focus. Wait, was she still talking? I saw her lips moving but heard nothing. It was like I could see the shell of myself sitting there listening to her but the real me was stuck behind a glass that the shell could not see and I was banging on the glass yelling "Mayday, Mayday, Pull up! Pull up!" So I cleared my throat. I cleared it so hard and so loud that it stopped her in midsentence. I put my face in my hand and peeped through my spread out fingers.

"Grandma," I said. "No."

"No what?" she replied.

"No!" I said louder. "There will be none of that."

"Well I know how it is—" she started.

"No," I said again. "No, no, no, no and no!"

"Well have you guys talked about it?" she inquired.

"No!" I said. "Well how do you know you don't?" she started again.

"No," I said again.

"Well do you know what the good Lord says about it?" she asked.

"He says no, and so do I," I said, hoping that the conversation would now end.

"Well, yes and no," she said. "God made sex. It is a beautiful thing in..."

"Grandma!" I finally yelled and then put my hands over my ears.

"Well I was just going to say it was a beautiful thing in marriage!" she snapped.

"I get it," I told her abruptly.

"Do you really?" she asked and accompanied the question with a penetrating stare.

"Yes." I was so embarrassed by this point that nothing on earth could bring me back.

"Well that's all I wanted. Guess I'll let you get back to making your lunch." She said as she laboriously got out of the chair.

"Thank you," I said through clenched teeth and squinted eyes. After Grandma left I couldn't get the thoughts out of my head that she had put in. Me and Brevin? Brevin and Me? No, never...I couldn't even bear the thought. I didn't know a lot of things but there was one thing I did know. This girl was saving all of that for marriage. There were so many things that I have done that were not pleasing to God, and I have a lot of questions for Him when I meet Him, but there was one thing that there will be no question about, and that was it. This girl was pure, and she was going to stay that way.

But Grandma did get my mind to thinking. Did Brevin feel that way too? Was he pure to begin with? And then all of these crazy thoughts started crowding my brain to the point that I couldn't take it anymore. What was I supposed to do with all of this now? Should I ask him? He has been my boyfriend for all of two weeks and he was already saying he "loved" me. How many other girls had he "loved"? Now the thought of Brevin coming over brought up other feelings that I hadn't felt before. I was still excited to see him, but now I was also scared. I didn't know what I was going to say, or if I was going to say anything at all. If it had been Grandma's intention to compel me to start thinking about these things, she had certainly succeeded, and she knew it.

Maybe she was right. Maybe this was something that I should think about so that I would be ready to stand my ground if the time ever came. But with the Brevin I knew, I didn't think it ever would, so I decided to let it go for now. We were just getting to know each other, there was no need to rush into *that* conversation. We were just having fun.

When Brevin pulled up I tried not to seem overzealous. Why couldn't I just be myself? I didn't want to seem too excited to see him but I didn't want to be too lax either to make him think that I hadn't missed him. I was going to wait on the porch but I thought that was doing too much. I was going to wait up in my room and let someone else answer the door and call me down, but my options for the "caller" didn't look good. After that conversation with Grandma this morning, there was no way I was going to let her answer the door. Dad was coming around but I was not sure that he had accepted Brevin quite yet. My safest bet was Grandpa but there was not guarantee that he would ever get up to answer the door. As a matter of fact I was quite sure that he wouldn't. So I waited in the kitchen. I would set the table and just yell for him to let himself in. That seemed like a perfect mix to me.

I kept looking at the time. What was it about this boy that was driving me perfectly mad? Finally I had to place my phone far away enough from me that I could still hear it but not see it in order for

72

me to concentrate on what I was doing. Finally the wait was over and I didn't know how I felt. I was a mixed bag of emotions.

"Come in," I yelled as my phone vibrated. Why was I so nervous? What was it about this boy that caused me to want to look perfect, to act perfect, to be perfect? Breathe. Remember what Mom told you the first time you actually "liked" a boy. Be yourself. Be yourself. Be your...

"Hey beautiful."

I looked up. He was here. My beautifully sun-kissed, blue eyed boy. And he was here for me. And he thought that I was beautiful.

"Looks good," he said innocently. "What are we having?"

I walked over to him and gave a hug. He smelled like a mix of clean linen laundry detergent, some men's sports deodorant and body spray. In other words, my man smelled good. Too good. As the hug deepened I heard Grandma's words from this morning's conversation and I jumped back. I had to keep my cool. Stand my ground. Not give him any reason to think anything else. I could handle this.

I guess he noticed because he asked me if I was ok. I was, physically. But mentally my mind was racing. It was going a mile a minute, filled with thoughts about him calling me beautiful, about whether when he said "looks good" he had referred to me or the food, about the fact that he told me how he loved me and I still didn't know how I felt about that, about this hug, and ugh! I just wanted to scream!

I asked Brevin to have a seat and told him that I would be right back. I needed to relax. I ran into the bathroom, checked to make sure the toilet seat was down (years of being a twin of a boy had trained me for that) and sat down. Was all of this normal? Is this what being in love was? Trying to make sure that everything was perfect all of the time? Being forced outside of your comfort zone while making sure your feelings and emotions stayed under control? If this was it, I wasn't sure I wanted any part of it... but I liked him. I liked Brevin so much that I wanted to do all of those things even if it was confusing.

My Mom's words kept ringing in my head. "Be yourself." She and Dad met in college. He was from Michigan and she grew up here in Virginia. She went to the University of Maryland on a partial track and field scholarship. Dad wanted to get as far as possible away from home. He grew up in a strict Catholic home and went to a private Catholic school his whole life. His family all but disowned him when they found out about Mom. Shortly afterward they stopped acknowledging his existence. KJ and I have never met them. Dad doesn't talk about them much. At the risk of sounding creepy, I have to say that my Dad is a nice looking man. He is a catch. He is a great provider, a hopeless romantic, and loves my mother. Some might say that he is a push-over when it comes to her. But in his words, "She rocks my world." He had always been captivated by her. Always. You could see it in his eyes when she walked into the room. That captivation was transferred in a fatherly form to Rylie and me. We were Daddy's little girls, me more than her. He just had this way of making me feel special and that is why we were so close. So if my mom could pull a husband like that, then her advice must be golden.

I breathed. I would just be myself. I took a quick peek in the mirror and headed back out to the kitchen. When I arrived Brevin was still there, just twiddling his thumbs, waiting for me to come back.

"Kennedy," he said in an unsure tone. "Are you alright?"

"Yes, I'm fine," I responded as I put lunch on the table. "Just thinking too much." I sat down caddy cornered from him and smiled. Instead of eating his food he grabbed my hands and reiterated how much he had missed me. I returned the sentiment and after a moment I encouraged him to eat. He must have really been hungry because he devoured his food before I'd eaten half of mine. We made small talk in between each bite and slowly but surely things started to feel the same way they had before he'd left… comfortable.

Time definitely did not stand still for the next two weeks leading up to school starting. It was a good time for us. Dad was thoroughly enjoying his new job. We lived in one of the fastest growing areas in the United States. The school district had already committed to building three new high schools and two middle schools over the next ten years because of this. So it was a realtors' dream. The houses could not be built fast enough for most of Dad's clients and he was selling those bad boys like hotcakes. I could tell it made him feel good about himself and that made me very happy. I was still walking with Grandpa every day, going to church on Sundays with Grandma while somehow avoiding her "topic of choice" (my relationship with Brevin), and KJ was still splitting his time between football and Mia.

We saw him when it was time to eat, shower, and ask Dad for money. Aside from that, he was pretty much gone. But everyone seemed to be at peace with that, including me.

Then there was Brevin. We spent every day together. Whether it was at his house, my house, the park, or at church, not a day passed during which we didn't see each other, and we texted or called each other in the times between our next meetings. And then all of a sudden it was the Saturday before school started and everything was going to change. He knew it, and I knew it. It wasn't that is was necessarily going to be bad. It was just going to be different, at least for me. I was going to school with over 1,400 kids, and I was only familiar with a few. There'd be KJ (who had met a ton of friends already thanks to football and hanging out with Mia), Julia, Isaiah, Trey, a few kids from the youth group, and Brevin.

I hadn't had good experiences in school, and who was to say that this school would be any different. And even though Brevin had given me no reason to think this, I still couldn't help but wonder if maybe he would change his mind about me once other kids started chiming in about how I wasn't all that. Maybe he would start to believe it too.

KJ played his first game on Saturday. It was a pre-season scrimmage and a toss-up as to who was going to start. KJ had come in and demonstrated to these Virginia boys how he played football in California. Not all of the players liked him or his style, but the coaches did. In his mind that was all that mattered. He'd heard some of the guys call him a cocky, arrogant, conceited douchebag, but he was ok with it, probably because he knew to some degree it was true.

"The only difference between me and every other cocky, arrogant, conceited douchebag out there is that I can back it up," he said. "I put my money where my mouth is. It will stop bothering them when we start winning. Then I'll be their hero." Secretly, I hoped he was right, although I really never said anything except that he should maybe tone it down.

"For what?" he'd answer. And that would be that.

Trey was a lineman and Isaiah was a wide receiver. They had his back and that is all he needed, KJ said. The real issue was Markus Wiseman. Wiseman had a gripe with KJ. He had waited three years to be starting quarterback and here came KJ, vying for his position. The team was divided. Some players that started off rooting for Wiseman switched sides once they saw KJ play. They felt that he was downright better than Markus. The other group stayed with Wiseman out of loyalty. Some of these guys had played with him since elementary school. They were familiar with him, used to his style, and didn't want to try anything different. But it was really up to the coaches. Today would decide his fate.

KJ was ready. I could tell because before every game in Cali, he would sit up in his room, watching game film, and listen to music. He didn't want to talk to anyone, he just wanted to focus. And that was what he was doing this morning. He even ate breakfast in his room.

Dad, Grandma, Grandpa, and I were going to the game. Brevin would meet us there.

"Sit with me," he'd said earlier. "There are some people I really want you to meet."

The game started at 1:30 but everyone wanted to get a good seat, so we got there around one. There weren't very many people present, mostly just parents from both teams. Brevin was nowhere to be seen.

I sat down on the bleachers with my family and saw KJ warming up on the field. He wasn't his usual self. Something was missing. His cockiness was gone. He wasn't going to start. I could tell from the look on his face. But as he tossed the ball back and forth, his expression went from disappointed to determined. I'd seen that look in eyes several times before. He was going to make the coaches pay for not choosing him. He'd show them. The glazed over look in his eyes was just the calm before the storm that was brewing, and I couldn't wait to see him pull it off. It was one of the things that I admired about him. KJ was a fighter when he wanted to be. He seemed to thrive when he was challenged. If something was too easy for him, he didn't give it his all. If something was too hard, he felt the need to prove to everyone that he could not only handle the challenge, but exceed it. I knew that was what he was going to do on the field that day, and I was looking forward to it.

"My big brother," I mouthed under my breath. I couldn't wait to see what he was going to do next.

Brevin arrived a little after the game started, greeting my family and sitting down next to me.

"What number is KJ?" he asked.

"He's number seven," I said while pointing to the sideline.

"Aww," he said, disappointed. "Didn't get the starting position, did he?"

"No, not today, but watch what he does," I said. I had confidence in my big brother and I knew that if he didn't start this game, he would the next.

"Remember that group that I told you that I wanted you to meet? They are right over there." He pointed. "Wanna come up there with me?"

"Sure," I said. I looked over at Dad for the silent ok. He nodded. I grabbed Brevin's hand so he could pull me up and led me up to where his friends were sitting. I heard the announcer behind me and a small roar from the parents and handful of kids. I wondered about KJ and how he felt being on the sideline, and then I realized I was being introduced.

"This is Q," Brevin said first. "We've been friends since the first grade. Started playing basketball because of him. We've been tight ever since." A scrawny big-headed black boy poked his head around and looked at me.

"Oh, I see you Brev," he commented and then put his hand out to shake mine. I obliged him as Brevin moved on. He introduced me to Evan, a cute dark haired boy that looked Asian, and lastly to Jason, a quirky little brown hair boy.

"This is my girlfriend, Kennedy." It was the first time I'd heard him call me his girlfriend. I knew we were together, but hearing him say it made it official.

"Nice to meet you all," I said.

We sat down to watch the game. I was hoping KJ would get in the second quarter, but it didn't happen. Watching the first string quarterback made me nervous because he was good. I felt for my twin. I knew that he wanted this so badly. I couldn't see his disappointment, but I could feel it. I prayed that he would not only get a chance, but that he would show the coaches what he was really made of. I don't know if God listens to prayers like that. I have often wondered if he does. What if someone else was praying for the first string quarterback to keep his starting position? How would God choose?

Before long it was halftime. Breven asked if he could buy me something and I said sure. I was hungry but I didn't want to come off as a hog. Not just in front of Breven, but in front of his friends too. I wanted to make a good impression so I asked for some nachos and a bottle of water. He told me to stay seated and that he would be right back. I wondered if his friends would start to interrogate me in his absence. It was about five minutes later that Q hit me.

"So Ken..." he said. "May I call you Ken?" I wasn't really fond of it, but I wasn't quite comfortable to say so, so instead I said, "Sure."

"So Ken..." he said. "What intentions do you have with our Brevin?

I know the expression on my face said, "What the heck?" Instead of playing along, I laughed. Was he serious?

"Do you find me amusing?" he asked. The expression on my face was blank. Who was this kid? This was creepy. Not only were his questions weird but he said them in a monotone voice with a serious expression on his face. Evan finally broke the awkward silence and told me not to pay attention to Q and for Q to leave me alone. Q responded in his creepy way.

"Whatever do you mean?"

Evan just stopped, stared and said nothing. Then the silence was back. Jason asked me normal questions about my life such as where I was from and a few questions about KJ. Just when things were perking up conversation-wise, Brevin was back.

"Long line," he said while handing me my nachos and water. He had two hotdogs, nachos, and a soda. Obviously he wasn't embarrassed to eat in front of me. He noticed the silence as he finished his hotdog.

"Q, what did you do?" he asked. Before Q could answer, I jumped up. Number 7 was in the game! KJ was in the game! I yelled for my twin. I knew he couldn't hear me, but I was sure he could feel my excitement.

He played the whole second half of the game, and boy did he play. He completed 21 for 29 passes, 328 yards and threw three touchdowns and ran the ball in himself for one! The stands went wild. This was way better than the 2 touchdowns the other quarterback threw. The score was 7-14 us at halftime, now the score was 7-42 with a minute left in the game. That's when the coach took KJ out and put in another quarterback, probably to give their star player a break.

Grandma, Grandpa, Dad, Brevin, and I could not stay in our seats. Even after they took KJ out we were all still standing! If that performance did not win KJ the respect of his peers, coaches, and the starting spot, then nothing would. Marcus Wiseman had been moved to second string and he knew it. You could tell by the way he sat on the sideline, helmet in his hands, legs stretched out, and back slouched. He didn't get up to cheer for KJ. Not even once. I started to feel sorry for him, but it was hard because I was so excited for KJ. Every time the commentator said Kendall James Morgan to whomever for the score, I beamed with pride. I was so proud of him.

Mom would have been so proud of him. She would have out-yelled any of us. That's just who she was. It didn't matter what we did. Her support and encouragement were unparalleled, regardless of whether we were good at it or not. But if we were good at it, all of the other parents might as well go home because she would make it all about us. She always had.

And Rylie, well she would have been out of control! Dancing and cheering with the cheerleaders, swinging on the beams on the bleachers and probably making googly eyes at Brevin. I chuckled to myself at the thought. She was so much like Mom. Carefree and confident - something that I envied about her and needed to learn in my life now.

Then there was my twin who taught me so much without him even knowing it. He was the type that did not let his circumstances get him so down that he could not rise to the occasion. I'd known that about him, but the conversation that we had the other day about Mom, Dad, Grandma, Grandpa, and myself confirmed it. There were a lot of things about KJ that I didn't like, I envied and prayed that one day some of this quality would rub off on me.

I didn't see Mia until after the game. I hadn't even known she was there until I saw her talking to Dad. She was quiet when she came by the house, which was rare. Brevin told his friends goodbye and I waved as he walked me back down to my family. Mia spoke to both of us and then was on her way. Dad said they were waiting for KJ and wanted to know my plans. Brevin politely asked if he could take me to the park. Dad told him to be careful. No texting while driving and keep his eyes on the road. He told Brevin he had grown to trust him and emphasized that Brevin must never take advantage of that trust because once he did, that would be it. Brevin assured him that he we would be careful and led me to his car. It was an unexpected pleasantry. School was starting on Monday and this was technically my last day of freedom. I'd have to prepare tomorrow after church for what lay ahead of me and go to bed at a decent time. This was it.

Mary Elizabeth Goodwin Park was called M.E.G for short. I only heard it referenced to by KJ, Isaiah, and Trey when I eavesdropped on their conversation about where they were taking their "girls." It was the make-out spot around here. So imagine my surprise and lack of excitement when that's where we pulled up. All the fears about what Grandma had said and was trying to say thereafter flooded my mind with worry. Not Brevin. Surely he wouldn't think that, that I'd, that we'd... we were Christians right? We didn't do things like that. Then I started thinking of KJ. He was a Christian too, wasn't he? And according to my spy work, he'd brought Mia here several times, and she was willing to go. What was I going to do?

"Kennedy. You gonna get out of the car?" Brevin asked so sweet and innocently. You would think that a girl would be happy to have a boyfriend that would think to bring her to the park to hang out, but I wanted to puke. I didn't know what Brevin's intentions were. I trusted him, at least I thought I did, but this would be the test.

"Kennedy," he said puzzled. "You gonna get out of the car?"

"Yeah," I said reluctantly. "Sorry, I had something on my mind."

When I got out of the car I noticed Brevin had a picnic basket in hands. We had just eaten at the game, and I wasn't that hungry, but I thought the sentiment was nice. As he led me over to a huge tree so we could sit under the shade I'd realized that I was probably making a big deal out of nothing. This guy was different from other guys based on what I'd seen in school, what I have seen from KJ, and of course what I'd seen on TV. Brevin was one of a kind. What had I to be concerned about?

He pulled out a blanket. What?

Brevin put his hand out for me to grab so he could lead me to it. I frowned.

"What's wrong?" Brevin asked. "You've been acting strange since we got here."

I just looked at him. I couldn't speak. I knew what I wanted to say, but I didn't know how to say it.

"Don't you trust me?"

I sighed. And that sigh opened a whole topic of conversation that I was totally unprepared for but knew needed to take place.

Brevin talked about me holding back about Rylie. While he understood, he couldn't help but wondering if I would have told him

80

if my Dad hadn't gone to church that night and talked to his parents. He never wanted to force me to confide in him, but he wished that I would trust him with my secrets.

He also brought up my odd behavior from when he returned from camp. He didn't have anything to hide. He really liked me, but he was starting to question if I felt the same way. I immediately interrupted him when he said that. I let him know that I did really like him but I was afraid. I was afraid of being hurt, and I didn't understand why he liked me. I took the opportunity to tell him what Dad said about him being a senior and me being a sophomore. I told him about the bullying in California. He didn't understand. He said I was beautiful and that they were jealous. Maybe they were, I expressed to him, but in California, girls like me were a dime a dozen. You had to have something else, something that I apparently lacked. I also told him about what Grandma had said. His eyes widened. And when I explained why I freaked out about the blanket, he laughed. I wanted to laugh too but something about it embarrassed me, so I just looked down at the ground. He grabbed my hands.

"Kennedy," he said. "I have never felt the way I feel about you before. I don't care about what those girls said about you in California. And with all due respect to your father, I don't care what he thinks either. And as far as your grandmother is concerned, I understand her concern, but you don't have to worry. I have committed to wait until I am married. My commitment to Christ is the most important commitment I have. My commitment to you is the second."

Was this guy for real? I felt safe. He made me feel safe. I walked over and sat on the blanket and waited for him to join me. He did. And by the end of the evening I had experienced my first kiss. It was quick and to the point and it was mine. Brevin had kissed girls before. I couldn't help but feel a tinge of jealously as he debriefed me on each encounter. But he was mine now. He made a commitment to me. And I committed that I would open up more, not hold back. He wanted me to share my feelings. He wanted me to share my thoughts, and I agreed that I would. I was starting to trust him, and it felt wonderful. No more holding back. I was free to be me.

Before we knew it, it was time to head back to the house. I was literally floating the way I always saw girls act on TV. I was giddy and excited. It felt as though I floated up the steps and into the house, passing Grandma, Grandpa, and Dad who were in the kitchen playing cards. I floated up to my room and somehow managed to close the door. It was a good night.

CHAPTER 6

School was exactly how I'd pictured it: busy. There were people everywhere, each of them on their own missions, trying to find their friends or trying to find their classes. I was just trying to keep my balance and find my place.

Schedules and locker numbers were distributed in homeroom. Brevin had a pre-season basketball captain's meeting so he had left for school early. Who knew where KJ was. We'd walked to school together, and he'd told me not to be nervous. He already knew everybody who was anybody and I was lucky to be his sister, he said. He had already paved the way for me, and he said I could text him if I needed him. Since homeroom was by last name and grade, we at least knew we had our first class of the day together. He told me to stay close and said I would be fine. As soon as we walked through the door, however, he saw some football players and I became a non-factor.

As I pushed my way through the busy halls, looking at the door of every classroom, I realized this was a new start for me. I didn't have to be afraid. No one really knew me here and I could be free to be me. With that revelation came a sense of freedom that I only felt when I was with Brevin. I had no expectations. I could fly under the radar my next few years here and I would be perfectly fine. I didn't know how plausible that was since I was KJ's sister but I was trying to look at everything in a more positive light.

I noticed everything. I didn't get the usual greeting I had become accustom to since *Finding Nemo* involving Mom and Dad going to each of our rooms, shaking our beds, and yelling, "first day of school!" I didn't get to go back-to-school shopping with the most stylist woman I knew, and have her flat-iron my hair and give the usual speech: "Walk in with confidence, Kennedy," she would say. "No one can make this a bad year for you but you." She would give that look that said *you've got this* and *I believe in you.* Then she would smile, give me a kiss, hold my hands. The whole experience was customized just for me, KJ and Rylie. She was all in for us. I hadn't appreciated it as much as I should have until now. But instead of crying about it, I learned from those moments with Mom and gave myself my own pep talk as though she was talking to me. I looked at myself in the mirror and prayed and encouraged myself in the Lord. Even though it was hard, it made me feel strong and I found peace in that.

"Aren't you Brevin's girlfriend?" an unfamiliar voice asked. I looked in front of me and saw a tall African boy. His hair was lighter on top than it was on the sides. He had on thickly framed glasses that I couldn't tell if they were really needed or just worn for fashion. He wore a bright pink shirt that said "Don't Laugh, This Is Your Girlfriend's shirt" and dark skinny jeans with colorful sock and turquoise Van shoes.

"That depends on two things," I answered confidently. "Who is asking, and if you are going to let me go into the classroom that I was trying to find." He laughed and stuck out his hand.

"Brees," he said. I shook it.

"Kennedy Mason. KJ Mason's sister, and yes, Brevin's girlfriend." Apparently my identity rested on them, which I liked despite myself. It took some of the pressure off.

KJ sauntered in as the bell rang, sitting down next to me and immediately to other classmates. How did he know these people? I figured we would be in the same homeroom since they did it by last name. What I didn't expect was that he would sit right next to me. Maybe my big brother was really back. He was growing up a little. After the teacher took roll call he handed out our schedules.

1st Block: U.S. History- Piven, Room 803
2nd Block: H English - Boyd, Room 724
3rd Block: Chorus- Joyner, Room 131
4th Block: Spanish II- Meza, Room 154
5th Block: Algebra II-, Room 117
6th Block: PEACE- Boyd, Room 724

7th Block: Biology- Willis, Room 124
8th Block: Health & PE- Edmond, Gym

I barely had the chance to look at it before it was snatched out of my hands. KJ. My big brother was back alright. He laughed.

"What's so funny?" I asked as I snatched it back.

"We haven't had a class together since elementary school. What are the odds?"

"What?" I asked as I peeked at his schedule. U.S. History was the same. I wasn't sure if that was a good or bad thing. But secretly I felt relieved.

"I see Dad got you to take that PEACE class." He retorted.

"You should have taken it too. It would have been good for you."

"I'm getting a scholarship. I don't need it." That was KJ's answer for everything college related. PEACE stood for "Preparing Everyone in Advance for College Education." It was a club that taught students everything they needed to know in order to prepare them for college. They even did college tours. Dad thought it was a good idea, and so did I.

My locker was right next to KJ's. I guess they did those in alphabetical order too. I didn't really have anything to put in it but they let us go and try them out to make sure we could open them. Just as I twisted to the last number of the combo my phone buzzed. It was Brevin.

Brevin: Where are you?
Kennedy: At my locker
Brevin: What number?
Kennedy: 1114, on the bottom floor.
Brevin: My locker is upstairs. On my way.

Brevin showed up shortly thereafter. I don't know what it was about him that was different from every other day, but my boyfriend looked good! I spotted him down the hall, light brown hair flowing and blue eyes shining. Dark denim semi-baggy jeans, polo striped shirt and tennis shoes. I was disappointed that Q was with him. Something about Brevin's friend rubbed me the wrong way.

"How's it going?" he asked.

"Ok, I guess," I responded. "Being known as KJ's sister and

85

Brevin's girlfriend isn't all that bad."

"Oh, you didn't know?" Q said in a monotone voice. "B's the king around here." Brevin just smiled.

"Let's see your schedule."

Brevin gave me the run down about my teachers. Apparently I got the best. Especially Mrs. Boyd. He thought I would really like her.

"I think we have Spanish together," he said, pulling his schedule out of his pocket. I was excited to find out he was right. He seemed excited too. We had lunch together on "B" days but on "A" we did not. I had third lunch both days. On A days he had first. My only hope was that I had lunch with KJ so that I didn't have to sit alone. I was glad to hear that I didn't have it with Q. I'd rather sit alone.

The announcements came on instructing us to head back to class.

"See you later," Brevin said, kissing me on the cheek. "Text me if you need anything." I smiled. I knew that I wouldn't, but it was nice to know that I could.

Mr. Piven, the history teacher, was a short tiny man who was balding but looked like he was trying to hair. He had a lot of energy, was loud and rambunctious. He reminded me of an angry little leprechaun. KJ sat next to me in history, although he didn't speak to me. Everyone already seemed to know him or was trying to get to know him; he was pretty busy talking to everyone else, but that didn't matter to me. He was still there.

When I arrived at Mrs. Boyd's class, she wasn't there, but Brees and Julia were. They quickly motioned for me to sit next to them, which pleasantly surprised me. God did love me. I was even more excited to find that I had lunch with them. He really loved me. Now I didn't have to sit alone. I thanked Him silently and listened to their lively conversation.

Mrs. Boyd walked in right before the bell with a stack of papers in her hands. She was a lovely, dark skinned lady with long dreadlocks who looked to be in her early thirties. She reminded me of Mom. It was bittersweet. After she gave us her spiel, we played Jeopardy! I met several different kids in the class. It was nice.

I couldn't help the nervous excitement that seized my body when I realized that my favorite and most important class was next. Chorus. How would I fare against the kids in this class? Would the teacher believe in my vocal abilities as my Californian teachers had? Would I be accepted? The nervousness shifted a bit when I realized that Brees and I were heading to the same class. He was excited as well.

As we walked to the chorus room he grilled me on my vocal ability. He was sure that Mrs. Joyner would love me, and he encouraged me to join the show choir. That was his favorite.

Ever since we moved to Virginia, I had yearned to sing, but hadn't had the opportunity except for when I was in the shower, or sitting in my room listening to my IPod. It was a part of who I was and was something that I loved. Not only was I good at it; it was therapeutic for me. There was nothing that I'd rather do than sing. In my dream world, it was what I planned to do with the rest of my life. It called to me, and I was finally going to be able to answer it in the best way I knew how.

Mrs. Joyner was a stocky, tall lady with blond and brown spiky hair. She was serious about her craft and didn't even crack a smile in her spiel. She didn't want any funny business, and if you thought her class was a joke, she suggested that you go and have a schedule change because she was not having it. She waved her finger and neck for emphasis. As the bell rang for lunch, she told those of us who didn't want to work not to come back, but instead to go to guidance counseling to drop chorus and pick up something else. She only wanted those who were passionate about chorus in her class, saying she didn't care if she only had one person in the choir. If you were not serious, this class was not for you.

As Brees led the way to the cafeteria, I expressed my concerns about Mrs. Joyner.

"Will some students really not come back?" I asked.

"Yup," he said. "But after they leave, she calms down a little bit. But she wants to win. She wants to win every competition and blow out every concert and does what it takes to get there." I swallowed hard.

"You're not thinking about dropping out, are you?" he asked with wide eyes.

"No," I said emphatically. "Not even a chance."

Mr. Meza gave his spiel in Spanish. I caught a couple of words here and there but for the most part, I was lost. It was hard to pay full attention with my gorgeous boyfriend sitting beside me. He wasn't paying attention to me, though. It was like he was drinking in every word that Mr. Meza said. I should have been, too, but I was too busy paying attention to Brevin.

Brevin was excited to hear about how my day went. He laughed when I told him about Mr. Piven, and smiled in acknowledgement when I told him about Mrs. Boyd. "You sing?" he asked in amazement, when I talked about Mrs. Joyner. I guess I had failed to mention that to him. He seemed a bit disappointed that I had kept such a huge part of my life from him, especially after we had just discussed the topic at our picnic on Saturday. I don't know why it was so hard for me to open up about the things that I felt were precious to me. This was all new to me. I was used to keeping things inside. Besides my family, I wasn't used to people caring about what I cared about, and all Brevin wanted was to be let in. He brought it up that evening after dinner when he called. He seemed annoyed. This was a new side of him that I hadn't seen before. It was kind of cute and flattering that he wanted to know me—all of me—to the point of frustration. I didn't want him to be frustrated, though. I just wanted us to be alright.

"Why didn't you tell me about your desire to sing on Saturday? I thought we put all of our cards on the table that day. Is there anything else?"

"No," I said. "Brevin, I don't know why I didn't tell you. This is all new to me. I'm trying."

Silence.

"Are you mad?" I finally asked to break the silence.

"No. Not mad, just concerned."

"Don't be," I said, trying to smooth things over.

Silence again.

"I've won awards," I started. "Lots of them. I've never told anyone this and I only realized it last year, but I'm going to go after it… a singing career. I know that everyone wants to move to California and become a star but I am going to. I am not just going to be one of those people who just want it. I'm going to do it. I figure that I could move there, go to community college to major in something part-time, but pursue singing full time. When I sing, it's like the whole world is lifted off of my shoulders. I'm nervous about fitting in here in the music department but am determined to make a name for myself in it. It is who I am. It is what I do. The Bible says to delight yourself in the Lord and He will give the desires of my heart. My mom used to tell me that God put the desire to sing inside of me, so I can bless other people with my voice… and that's just what I intend to do."

Silence. It was the first time that I had brought Mom up in casual conversation. It was the first time that I heard myself express my dreams and goals out loud. It felt good to open up, it felt good to get it out, it felt good not to be afraid to say how I really felt, and it felt good to tell him.

"I think that's great," he said. "And I believe you. Although I have never heard you sing. Are you sure you're good?" He laughed. I laughed too.

"I hope so, or else I'm going to be in trouble," I responded.

"Not just you," he said, "but the whole school will be too!"

"Shut up," I said in jest as he continued to laugh.

"But seriously," he said. "I can't wait to hear you." I smiled.

"And I can't wait to show you."

~

The next day in school was just like the first, meeting my teachers, them giving their spiels, and meeting new people. I didn't know anyone in my Algebra II class, which was fine because Mr. Ullery put us to work right away. Julia and Brees were in PEACE with me, as well as many other multiethnic kids. I was surprised to see Mia in my Biology class. She gave me a half smile and went to find a seat next to a group of boys who were goofing off in the corner. They seemed to be familiar with her but she seemed to have no time for their immature antics. Not long afterwards she rolled her eyes and turned away from them as they all yelled "Drew" and put their hands up. I turned my attention to the door and saw a very cute brown haired, brown-eyed boy stroll in. He was even cuter when he smiled. I blushed in admiration and found myself watching him walk over to the boys to find a seat. He must have noticed me staring because he put a smirk on his face and nodded his head as if to say hello. I jumped in embarrassment and put my head down. What was I doing? There was nothing wrong with looking, right? I was just admiring and acknowledging God's creation. Just as I convinced myself that I had done no wrong, class began.

We didn't dress out for PE that day, but I noticed that it seemed as though my whole Biology class went to PE together. Mia was there, and so was Drew. This time I made sure to preoccupy myself so as to not stare at him again. Just as I settled into "Rihanna radio" on Pandora on my IPod, I heard a voice. It was Mia.

"Hey," she said. I took my headphones out of my ears.

"Hey," I replied.

"This is so boring," she said in a sleepy voice. I didn't say anything for a moment. I think I was still in shock about the fact that she had spoken to me to begin with.

"Yep," I finally replied.

"So, you really like Brevin huh?"

"Yep."

"A lot of girls here do," she went on. "So you should watch out." Oh. Two of us could play this game.

"I've seen a lot of girls talking to KJ too," I said. "So you better watch out as well." She rolled her eyes hard and just stared at me. I could tell it was messing with her. Just then another voice came into play. I looked up. It was Drew.

"Mia," he said. "Why don't you introduce me to your friend?"

"Who?" she said dizzily. I cleared my throat. "Oh," she said. "Her. That's my boyfriend KJ's twin sister, Kennedy. She is dating Brevin Johnson." I smiled and stuck out my hand to shake his.

"I'm Drew," he said. "I think we have Biology together as well."

"Pretty much everyone here does," I said. "It's like they just grouped us together and gave us the same last two classes."

"True," Drew said. "Well, it was nice to meet you."

"Nice to meet you too," I replied.

"Bye Mia," he said and walked away.

I didn't trust Mia. Not one iota. But something in me made me say out loud, "Well, he is really cute."

"Ewe," she responded. "But I forgot that you like white boys." That was interesting considering that she herself was white.

"Well," I said inquisitively. "What do you like?" Her reply struck me as both simple, yet intelligent, which is something that I didn't anticipate. I had always thought she was a little ditzy, but she was starting to prove me wrong.

"I like KJ." That was it.

For the next four weeks, school became, well, school. I felt like I had been there all of my life. I was familiar with the teachers, my classes, and some of the students. I actually enjoyed school for the first time in a long time. At times I felt guilty for being glad that we moved to Virginia, due to the circumstances. But things were going well for the first time in a long time. KJ was excelling in football, Dad was excelling at selling houses, and I was enjoying it all. I felt like I belonged, and it felt good for my family to be back to functioning as a family. Grandma was fulfilling Mom's role and Grandpa was an added bonus. I still kept my pact, though. I tried to go talk to Mom every day. Some days the conversations were longer than others depending on what was going on that day, how much homework I had to complete, or if there was a game. I always went in to at least tell her hello, give her a kiss, and tell her that I loved and missed her and wanted her to come back. It wasn't scary anymore. It was what I did. And even though I didn't see a change in her, I felt a change in me. She was back in my life again, and I would take that.

Chorus was going well. I hadn't had a chance to show off my talent yet, but the time was coming. Show choir tryouts were next week and Brees and I had been practicing a duet. The theme for the show was a modern hip-hop young love story. We were singing "My Boo" by Alecia Keys and Usher. I was nervous because today was the first time Brevin was going to hear me sing. He was taking me to the movies after rehearsal at Brees' house and asked if he could listen. Brees said sure before I could answer.

It wasn't that I didn't think that we would do a good job. I knew that we would do a great job. The melodic flow of his tenor voice danced with the alto in mine like they belonged together. We were able to correct one another and made each other better singers. I know it's cliché to say but it was like we were a match made in heaven. We became close friends quickly and even though Julia didn't sing, she quickly became one of my best friends. We were the three musketeers. It was nice.

Brees' house was huge. It had a modern feel and perfect for his large and expanding family. He had five brothers and sisters, and his sixth sibling was on her way. His mom was a dentist and his father worked for the government.

"It is top secret," Brees said. "He works for the U.S. Embassy for the country of Cameroon, which is where we are from."

His house always smelled like cinnamon because his mom boiled cinnamon sticks whenever she cooked. Her African food quickly became the highlight of my week and she always encouraged me to eat.

"You're too skinny," She would say. "In my country, the bigger you are, the better. Eat."

Brees and I were in his room finishing up when we heard the doorbell ring. I was nervous. Brees assured me that I would be fine. It was good for us to perform in front of someone before tryouts. Brees' whole family would be joining Brevin as our audience. I always got nervous before a performance, but this was different. I felt physically ill.

"Sing it to him," Brees said.

"Huh?"

"Sing it to Brevin. I mean, come on. Look at the words. This is your story. We have to sell it to Mrs. Joyner. Sell it to him. See if he buys it." Brees was correct. The words were my story, and could continue to be. I was ready. We came downstairs and I pretended that I was on stage. I would sing this to Brevin. I stood right in front of him as the music began. Brees would start.

There's always that one person that will always have your heart
You'll never see it comin' cause you're blinded from the start
Know that you're that one for me, it's clear for everyone to see
Ooh baby, oh, you will always be my boo...

We walked around each other as he continued to sing and looked into each other's eyes just like we practiced it. We had to make it believable even though we not even in the least bit attracted to one another in that way. When it was my turn, the nerves rose up again, but I looked at Brevin, opened my mouth, and belted it out.

Yes, I remember boy, 'cause after we kissed I could only think about your lips
Yes, I remember boy, the moment I knew you were the one I could spend my life with
Even before all the fame and people, screamin' your name
I was there, and you were my baby...

As Brees and I harmonized our way through the rest of the song I was so caught up that I didn't notice that the expression on Brevin's face had changed. It wasn't until the end of the song that I felt him staring at me. And when I glanced over I noticed the smile on his face...the widening of his eyes...he couldn't keep them off of me.

92

My Oh, my oh, my oh, my ohh,
My boooo!

We sang in unison and finished it up. It was the best that we had ever done. We knew it and it was apparent to everyone else. Brees' family were standing to their feet clapping. Brevin hadn't moved. He was still staring at me. Just me. It made me blush and then smile.

"You know that could be us." He said as we pulled out of the driveway.

"What?" I asked. I knew what he was referring to, I just wanted to hear him say it.

"The song. Especially the part about all the fame and people screaming your name. Just remember that I was there before any of that, I was there before you became a star." I smiled. "You were fantastic," he said, still beaming. "You were right. You were made for this."

"Thanks," I said appreciatively. "And what were you made for?"

He paused for a second before answering.

"You."

Fast and Furious 7, was awesome. We laughed, jumped in excitement, and had a really good time. I was surprised when he pulled up to The Cheesecake Factory for dinner. I figured we would just go to Moe's or Chipotle, which were two of our favorites. We always argued over which one was better. I was a Chipotle girl myself. I started to question him but after dating for four months I was starting to understand my boyfriend just a little bit more and decided to go with the flow. It was better that way. I knew that I would get my answer soon enough.

I noticed the flowers on the table after we ordered. At first I thought it was a centerpiece, but upon further inspection I realized that there was a card and that flowers in restaurants were usually in vases, not laying on the table. Brevin seemed delighted when I finally got the hint. That boy was a sweet romantic one. Sometimes I felt just a little too sweet, or just a little too romantic, if there could be such a thing. I didn't feel like I deserved all of that, but I certainly appreciated it. What girl wouldn't?

"Are these for me?" I asked. And I thought that Mia was dizzy.

"Of course," Brevin said. "Read the card." I pulled the card out and saw seven little words that I hadn't expected but was excited to yell "yes" to. I had been so busy with Brees that I had all but forgotten about this. Brevin asking me in such an awesome way made me feel like the luckiest girl in the world.

"Of course I will go to homecoming with you!" I'd never been to homecoming, but I knew that you went with a bunch of friends, dressed up, went out to dinner, and danced the night away. I also knew there was a homecoming court, a homecoming football game, and all types of homecoming activities. Had I been in California, I wouldn't have participated in any of that, let alone had a date. I was super excited about it. I would have to text Julia. This would call for a girl's day of shopping and pampering.

I walked into the house floating again from an evening out with Brevin. This was a usual occurrence, but what I walked into was not. KJ's back was to me, but I could see Dad's face. It looked tired and weary. Since he began a job his countenance had changed. It was brighter, more jovial, younger. But tonight, that look that the he had after the *Event*, that look that he'd worn for almost a year, was back. Something was wrong. My first thought was Mom. I fixed my mouth to speak but KJ spoke before I could. According to KJ, Dad was on the phone with a friend from California. KJ overheard him talking about a woman, Vanessa, a co-worker that had been hitting on him.

"I heard you Dad," his voice cracked. KJ was crying. I could tell... and he never cried. "You said how it had been a long time... a real long time since you and Mom were *together*. I saw how you looked at Vanessa last week when I stopped by the office. I have overheard your phone conversations with her. I saw your texts setting up time to go out to dinner. I gave you the benefit of the doubt. I knew that *my* dad would never do anything like this. Not to Mom, not to us. The man who is trying to turn me into a man...not him, not ever."

My mouth dropped. Surely KJ was mistaken... surely...

"She is sick!" he screamed over and over again through snot, spit, and tears. I had never seen him so emotional, ever. "How could you?" he continued. "I don't respect you, you are the worst husband ever, the worst father ever! What kind of an example are you? What are you teaching us? To kick people when they are down? To leave them when they need you most to fulfill your own selfish desires?"

Dad tried to speak. "Son, I, I..."

94

"Come on Dad," I pleaded with him in my mind. My heart was beating quickly, then and slowly with anticipation. *"Tell him you didn't do it, Tell him he is mistaken, you wouldn't have, you couldn't have...DENY IT, COME ON!"* He didn't.

My heart sank. Tears streamed down my face. I felt my world crashing down around me. My life hurt. It felt like the *Event* all over again. I couldn't breathe as I watched him form the words I didn't want to hear. Brevin was wrong. God didn't care about me and my family. We were His stomping ground.

"Daddy...no." I was unaware that I had spoken aloud until KJ and Dad stared at me. I could tell that they did not know that I had come in and witnessed everything. "God, no." I pleaded with the higher power who I felt was determined to ruin my life. With no one else to plead with, I felt hopeless and lost. I put my hands over my ears and closed my eyes. I didn't want to hear it. I didn't want to see it. "No...no...no...." I mumbled aloud.

I felt a hand on my shoulder. It was KJ. He had walked over to join me. My father turned. He looked ten years older and defeated. It was like he could not do anything right. I felt sorry for him. He'd lost a daughter and a wife at the same time. And now he felt like he was going to lose us too. So there, we were in a standoff. It felt like it was us against him. He stood in solidarity on one side of the room with us, a united front, on the other.

Dad finally spoke, and KJ, well, he lost it.

"I am sorry, son..." he started. "I've been careless. I didn't think..." he did not get to finish. KJ walked right up to him and punched him in the face. I screamed.

Dad's nose bled. He touched it, saw the blood, and gave KJ a look that said you shouldn't have done that. But KJ didn't care. He didn't stop. He looked at Dad and said, "I...hate...you." Then he spit in Dad's face. He was challenging him, and Dad took the bait. The fight was quick. Dad took his forearm and put it against KJ's neck and forced him to the wall. A picture fell. I screamed again but couldn't move. KJ struggled to get free and punched dad squarely in the stomach. It knocked the wind right out of him. Dad sunk to his knees and KJ left.

~

No one went to church the next morning. Grandma decided to have it right here in the house. She was listening to "Better" by Kirk

Franklin. The lyrics spoke to me, even though I didn't want them to.

If I could, I'd get away
Far from all this trouble I see everyday
Nobody wants to show their face
This is like a, like a masquerade
(Jesus)
I know you love me
I know you care
But while I'm hurting I just need to know you're there
Watching over me and I feel you're telling me
Count it all joy and always remember, life will get better
It's gonna get better
No matter the weapon, it will not prosper
Things will get better, it's gonna get better…

At this point, God and I were not on speaking terms. I wasn't angry with him. I was hurt. Just as things had started to get better, just as I started to live the life that it seemed I was made for, things went downhill. What if Dad did cheat? What would happen to us? What would happen to Mom? Would Grandma and Grandpa put him out? Would he leave? Where would KJ and I go? Would we have to move again? And if Dad did leave, would we ever see him again?

I was in a deep dark place and I wasn't sure how I could get out. I called Brevin as soon as his church let out. I told him everything and he came right over and picked me up. We would go to Mia's. I knew for sure KJ would be there. He wasn't. We learned that Mia was out of town for the weekend. She'd left on Friday, so there was no way he was with her. When we got back in the car, I lost it. Brevin grabbed me and pressed my head to his shoulder. This could not be my life. When we got back home Dad was gone. He was out looking for KJ too. The police said that he had not been gone quite long enough for a missing person's report, but in an hour or two, he would be.

It was a rough night. I don't think anyone slept…except for Mom who was completely oblivious to what was going on. So she lost Rylie. We all did. Why did she get to escape? This was all her fault. Everything was. We would have a very serious conversation one day about everything if she ever snapped out of it. She'd made everything

96

worse for all of us, and she got to disappear into her pain while the rest of us had to deal with ours.

~

Monday morning Dad didn't go to work. He said I didn't have to go to school, but I wanted to. Not only to see if KJ showed, but to try to get away from the chaos that was my life. Brevin, Brees, and Julia would be there. So would KJ's closest friends and Mia.

No one had heard from KJ. He wasn't at school. Mia didn't even know what had happened. She hadn't heard from him, which she thought was strange; but she hadn't even known he was missing. I could tell she wasn't lying. For the first time I had actually hoped he was with her. I asked her not to tell anyone. I asked the same of Brees, Julia, Isaiah, and Trey. I didn't want the whole school to know. It wasn't time for rumors and child's play. This was serious. This was my life. A little privacy was in order and I felt comfortable that they understood that.

School didn't help. I had nothing. No twin's intuition, no leads - nothing. I felt sick, so Dad picked me up before lunch.

"Heard anything," Dad asked in quiet desperation.

"No," I sighed. "I am assuming…"

"No," he answered. I hung my head. Dad put his hand on my knee. "I didn't cheat on your mom, Kennedy. I would never…" his voice trailed off. "I'll admit, I did enjoy Vanessa's company. I miss your Mom so much." A single tear ran down his face. I grabbed his hand and really looked at him. His hair must have been 50 shades of gray. "Vanessa was showing me some attention and maybe I let it go too far with the texting, lunches, and dinners, but I never crossed the line… never. I can't say I hadn't thought about it, but I didn't do it. I am human. And as much as I would love to be superman…" He breathed. "My shoulders just aren't broad enough. Anyway, it is important to me that you know that."

I didn't know what to say. What do you say to a man whose world has been chewed up and who is expected to put it back together again? I didn't know if I should say, "thanks for telling me" or lie and say that I'd never doubted him… because I did doubt him. All I could do was force a smile. He forced a sad one too, and we drove in silence the rest of the way home.

It wasn't until Wednesday evening that we heard something. The police called. When I found out it was them, my heart sank.

"No, not again," I heard my dad say. I knew what he was thinking. Grandpa took the phone call. Even Grandma couldn't even bring herself to take it. Take one grandchild and she will survive but take more and, well, her expression said it all. Grandpa was indifferent while on the phone. He always was.

I pleaded with God again, repented for my sins, asked Him to forgive me, and begged Him to please do one more thing for me. Even if He never did anything else for me again, please let my brother be okay. Grandma sat in a chair with her hands on her face, and Dad leaned against the wall. No one said anything when Grandpa hung up and walked out of the door in silence. Nobody moved. About sixty seconds passed and then he came back in, KJ behind him. I let out a shriek and ran into my brother's arms. His hug had never felt so good. Grandma let out a huge sigh of relief and began to cry. KJ apologized. Told her not to cry. Admitted that what he had done was careless and selfish. He promised that he would never do that again. When Dad finally spoke, he asked KJ where he had been. Grandpa answered for him. KJ had been staying at a men's shelter. He passed for eighteen so they didn't ask him any questions. He was found by the police who had been on the case for a few days.

It felt good to be able to breathe again. I had felt suffocated since he left. Grandma got up and asked KJ if he was hungry. He was. She started cooking. It was her therapy. We hadn't eaten well while he'd been gone.

Dad and KJ still didn't speak. We ate dinner in silence and went about the rest of our evening. I had homework to make up, Dad had clients to contact, Grandpa had television to watch, and Grandma had hymns to sing. I hadn't told Mom about KJ being gone. I didn't think she could handle anything else. Each day that I walked in while he was missing, I put on a brave face. If she really could hear me, she wouldn't have known the difference.

I texted Brevin to let him know KJ was back. He didn't ask for details. He just reminded me that prayer works, that faith works, and that God did care about my family. He said that tough times come to make us stronger. Over the past year and a half, I had gained enough strength to last a lifetime. I was hoping that I was done.

As I settled into my bed I could hear KJ defending himself on the phone. He must have been talking to Mia. She called every day that he was gone. I could hear the fear in her voice when she asked if he was home yet and I knew she could feel the pain in mine when I had to tell her no. He was telling her not to cry, to calm down, that he knew he was wrong, and that it was careless. He must have practiced his spiel because he told Grandma the same thing. He said he didn't care if he ever talked to Dad again. It sounded like Mia was trying to defend Dad because KJ yelled at her and told her there was no excuse for what he'd done and that he didn't have to ask Dad anything because our father hadn't denied it. What KJ didn't know was that Dad had denied it. He'd denied it to me, but KJ hadn't even give him a chance to. I believed Dad, and Grandma and Grandpa believed him too. Dad and KJ would have to talk soon, but for right now I was just happy he was safe. I could finally get some sleep and focus on Homecoming for the next two weeks.

KJ found me at lunch and said we needed to talk. He was freaking out. Since he wasn't talking to Dad and just came back to school without an excuse, he couldn't practice for the rest of this week and was forbidden to play in this Saturday's game. He needed a doctor's excuse or a note from a parent that said it was a family emergency. He had none.

I was stunned that the school didn't know since Dad had filled out a missing person's report. How did they not know? I told him not to worry and that I would take care of it. He would have a note by the end the day. He hugged me and told me what I already knew. I was a great sister. I immediately texted Dad and told him the situation. He said he would fax in a note. I also asked him how the school didn't know KJ had been missing. He said he would take care of it. This was something that KJ needed to know. I understood his anger and his frustration but his practiced pitch should be told to Dad as well. He owed Dad an apology and the opportunity for Dad to explain himself if he wanted to. He at least owed him that much.

After school KJ came to my locker.

"Did you take care of it?" he asked desperately. I gave him the fax. He gave me a kiss on the cheek. "I owe you."

"We'll talk about that later," I assured him. He owed me alright, and I would make sure he paid.

I hadn't practiced with Brees since KJ had gone missing. Tryouts were this Saturday so we had to practice tonight and tomorrow night. Brevin said he would take me, stay and work on his homework at

Brees' house, and then take me home. It was twofold, he said. He got to spend time with me and get his work done at the same time. It didn't hurt that Brees' mom was making foo foo, Cameroonian chicken, and okra soup and had invited us to stay for dinner.

Julia texted me while we were on our way. Brees had asked her to homecoming. I'd thought he would. We decided to go shopping on Saturday after show choir tryouts. It would be a girls' day. I hadn't had one of those in a long time. As a matter of fact, the last girls' day I had was when Rylie was still alive, during her ninth birthday. There is no way that I would have thought it would be her last. I hadn't wanted to go but Mom insisted, saying I needed to grow up and stop acting like I didn't want to hang out with Rylie. She was my little sister, after all. She wanted us to be close. It wasn't that I didn't love Rylie. I did. We were just so different. I can finally admit to myself now that I was jealous of her. Everyone loved Rylie. Her personality was so bubbly and she could talk to anyone. We went to the mall on that last girls' day. Her magnetic personality and baby doll look caused all of the women who worked at Superstar, a birthday place that allowed you and a few friends to have the ultimate birthday experience, to say how cute and how funny she was. She chose a spa day and wanted me to go as her guest. I was too smug to see how much she loved me. But now I know that she wanted to be just like me, while I was busy wanting to be just like her. I actually had a really good time that day. Who would have thought that that memory with her would be one of my last?

When I got home, I found the usual "suspects" in their usual places. I knocked on KJ's door, and it was half open. He looked and motioned for me to come in. I sat on his bed as he told Mia he would talk to her later. I didn't really know how to start this, so I told him that I came to collect on what he owed me.

"Already?" he said with this perplexed look on his face. "Alright, shoot."

"He didn't do it."

"Who didn't do it?"

"Dad"

Silence.

"How do you know?"

"He told me."

"Kennedy, you are so gullible. Of course he's going to tell you that. What would he do? Where would he go if Grandma and Grandpa put him out? He doesn't want to lose us. I saw his texts and heard his phone calls Ken."

"All he did was let his good be evil spoken of." Took that one right out of the Bible.

Silence.

"KJ…" I continued. "Dad told me everything that he did. He repeated everything that you said. I know all of that is true, but he did not cross the line." Silence. "He said he was tempted, but he didn't do it. Haven't you ever been tempted to do something but you didn't cross the line? You have to understand that. You didn't even give him a chance to explain himself. He messed up, true, but I want you to forgive him."

Silence. KJ just stared at me.

"This is what you owe me," I said.

"I have homework to do," he said. Homework, I thought to myself. Really? KJ is a minimalist when it comes to schoolwork. He does just enough to get by. A "C" is an "A" to him, giving him just enough so that he can still play sports and keep our parents at bay. I'm an A-B student myself. I actually like making good grades and the financial incentive my parents used to offer didn't hurt either. But even if they hadn't (which they hadn't since Mom 'left'), I would do it anyway. This was just another way that my twin and I differ.

KJ got off the bed, walked me out of his room, and began to shut his door. I pushed back.

"He's the one who made sure the school didn't find out that you had run away. That you really didn't have an excuse. That it all really was unexcused. He's the reason you still get to play. Doesn't that mean anything?" He paused in mid-shut.

"I'll think about it," he said, and then closed the door all the way.

CHAPTER 7

Homecoming week was busy. Every day was a different day to dress up to show your school spirit. Monday was pajama day, Tuesday was salad dressing day, Wednesday was 80's day, Thursday was super hero day, and Friday was spirit day. There were pep rallies, bonfires, tailgating, powder-puff football, the homecoming game, and then of course the homecoming dance. Brees and I would also find out if we'd made it into the show choir, and if we had, what parts we had received. Our tryout was pretty amazing. Neither one of us thought it was our best performance, but it had gone very well.

Julia and I made appointments to get our nails and hair done, as well as to get our eyebrows waxed on the Saturday afternoon before the dance. I wasn't crazy about the eyebrow appointment, but Julia assured me it would be worth it. We had a great time on our girls' day. Julia's sister Eleesia took us to the mall and picked us up when we were done. We had a blast trying on dresses, laughing at each other in terrible gowns, and oohing and awing at the fabulous ones. Dad was very specific about the instructions for me. Nothing too short or too revealing. He said he was confident that I knew what that meant and if I didn't he would promptly have me take the dress back and then come back out to shop with him and Grandpa, and if that didn't work, then I didn't go. I took the hint to heart and made my selection with his words in mind.

Julia chose a short Blush cover dress that was one shouldered. That shoulder had a pretty ruffle that flowed from the top of the sleeve across the middle of the dress to the other side. I loved it. She topped it off with a pair of Blush open toed heels, a pair of black teardrop earrings, a sparkly arm bracelet, a huge Blush colored bauble ring, and a black clutch. Her hair would cascade down the opposite side of the ruffle. She was going to look fabulous.

I chose a bluish-purple (I said it's blue, but Julia argued me down that it was purple) halter Maxi dress with knitted lines across the top. It cinched in at the waist and had a full sheer skirt that met my feet at the floor. A blue slip hit my knees beneath the dress so that you could only see through it from the knee down. I would get my hair flat ironed and then pulled back in a sleek ponytail. I chose a gold bracelet and large gold shimmery hoops with a matching clutch. My shoes were gold pumps with satin bows that I would tie around my ankles. I would look fabulous. It was exciting to think about and look forward to. All I had to do now was get through this week reasonably unscathed, and everything would be good. Brevin would borrow his mom's SUV and six of us would go to dinner. Brevin and I, Julia and Brees, and Q and his "friend" Jess. Brevin said we would meet the rest of his friends and their dates there.

My family loved my dress. Even KJ said I looked nice. He and Mia were going to ride with some of her friends and their dates alongside Isaiah, Trey, and their dates. He wasn't excited about it, though. His mind was where it always was: on the game. There was no way he would let his team lose their homecoming game. Right now the team was 5-0 and he intended on keeping it that way.

He may have intended on winning the game, but the battle at home was still being lost. Dad and KJ still were not on speaking terms. As excited as I was about all of the events at school, my mind began to settle on Mom. She wouldn't get to see me go to my real first dance with my first real boyfriend. That thought saddened me. I would go into her room and show her before I left. I would have that moment with her, and even if she couldn't enjoy it, I would. I wouldn't let the devil steal my joy. No, not this time.

Monday came and Brees and I sprinted to the choir classroom to see the results, nearly breaking our necks in the process. We were super excited and super nervous at the same time. We both had on those footed one-piece pajamas. Running in those on a newly waxed floor is probably not the best idea.

There was already a crowd gathered when we arrived, and people promptly began to congratulate us. We had gotten the leads! I jumped up into Brees' arms and we screamed like two six-year-old girls. This would be the beginning of a great week. Of course not everyone was happy for us. But we had earned our spots and were determined to prove it.

On Wednesday we found out that Brevin was nominated for the homecoming court. This was a seniors-only privilege. I was excited for him. He gave off the air that he didn't care, but I knew he did. My only reservation was whether he was okay with going to the dance with a sophomore. I worried that it bothered him and that his peers would say something, but if he did have reservations, he hid them well. There were a few occasions when I wanted to say something but then I decided that I'd rather not. Living in my fantasy world where everything was nice and cozy and tied up in a neat little bow was good enough for me.

Friday night KJ threw three touchdowns and ran the ball in himself for the final play. Dad, Grandma, and Grandpa could hardly contain themselves. The score was 28-7. Halftime would be the moment of truth. This is when they would announce who won homecoming king and queen. It was the first time that I felt a little jealous. Brevin had to escort a very pretty girl named Emma to the middle of the field. I felt a pain as they smiled at each other and waved to the crowd. And when I saw them holding hands my attitude kicked in. Brees and Julia tried to assure me that that this was what all of the couples did, that it meant nothing, and that I needed to calm down. I did on the outside, but on the inside I was fuming. Brevin not winning was bittersweet and her not winning was even better. Of course I wanted my boyfriend to win, but if he had, they would have hugged each other and then all of the other girls would have hugged him too. Then at the dance they would all want to dance with him and I wasn't sure how much of that I could handle. I was ready to have my man back.

Saturday was a whirlwind adventure of hair, nails, and make-up. Julia came over to my house to get dressed and to wait for the boys. We would pick up Q and Jess on our way to the restaurant. They chose a quaint little spot called Magnolia's. I'd never been there before but I was really excited to go. KJ looked nice. He wore all black with a white tie. Leave it to him to find a way to stand out. Since Brevin was the only person that I had told about my mom, it was a little nerve-racking having Julia over. The topic would come up eventually, and I would tell both her and Brees when the time was right.

Once I was fully dressed, I broke away and went into Mom's room so she could see me, so she could hear me, and I could feel her. I sat on her bed and told her all about my night - who I was going with, where we were going, and how excited I was. I told her how nice KJ looked and how I didn't know which accent color to use with my outfit. I had always thought that silver was the best accent color for blue but my dress what kind of bluish purple and when I put on the gold, I knew it was the right choice. Then a wave of emotion hit me like never before. I laid down and put my face on her face and before I knew it, tears started to come out of my eyes.

"It's my first real dance," I said between sniffles. "I promised myself that I would have a good, no, a great time. We have been through so much, and Brevin says that I deserve some happiness, but that I owe it to myself to make it happen. I pray for you, sometimes so long that my knees begin to wobble. This is the time in my life when you are supposed to be here for me! I know that sounds selfish, and I know I should be grateful that you are still here." I paused, determined to get myself back together. "I am so sorry that this happened to you. I want you to know that I love you very much and that I will have a great time tonight and that it is ok. I hope you are happy wherever you are. Just do not forget to come back to us, please. We need you too."

I got up and grabbed some tissues to wipe her face where my mascara had run. As I started to pull away, something miraculous happened. Mom took her hand and raised it slowly to my head. I had a hard time holding my breath. I couldn't help but wonder if this was reality or another daydream? I shivered slightly as she started at the top of my hair and moved it down, intently touching every crevice of my face. As I unsuccessfully fought tears for the second time I watched the pain in her eyes turn to longing. She wanted to come back to us. I placed my hand on top of hers to help guide her. She squeezed my hand slightly and closed her eyes as it moved from my face to her chest.

I went into her bathroom to get myself together again. I sighed heavily, half from disbelief and the rest from relief. I said a little prayer and praised God for His faithfulness. I wanted Him to know that I was grateful for that experience with Mom. It was what I needed to move forward in faith, and what a blessing for Him to give it to me tonight. I didn't want to keep the others waiting, so I headed back to my room so I could fix my makeup. On my way to my endeavor I ran into dad. He saw me as I closed the door to their room. I guess he could tell that I had been crying because he gave me a big hug.

"You are beautiful," he said genuinely. I smiled.

"I messed up my makeup, though," I responded.

"You don't need it," he said. Then he put his hands on my elbows. "I want you to have a good time tonight. Do not worry about anything. Let Daddy take care of all of this. You be a carefree teenager tonight and have a responsibly great time."

"I will," I said. He hugged me again. Just then I heard KJ's voice.

"Can I get in on some of this?" His voice not only surprised us, but himself as well. The look on his face denoted that he couldn't believe he said that out loud.

"Of course," Dad answered. And we all hugged. We used to do this all the time before the *Event*. All five of us would come in for a group hug. It could be serious or silly. It was a sign of unity. I would have never thought in a million years that only three of our family would be left. This was significant and special, an indicator of forgiveness and change for all of us. I decided to keep my encounter with Mom for myself until they needed it. Right now, just having each other was enough, but God had given me a special gift and I was determined to hold onto it.

Brevin and Brees had impeccable timing. After getting blinded by the myriad of pictures Grandma took, we were free to go. Brevin was given strict instructions by his mom to take pictures on his phone to send to her before we went to the dance. We also had to stop by Julia's house so that her mom could do the same. We finally picked up Q and Jess and, after Jess's mom snapped a bunch of pictures, headed out to dinner. Brevin opened the door for me and told the others to go ahead and get our table. We'd be there shortly.

"First," he said softly, "I want to tell you how beautiful you are. You are beautiful without all of this, but when I first saw you, I almost cursed. I still can't believe you are mine." I blushed and looked down. "Second," he said as he pulled out a beautiful purple and gold corsage, "this is for you." It was purple calla lilies with baby's breath and gold glitter sprinkled over it with gold ribbon. I knew he had spoken to Julia as I had told him my dress was blue.

Nevertheless, it matched perfectly. "Third," he said, his voice more serious now. "I just wanted to make sure you were okay." I knew immediately what he was talking about. I wasn't sure if it was just my imagination, but at Julia's house and then again at Jess' house, I'd felt like he was holding me a little closer, being a little more clingy than usual, especially when their moms were around. He was trying to protect me. Now I knew it was true.

"I am great," I assured him. "I spoke to mom before I left. Showed her my dress. It was good." I gave him a kiss on the cheek. "Thanks," I said. He took a deep sigh of relief.

"Let's eat, then." I smiled on the inside, knowing that it showed on the outside. We walked hand in hand into the restaurant and into the rest of the night.

Brevin was a surprisingly good dancer. I liked it. When he took breaks, I danced with Brees and Julia. We had a blast. We did the Cupid Shuffle, the Harlem shake, and any other dance craze that you would think of. Brees was a great dancer. He taught me how to do the Dougie right there in the middle of the dance floor. I know I looked like a fool by the way they were all laughing at me, but I didn't care. I was having a great time.

Q and Jess just sat a table the whole night watching everyone else. When Brevin took a break, that's where he sat. I felt sorry for Jess. Who would want to sit and look at Q and listen to his mundane sarcasm? When I asked them why they weren't dancing, Q simply said that he did not dance. KJ didn't dance either, although Mia did get him up for a few slow dances.

By the end of the night, our heels were off and our hair was unkempt, but we'd had a blast. When the DJ said it was the last song most of the students protested and begged him for more. The school officials ushered everyone off the dance floor as the last note of the last song played. My first homecoming had come and gone in a flash, and it was fabulous.

The school year began to roll right along. The week after Homecoming, Show choir rehearsals began and between that, homework, seeing Brevin, and church, my life was pretty full. I rarely had any down time which was how I liked it. The football team won districts but lost at regionals. KJ really made a name for himself in the high school football world here in Virginia. He was voted 1st team quarterback out of every school in the state. He and Mia were still going strong which was a surprise to me. I thought it was just a summer thing based on his track record.

Show choir was going well too. It was a little difficult at first as I had to learn Mrs. Joyner's teaching style, but I got it eventually. Brees and I had amazing chemistry on stage. He was so easy to talk to, as was Julia. The three of us could get on the phone together and talk for hours about nothing. Those were the best conversations. It wasn't until the week before the show choir performed in December that one of our conversations turned serious. I'd known it was coming, and it was time.

"Are your parents coming to the Show?" asked Julia.

"My whole family is," Brees answered.

"Yeah, mine too," I said.

"Your mom too?" Julia asked.

I stopped mid-thought. That question had thrown me for a loop.

"Yeah," Brees chimed in. "Will she be flying in from California?"

It was obvious that this had been discussed. Whether it was together or not was irrelevant. I hadn't told them, so they came up with their own theory. They were my friends. They deserved to know the truth.

"She doesn't live in California," I told them. There was silence on the other end. I knew they thought she was dead and were regretting their decision to bring it up. I quickly put them out of their misery by telling that she was here in Virginia with us, but that she wasn't well, and that is why they had never met her.

They quickly apologized but also had questions. How sick? What did she have? What is wrong with her? Will she be ok? I answered all of their questions with the sketchiest of details so that I didn't have to relive anything that would trigger an emotional response for me. I had been doing well. I could never forget, but I could manage.

All I told them was that my mother had had a breakdown and that the nurses were helping her get herself back together. Their responses were, "Oh Wow" and, "I am sorry to hear that." I was glad they didn't ask any follow up questions because I didn't want to answer them. I think they knew that. All I asked for in return for the information that I trusted them with was that they pray for her. They assured me they would.

We would perform the Show several times, once in front of the school, once in the evening for parents, and then we would take it on the road. There was a district Show choir competition between the eight local high schools. First and second place moved onto the state competition in Virginia Beach, VA in which we would go against at least 100 schools in the state. The top two from there would then go to the finals in New York City to face schools from all of the country. This was Mrs. Joyner's dream. Just to make it to New York City. She said that with the talent she had this year, if we really pushed ourselves and listened, we could make it. I couldn't help but make it my dream too. This was every performer's dream. To perform in New York City! I'd never been there, but I was certainly stoked to go. We could do this. The Show was good—really good

Because of our performance of "My Boo," by Alicia Keys and Usher, Mrs. Joyner elected to write it into the Show. We also sang "Call Me Maybe," by Carly Rae Jepsen, the first song Keith and Roxie (Brees' and my characters) sing when they first meet. Brees did not love the name Keith, but Mrs. Joyner said it was very masculine name and Brees needed to stop crying and move on because it wasn't changing. I loved the name Roxie. It almost gave me an alter ego, allowing me to see a side of myself that I didn't feel like I had. Roxie was edgy and confident. She knew what she wanted and went after it. She had a drive and determination that I could only pray for. She had found her voice. It made me want to find mine.

The second song, "Crazy in Love," by Beyoncé was the next step in a typical teenage love story. It conveyed where I was in my relationship with Brevin. Next, as in all relationships, there must be some drama, as in that late 90's classic by Brandy and Monica: "The Boy is Mine." Melissa starts showing Keith some unwanted attention which makes Roxie insanely jealous. She confronts Melissa, which results in the song. Melissa knows that she has gotten under Roxie's skin and stages a situation that makes it look like Keith likes her too! Roxie's heart is broken and she breaks up with Keith. Despite his many efforts, she sings, "We are never getting back together," by Taylor Swift and she means it! Fast forward ten years down the road, Roxie and Keith meet unexpectedly and sing together one last time. They have very different lives and recognize the love they had can never be again, but they will always be each other's boo.

I was super excited about the Show. I told Mom about it every night. The encounter had renewed my faith even though she hadn't done anything like it since. I didn't forget what God had done for me, but I wanted more. Every time that I didn't get it, I started to feel like it had just been a tease. The night before our performance in front of the school, I realized that she was not going to be there. I mean she *really* wasn't going to be there, and I think it broke my heart. It was the second performance that she wouldn't be at. The first was a Christmas program in California. That had been hard, but I'd managed. This time, for some reason, it really hurt. I wanted her to be there.

The only person I could turn to was God. He was the only one that could help. He had already shown Himself through her smile and the touching of my face. Surely He would come through for this too. I went to my Bible. I knew there were a couple of verses that spoke about faith. I did believe, I could do this, God could do this, and God would do this. All I had to do was believe. I looked in the concordance and found the word "faith." There were several verses, but the one I was looking for was found in Matthew 17:20. It was right after the disciples asked Jesus why they couldn't drive out a devil. His response was exactly what I was looking for. It read: "He replied, 'Because you have so little faith. Truly I tell you, if you have faith as small as a mustard seed, you can say to this mountain, "Move from here to there," and it will move. Nothing will be impossible for you.'" All I needed was to have faith, not even a lot, just a little -the size of a mustard seed. Then nothing would be impossible to me. Nothing.

Later that evening, during my nighty conversation with Brevin, I asked him if he would pray with me.

"About the Show?" he asked. "Are you nervous? Are you afraid?"

"No and no," I responded. "I want to pray for my Mom. That she will be better, and that she will come." There was silence on the other end.

"We pray for your mom all the time," he responded. "Of course we can do that."

"No," I responded. "This time is different."

"How so?" he inquired.

"This time, I want to pray with faith that she really will be healed."

"But we always pray that she will be healed," he said.

"I know," I said. "But when we pray, I believe that she will be healed…eventually. But I want to really believe. I want to have that faith of a mustard seed. I want us to have that faith of a mustard seed

110

that tomorrow night, when I look out at the crowd, she will be there…for real."

We sat in silence for what felt like a long time after that, so long that I asked Brevin if he was still there. He was.

"Tonight," he said, "we will pray for your mom with the faith of a mustard seed, we will pray with expectancy. It will not be lip service, but faith service. It's time that we did this thing right and put our faith truly to work. The Bible says that when two or more are gathered in His name, He is there in the midst. The Bible also says that He will do exceedingly above all that we dare to ask and imagine, so that we might receive."

So right there, at 8:59 p.m. in my bedroom, on my cell phone with Brevin on the other end, I prayed like I had never prayed before. I had prayed before out of desperation. I had prayed out of grief and hoped that God would come through. But this time I prayed in faith, knowing that He would come through. The peace I felt afterwards was amazing and indescribable. I couldn't wait to go to sleep so that I could wake up to the miracle we had prayed for. No one could tell me that it was not going to come true. It was, and I knew it.

The next morning seemed to come just as quickly as me closing my eyes. Unsure of what my next move should be, I laid in bed in quiet anxiousness. Should I run to her room or let her come to me? All the while I was fighting this sense of dread that was filled with the "what ifs," the disbelief, the snap-out-of-it-this-is-the-real-world-it's-not-gonna-happen. It had to happen. My mind was made up! I quieted the other thoughts that tried to take over and strengthened my resolve. I would go to her and she would be perfect.

I rolled out of bed, took a deep breath, and prayed as I walked. God was a good God, a faithful God, and I believed in Him and His Word. I had the faith. Now it was His turn.

I opened Mom's door and walked right up to her bed. My jaw dropped when I realized that she wasn't there. She was ALWAYS there! My emotions and my heart were racing all at one time! Where was she? Was she downstairs talking to Dad? Out on a walk with Grandpa? Making breakfast with Grandma? I raced down the stairs and yelled at the top of my lungs

"Dad! Dad! Mom is…" I slid into the kitchen and found Dad with a bewildered look on his face, sitting at the table, drinking his coffee. Grandma stood at the oven with the same look on her face. They knew. "Mom's not in her room!" I said emphatically and out of breath.

They both stared at me like I was crazy but said nothing.

"Well," I started, "where is she?"

"Calm down, Ken. The nurse has to leave early so she came early and is giving your mom her bath. She's fine."

"What do you mean by fine?" I asked as I slowly moved toward him.

"I mean she is with the nurse, getting her bath, like normal." Dad must have seen the look of disappointment on my face because he said, "You didn't think I meant she was better, did you?" I looked up. He shook his head. "Oh Ken, I'm sorry, I…" I put my hand up to stop him. I didn't want to hear this. Grandma offered me breakfast but I had lost my appetite. After I left, I could vaguely hear them questioning why today of all days I would think that Mom would be okay. It hurt them to see me like that, and they were worried.

But the day was not over yet. I had a lot to look forward to. Two shows, one for the student body, and one for the parents at night. God had all day to come through for me. And I was still confident that He would.

When Brevin picked me up for school I told him what happened, but that I was ok. I still believed that she would be better, today.

"Kennedy, I don't want you to get your hopes up," he said.

"What do you mean?" I asked.

He took a deep breath.

"I don't know how to say this. It's not that God can't heal your mom. He can. But what happens if he chooses not to? Are you going to be okay with that?"

"Chooses not to? Why would He choose not to? Why would He choose to have her suffer, to have us suffer? Haven't we been through enough? What are you saying? Why would you say that? I have faith. That's all it takes."

He could tell I was getting upset, and I was.

"I don't know the answers to all of your questions. But you can't put a time limit on God or dictate what he is going to do. I didn't say he wouldn't, I just want you to be ok if he doesn't."

I couldn't help but become angry, hurt and confused. All of the scriptures that Brevin had fed me, all of the youth meetings we attended where they talked about God and how He was kind and loving and all we had to do was believe. What was the point if, we couldn't act on it? I didn't say anything to him. I couldn't. If he didn't believe, I could believe all by myself. I didn't need him. This was between God and me. God had already shown me that He could come through, so my faith was strong. I wouldn't let Brevin ruin this with his unbelief.

Unwanted tears started to stream down my face. Brevin tried to touch my hand but I snatched it away. As far as I was concerned, if he wasn't for me, he was against me.

"Kennedy…" he tried. But I just turned my head and looked out of the window. I couldn't wait to get out of his car and get away from him. As soon as he turned the key, I was out of there without a word. I had classes to get to and a performance to prepare for. I didn't have time for this, and I didn't have time for him.

As I walked into the school I couldn't believe how abandoned I felt by him. I thought we were in this together. Out of everyone who loved and cared about me, I thought Brevin could understand my faith. But I couldn't allow myself to be around naysayers. I was fighting enough of that in my own head. I couldn't handle it from him as well.

The first part of the day went by in a blur. As I walked through the hallways, people talking and laughing, I felt like I was all alone. As the teachers taught, I remained unmoved. No one called on me. It was as if they knew.

Life kicked back in when it was time to get ready for our school performance. I was excited. There was a nervous energy in the air that I thrived on. I was about to do what I did best, and the whole school was going to see it, see me, for the first time. I was making my own identity. I would no longer be KJ's twin or Brevin Johnson's girlfriend. They were about to see me for who I really was, and I couldn't wait.

Brees pulled me aside and asked me if I was ok. Both he and Julia had noticed that I was in a mood and decided together that they had better leave me alone. I smiled.

"I'm good," I said. He smiled.

"It's time," he said. "Let's go."

The crowd was wild from the moment Mrs. Joyner stepped onto the stage to set up the story to the first note of the first song. When I glanced out into the crowd, I couldn't see anyone, just outlines of where people would be. I could hear them, though, and that put me in my zone.

When the show ended, the students were on their feet. Mrs. Joyner was on the side of the stage jumping and clapping. Brees and I hugged, both out of breath, sticky and sweaty. It was exhilarating. Mrs. Joyner came between us and grabbed our hands as we all bowed. It was wonderful and all I could think about was the fact that Mom would see the show tonight and that she would love it. After washing off and changing my clothes I remembered that I wasn't speaking to Brevin and that I was going to walk home. I was still upset with him, but I couldn't wait to get home to see what God had done while I was at school.

As I walked out I ran into KJ. He gave me a big hug.

"You did a great job today. Proud of you, sis." I smiled.

"Yeah," Mia chimed in. "I didn't know you could sing like that." That started it. As I made my way through the hall, other students, teachers, and administrators, all came up to me and told me what a great job I had done and how they hadn't known I had that inside of me. They told me it was amazing and they couldn't wait to see me perform it again.

With all of the compliments, all of the accolades, there was only one that I was waiting to hear from and she was at home. I walked out the door and headed home. I hadn't heard from or seen Brevin all day which was probably best. I was focused on my faith. I needed God to come through.

When I got home, I found the house very quiet and no one was around. I went straight up to Mom's room and found her there in her bed as usual. I told her about the performance today and my disagreement with Brevin. I told her that I looked forward to seeing her tonight, gave her a kiss, and walked out. I felt a pain as I shut the door. But I was determined to hold onto my faith. Yes, Mom was the same, but that didn't mean that she was going to stay that way. Have faith, I told myself. He will not let you down.

When Dad got home, I asked him if he would bring Mom to my performance. He gave me a look that asked, "Are you crazy?" and then shook his head and said no.

"Why?" I inquired aggressively. He paused.

"Kennedy, you know why. What is going on with you? Why would you even ask that?" He seemed annoyed.

"I just really want her to come," I said.

"I can't Kennedy. What if she has a spell and starts screaming and crying, what if she has to use to bathroom and goes on herself, what if she refuses to walk? There are just too many variables. I know you miss her. I know you want her there and I am so sorry that she can't be. But I will be there, and so will Grandma and Grandpa. I know we can't take her place, but we are going to try. Life is not fair Kennedy. It's not fair for you to be so young and to have to go through so much. It's not. And if I could change it, I would. But I can't, and I am sorry."

"Fine," I replied and went straight up to my room where I stayed until it was time to go. Grandma knocked and tried to get me to come out but I didn't say a word. Grandpa made his feeble attempt next. Nothing. They must have really been desperate because even KJ came. Nothing. I couldn't speak. I just couldn't. I had closed the door on my heart, thoughts, and emotions, and I was merely existing while maintaining a glimmer of faith that God would still come through.

When it was time to go, I noticed that she wasn't better. He didn't come through... I felt nothing. I couldn't. I went and performed the show as though everything was alright. It wasn't. I don't think I had ever been so broken. Never. Not the night of the *Event*, not when Mom left, nothing. And I couldn't feel. It affected me in a way that I didn't think was possible. It hurt... a lot. I felt like I was screaming. Screaming loudly, desperately. Everyone around me was smiling, patting me on the back, hugging me, and I am screaming. No one cared. To be let down by humans was one thing, but to be let down by God was another. I had lost my only hope. It was gone and so was I.

Everyone congratulated me after the show. KJ came again, which surprised me, and gave me another big hug. This one almost made me cry. I was going through so much emotional turmoil inside that it was hard for me to keep it in, but I did. Dad, Grandma, and Grandpa followed suit. When asked if I wanted to go out for ice cream afterwards I declined, telling them there was a cast party that I wanted to go to. Brees' parents would bring me home. Dad sighed. Grandma smiled. Grandpa said he was going with or without me. KJ was gone.

This was the first time I point blank lied since I could remember.

There was no party. I didn't have a ride home. I didn't want to pretend to be happy. I wasn't. And I wasn't in the mood to fake it. I just wanted to be alone.

As I packed up all of my things and said goodbye to everyone I started to realize how lonely I was. I couldn't believe how hollow in such a short amount of time I had allowed myself to get. At this point I didn't care about anything, least of all me. I started to wonder if this was the place that Mom had traveled to. A place where, if you didn't care about anything, then nothing could hurt you. That's what made it safe. I started to understand why she'd go there. There was nothing really to live for. Nothing and no one to stop the pain of being in this world. It made sense for her to run. I wasn't far behind her. I had never pegged myself as a quitter, but today I had discovered that there was no hope. There was nothing to believe in. Nothing for me.

The school emptied as I wallowed in my self-pity and left the dressing room. I didn't know where I was going or what I was doing. I felt so suffocated. Just when I felt like I was going to explode, I heard my name. I turned. It was Brevin. I stood. With each step he took toward me I began to break. Slowly at first and then more rapidly as time passed. When he grabbed me I was already a mess. I don't know how long we stood there, with me crying and let out all of the pain, hurt, and anger while he did everything in his power to be strong for me, holding me up, stroking my hair, and quieting my cry. By the time I finished, his shirt was soaked and I was empty. We walked quietly hand in hand to his car where I sat and cried some more. Why was this happening? Why was this my life? Why did God hate me?

"God doesn't hate you," Brevin said. I looked up. It was the first time he'd spoken. I must have asked the questions that I thought were in my head aloud. He grabbed my hand and looked me deep in my eyes.

"I can't even imagine what you have been through," he started. "And it sucks. It really does. Being a Christian doesn't mean that we will never have to go through anything. It means that when we do go through something, God will be there for us. You didn't just have one big blow, you've had two. And that really sucks. And I hate that this is happening to you, but part of having faith is knowing that no matter what it looks like, it will all work out for good. I know it's easier said than done, coming from the kid who hasn't really been through anything. But when my time comes, and it will, I am going to stand and believe that God will come through on His timing, not ours. Will your mom be healed? Yes, I believe she will. But it is not up to us to dictate when. It's up to us to have the faith and patience to wait until God says it's time. Until then, He will take care of you, He will sustain you. Hasn't He so far?"

I sat and thought for a moment. And after fighting through all the anger and disappointment, I finally started to remember...started to recognize that God had. Things were hard, granted, but things were also good. We didn't need anything. I had Dad, KJ, Grandma, and Grandpa. And Mom. I still had Mom. She was still alive. I had the best friends a girl could ask for in Brees and Julia. And I had Brevin. I had Brevin, who had brought me back from falling into the trap that Mom had sunk into. Brevin, the one who helped me regain my faith. Brevin, the young man who was my first love.

"Yes," I answered.

"Alright then," he said. "You alright?" I managed a half smile.

"I think so," I said. We sat in his car and talked until right before curfew.

When I got home Dad was waiting.

"Hey kid," he said. "How was the party?" I sat down next to him and told him everything. I thought he would be furious. He wasn't. He hugged me and I promised that I would never do it again. He wasn't happy but he wasn't angry either. He said he understood and that we are all dealing with this the best way we could, and for the record, I was doing a pretty good job. He was proud of me but warned me not to lie to him again. I told him I wouldn't and he said he believed me. I was relieved and blessed indeed.

CHAPTER 8

Christmas Break was coming up and I was super excited. We all were. Twelve days without any school, without any rehearsals, just a chance to relax. Districts for show choir were not until February, so Mrs. Joyner gave us a well-deserved break. She said we could perfect the show later. We had plenty of time. The news came as a shock to us because, as far as we were concerned, the show was already perfect…but what did we know? She had been to districts before and won, and she had even gone to regionals. She was gunning for state and the nationals, and she believed that we were the crew that could pull it off if we perfected our performance.

"Have a good break and rest up," she said. "You will need it!"

My biggest problem was what to get Brevin for Christmas. After all, he was my first boyfriend, and boys are the hardest to buy for. Trying to ask him what he wanted was no good. His answer was 'nothing'. All he needed was me. As much as I loved Brevin, his sweetness sometimes was a little too much. He was like that all of the time! Did this boy ever get upset about anything? Sometimes it was hard dating a super saint! I felt like he was the closest to perfect as one could get without being Jesus. I had a hard time believing I deserved him and understanding why he would want me. But, at any rate, I was very happy with him. Sometimes I thought he'd saved my life. I don't know what I would have done had he not shown up that night after my performance. It's something that I try not to think about.

My friends were no help.

"Get him cologne," Brees said. "Every man likes to smell good."

"How about a pair of earphones?" Julia suggested. "You know

those Beats by Dre."

KJ was no better.

"Get him a Bible. Never mind, he probably has a lot of those."

Grandma said he already had the best gift, which was me. When I told her that he said the same thing, she said, "my point exactly." Grandpa agreed with Grandma. And Dad said to get him nothing.

"If he says he doesn't want anything then don't get him anything. It's really my money anyway."

I wanted what I got him to be special. But time was running out and I had been to mall what seemed like thousands of times and always come back with nothing. He never even asked me what I wanted. He just kept saying how perfect the gift he'd found for me was.

Mom was still the same. It took me a couple of days after the performance to get back to my routine. I don't know why I was so afraid to go back in there. I just was. But I started to miss her, and missing her overrode my fear. I loved her so much. It didn't matter if she spoke to me or not. Just knowing she was there was somehow enough.

"Hey Mom," I said, sitting on her bed next to her a few days before Christmas. "It's our first day out of school for Christmas break. It feels like a relief. I've been so busy with school work and the show that I am ready to do absolutely nothing. I just don't know what to get Brevin for Christmas. I don't like anyone's suggestions, so I guess I'll have to figure it out on my own. I can hear you saying, 'just choose something from your heart,' and I am trying. I just don't know what." Then it hit me. "Choose something from the heart." I gave Mom a big wet one on the cheek. "Thanks!" I ran to my room to get to work.

Grandma and Grandpa were super excited for Christmas. It had been years since they'd had their whole immediate family together for the holidays. Last Christmas they traveled to California to be with us in Mom and Rylie's absence. The year before that they had traveled to be with their son's family for the holidays. They had two children: Mom and her older brother MJ, which stood for Monroe Willis Lee Jr. Uncle MJ was married and lived in Montana. Grandma and Grandpa always like to tell the story of when I was five and I found out that was where he lived. I asked innocently why he lived there and said, "They have black people in Montana?" To this day I have no clue where that came from. It was during a time when I was just discovering that I was a mixture of two cultures and wanted to understand how I got that way. My cousins Bailey and Christian (Uncle MJ's children) were all one color, as was everyone else who I knew at the time. How come we weren't? I didn't like feeling different, and as much as Mom and Dad tried telling me that it was a blessing to be more than one culture and that I was special, I couldn't help feeling like I wished that I was either one or the other. It wasn't until I began school and started seeing children who looked like me that those feelings subsided. In California, tan children like me were the norm. Whether they were bi-racial, Korean, Hispanic, Indian, etc., it didn't matter, so it no longer mattered to me.

Bailey was an eighteen-year-old college freshman, and Christian was the same age as KJ and me. He and KJ had always been close. Every time they saw each other it seemed as if no time had passed. He was the only one who got KJ to speak when we were at Rylie's funeral, the last time we were all together.

Aunt Ronna was their mother, who from what I understand, has always been a part of the family. My aunt and uncle were high school sweethearts who knew each other in grade school. She received a full academic scholarship to the University of Montana and Uncle MJ followed her there.

They were flying in on Christmas Eve and staying through the New Year, splitting up their time between Aunt Ronna's family and us. Grandma would cook us all Christmas Breakfast and they would come over so we could eat and open presents together. They would spend the remainder of the day with Ronna's family, and we were invited as well. It took a lot of wrangling, but Dad agreed to let me go over to Brevin's for Christmas dinner. We would exchange our gifts with one another over there.

Having everyone together on Christmas was awesome. It almost made me forget that Mom was not there. There was a lot of laughing, excitement, and love. My favorite gift had to be a calendar Bailey gave me. It had pictures on it from our past. She watched me intensely as I flipped through the pages. I saw old pictures of us with Mom and Rylie in happier times. On the side of the calendar were words of strength, I guess to keep me going when times got tough. I appreciated it and told her so. She said she wasn't sure if it was too soon, but in her studies she had found that we need to embrace our losses and focus on the good times to keep us moving in the right direction. She thought this would help. I gave her a big hug and thanked her for thinking of me. That's what reminded me that Mom was missing. As soon as we finished breakfast, I went up for our daily talk.

Brevin picked me up around 5, right before the rest of the family was heading out. As soon as they saw Brevin, they became solemn and started acting all tough. KJ said that Brevin had better bring me back the way he takes me and that Brevin knew what he meant. Christian puffed out his chest and said, "Yeah." I rolled my eyes at both of them and pushed through the little barricade they made at the door. Brevin followed.

"What was that all about?" he asked as we got in the car.

"KJ was just showing off," I said. "Don't pay any attention to him."

Brevin's mother was always so happy to see me. She had a bubbly personality and never seemed to be agitated or upset. She always had a smile on her face. Brevin's father was always even tempered. I had never heard either of them raise their voice. I guess that's where Brevin got it from. Samantha, his nine-year-old sister, was a ball of energy that brought back memories of Rylie.

It was a much calmer existence than I was used to. Christmas music was playing in the background and the house smelled like freshly baked cookies. It was a scene from out of a perfect Christmas movie, and I was right in the middle of it. There was a ham on the table with a bunch of fixings around it such as sweet potatoes, green beans, rolls, cranberry sauce, and stuffing. There was also a pineapple upside-down cake and a plate of Christmas cookies.

After a delicious dinner, we sat in front of the Christmas tree to exchange gifts. I had imagined a more intimate setting in my mind with just the two of us, but his entire family was there, all waiting to watch the exchange. It embarrassed me a little. I really did not want Brevin to open my gift in front of them, but I didn't know what to do. I tried to tell him with my eyes but he just kept smiling and saying, "What?" Finally I gave up.

"Open mine first!" said Samantha, handing me a gift. I was delighted to see it was a very pretty bracelet made of different color beads and string. "I made it myself!" I thanked her by giving her a big hug and told her how beautiful it was. Next his parents handed me a gift. I was pleasantly surprised to find that it was a DVD of my performance in the show choir.

"We loved it," Brevin's mom said. "You are very talented. We thought you would like this as a keepsake before you make it big!" I thanked them and gave them both hugs.

Next it was Brevin's turn. He handed me a medium sized box. I was anxious to see what was inside. It was a pair of gray UGG boots with silver bows on the back! It had to have cost him close to $200.

"I love them!" I said and immediately put them on. "They are perfect!" I ran to give him a big hug but thought twice about the kiss since his whole family was watching. His mom and dad sat on the couch with his dad's arm around her, both with huge smiles on their faces. Samantha was preoccupied with a doll she had received earlier.

Next it was my turn to give my gift to Brevin. I nervously handed him the package. He opened it slowly to find a rolled up piece of parchment with a ribbon tied around it and a CD. He opened up the paper and read it to himself. His eyes lit up.

"What is it?" his mom asked eagerly. "It's a song," he said in a soft voice.

"Wow," his dad said. "She wrote you a song?"

"Yes," he said. "And it is beautiful."

"Read it," His mom said. I was begging him not to with my eyes, but he apparently didn't get the message. Brevin jumped up and put in the CD of me singing.

"Really?" I thought to myself. "In front of your parents? This was something intimate to be shared by just you." I have never seen myself turn red, but if I could turn red, I knew it was in that moment.

"For Brevin. Merry Christmas," I heard my voice say through the speakers. Then the piano began to play, and my voice came through singing these words:

It seems that I've been crying for one whole year
You can't imagine how that feels
The loneliness had finally crept in
The nightmare had become real
I thought I walked the path all by myself
Looking for a place to hide
And just when I thought there was no one else
God placed you by my side

And I will be forever grateful
And I will be forever in love
And I will be forever grateful
To the Man up above
For sending me my love...

It seems that I'd been dying for one whole year
Pieces slowing fading away
Looking at reflections of myself
Hoping that I would be okay
Thinking that my prayers had done no good
Thinking that I was on my own
And just when I had given up on hope
You showed me that I was not alone

And I will be forever grateful
And I will be forever in love
And I will be forever grateful
To the Man up above
For sending me my love

I appreciate your heart...
I appreciate your love
I appreciate all that you are
My gift sent from above
Thank you Lord for sending my love

It seems like I've been running for one whole year
Trying to catch up with myself
You came along and showed me that it's okay
To slow down
And to take it day by day
To slow down
And to get on my knees and pray
To slow down
And that God will make a way...

As I heard my fingers hit the last note on the piano, I heard clapping. I looked and it was Brevin's parents. His mother was wiping tears from her eyes and his father looked thoroughly impressed.

"Were you playing the piano too?" he asked in between claps.

"Yes," I answered proudly. "It was my first instrument. I started when I was three. It was before I discovered my voice."

"It was lovely," Brevin's mom managed to squeak out. I thanked them for their kind words, but it was really Brevin that I was interested in. What did he think? As I turned my head from his parents I noticed him walking toward me. He planted one right on my lips in front of everyone. I tried to get away but he held me close. Once I realized I was stuck I relaxed into the kiss. As if I wasn't embarrassed enough, he had the nerve to tell me in front of them all that it was the best gift he had ever received and he loved me. I put on a nervous smile. I know he was waiting for me to say it back, but I couldn't. All eyes were on us. Samantha broke the tension by letting out a very guttural sounding "eww" which made us all laugh and relieved the awkwardness. I was so relieved when his mom asked if anyone wanted to play Scattergories. It took the focus off of me.

After four exhilarating games it was time for Brevin to take me home. I hugged everyone and thanked them for their gifts before heading out to the car. It had been a good night. I didn't want to ruin it by starting anything but I did request that Brevin never kiss me in front his parents again. I would die if he ever did that in front of mine and he would probably die as well… literally. He didn't seem to think it was a big deal but if I didn't like it, he wouldn't do it again. I also told him that he needed to work on reading my expressions better and that we needed a secret language or something like that. He laughed. He said we could work on that. I laughed too, although part of me was serious. Before I got out of the car he reiterated how much my gift meant to him and that now I could sing him to sleep. That boyfriend of mine, a little mushy, but super sweet. I loved every bit of him.

The rest of my break was spent hanging out with family, Julia and Brees, and of course Brevin. I went shopping with Aunt Ronna, Grandma, and Bailey. Grandma loved all of the after-Christmas sales. I went to the movies with Julia and Brees, and hung out with Brevin.

Brevin's seventeenth birthday was on New Year's Eve. He'd just made the cut off for school when he began kindergarten. He was always the youngest kid in his class, which was fine with me. (Had he been older, I don't think Dad would have let me date him.) We celebrated his birthday at church during the New Year's Eve service, where a party had been planned for him. There was dancing and food, and everyone seemed to have a great time! I'd bought Brevin a waterproof phone case for his IPhone, his name and a cross printed on the back of the case. He loved it, which was a great relief for me. Brees had helped me pick it out. Finding the gift was easy. Answering Brees' questions as we were shopping was the hard part. In California, there were a lot of kids who looked like me. In Virginia, not so much. But I had never felt like I was any different than anyone else. One time a lady in a supermarket started speaking to me in Spanish and I knew enough to say, "No hablo Espanol," but that was all. So I was in no way expecting questions from anyone, especially from Brees.

"So, what does it feel like?" He began. I'd had a feeling that he wanted to ask me something. He'd kept looking at me and then turning away. He would purse his lips to say something, yet say nothing. I knew it was coming. I just didn't know what.

"What does what feel like?" I asked as I put down a watch after looking at the price.

"You know…" He said as he quickly looked away.

"No," I responded, a little annoyed. "I don't. Wait…are you asking me what it's like to be a twin?" My mind rested in my discovery and was relieved that this would be easier than I had suspected. What twins doesn't get asked that multiple times in their lives? I had my standard answer ready when he interrupted what was going to be my twin spiel and said that that was not what he was talking about. Now I was thoroughly confused. My Sherlock senses were not as on point as I'd thought they were.

"Being mixed."

I didn't answer right away. I stared back as I thought. Initially my mind was blank. I didn't know if I was offended or if I should even be offended. My mind felt jumbled. Why did he ask me that? For what purpose? Was I supposed to feel a certain way? Was he serious, or was this a joke? Was it meant to be hurtful, or was he being curious?

I guess I took too long to answer because he followed up with, "I am not trying to be rude, Kennedy. I just really wanted to know. I've

125

been curious. You don't have to answer if you don't want to."

"It's fine, I guess," I responded. "I really don't think of it much anymore."

"Really?" Brees said. "Hmmm."

"What?" I retorted. "What does it feel like to be African?"

"Being African feels like sunshine," he said as he smiled. "I love the food, I love the traditions, I love the music, and I love the attitude. I love my culture and am very proud of it. That's where I'm planning to live after college. I want to go back."

"You don't like it here?" I asked.

"I like it here," he said. "But it doesn't feel like home to me. I want to go home."

"Hmm," I said out loud as I mauled over what Brees had said.

"Well, I didn't always like it," I began. "I never knew what side to really embrace," I lamented as I put down a polo shirt. "Mom's side embraced us and Dad's side rejected us. I can admit that when I think about it I feel angry and hurt. I remember the first time I had to circle in my race on a test. I didn't know what to pick, so I picked both. My teacher told me that the test couldn't read it so I had to choose one. I couldn't decide so I chose 'other.' I can't explain to you how it made me feel to choose 'other.' Almost like I didn't belong. When I asked KJ, he said he chose black. When I asked him why, he said that he looked black and felt black, so that's what he put. But I didn't feel anything like that. I didn't feel black or white. I just felt like me and no category for that. Mom was furious when I shared this with her. She made it clear that I was not other. I had a place and purpose and if I ran into that again that I should choose both or choose nothing at all. And if they had a problem with that, they could come see her."

I laughed to myself at that memory. My mother was a fireball and the school definitely didn't want that.

"But I never did," I confessed. "I chose black after that in part because KJ did, but also because that's the side that embraced me…even though I felt uneasy every time. I didn't want to disrespect my dad."

Brees was watching me. It was freeing to talk about it, so I continued. "The kids at my school weren't always nice to me. They would call me names and tell me that I didn't belong, but my parents always made sure I knew I did. They made it their mission to make sure I knew who I was and not to focus so much on what color I was, but to focus more on who God created me to be. I remember my mom standing up in church one day explaining that she was Christian before she was black. I took that and have held onto it ever since."

Brees put his arm around me and said I had gotten way too deep on him, but he appreciated me answering his question. We headed to the Apple store where we eventually found Brevin's present.

There certainly is truth to the saying that time flies when you are having fun. Before we knew it, it was time to go back to school. I was actually looking forward to it, to the show choir. It was exhausting, but I really missed it. I looked forward to taking our show on the road and seeing if we were actually as good as everyone said we were. I wanted to prove them right.

We only had three weeks of school before exams and the beginning of the second semester. Those three weeks were riddled with tests, quizzes, essays, study guides, and grueling practices for show choir. I barely saw Brevin outside of school since basketball season was now in full swing and we were both very busy. Of course we saw each other in Spanish class and at lunch every other day. We also managed to walk each other to class and religiously spoke to each other every night on the phone. Going to youth group also became hit or miss depending on what we had going on that particular Wednesday night.

I made it my business to go to all of his home games, though, and quickly discovered why he was the captain of the team. My man knew how to play basketball. He was really good. And as much as I hated to admit it, Q was really good too. Still creepy, but very good. They always seemed to know where each other were on the court. Brevin told me that they had played together as little kids. Brevin was a year older than Q and both of them had expressed that they didn't know what they were going to do without each other next year when Brevin went to college. I was starting to think about that myself.

Second semester seemed to start very quickly, and we began labs in science. I was placed in a group with two boys: the very cute Drew, who I'd noticed at the beginning of the year but paid very little attention to thereafter, and the very annoying Noah, who did absolutely nothing in class and was not expected to do anything to help us with the labs. Drew and I basically had to do all of the work ourselves which made us spend more time together. We had to get together from time to time to take care of Noah's work. It wasn't all business though, and we got to talk some and really got to know each other. He was cool, laid back, and easy to talk to. When the science fair came along we decided to do our project together and exchanged numbers. That's when the real problem began.

Brevin called me after a game one evening and he was in the middle of telling me a story about how Q stole the ball, passed it to him, and drove down the lane, when my phone beeped. It was Drew. I didn't think anything of it so I asked Brevin if I could call him back as soon as I took this phone call. It was for the science fair and of course he agreed, with no problem. While I was on the phone with Drew, it hit Brevin that he was my partner was for the project. It wasn't a secret. I'd told him we were partners when we first agreed to work together. He hadn't seemed to care then.

"Who was that?" he asked almost immediately after I called him back.

"Drew."

"Oh, so you guys have each other's number now?"

"Yeeesss..." I said almost timidly. "Is there a problem with that?"

"I guess not. It's only for the science fair, right?"

"What else would it be for?"

"Why are you evading the question?" He asked

"I'm not evading anything. What is your problem?"

"I just don't understand why you won't answer my question?"

"I did answer your question."

"No you didn't."

Now I was getting irritated.

"I have no clue what you are talking about then. Ask me again."

He was really mad now. I could tell by the tone in his voice. Mr. Even-keel who never got angry about anything was now mad and I didn't even know why.

"Oh now you don't know what I'm talking about."

"Brevin, really? What are we arguing about? The fact that Drew called me? Yes, he called me. So what! He asked me not to forget to bring in the poster board tomorrow because I forgot it today so we couldn't work on it during study hall. Is that a crime?"

Silence on the other end. I hated when he did this.

"Brevin. Brevin. Are you still there?"

"Yes I am still here. And you still have not answered my question. My question is whether or not you guys only have each other's number for the sake of the science fair?"

"And my answer is yes."

"Why didn't you say that the first time?"

"I don't understand why I had to. Is that a problem?"

"No. No problem. I just wanted an answer."

"Ok…and you got it. Now what?"

"Nothing, I guess. I'm getting tired. I'm going to bed. Goodnight."

He hung up. No "I love you," no nothing. This was a first for us. It was a first for him. I thought about calling him back, but then decided it would be better if I didn't. He wanted to sleep, so I let him. He needed time to think; so did I. But the more I thought and replayed the scenario in my head, the angrier I became. What was Brevin implying? Did he not trust me? Yes, I thought Drew was cute, but that was it. I'd never given Brevin a reason to doubt me. How could he be angry at me?

When I walked in KJ's room he was throwing a ball up against the wall and talking on the phone to Mia. Of course. I didn't expect anything less. He must have heard me because he rose up a little bit and told Mia to hold on.

"Can we talk?" I asked. He held up a finger and I waited. She must have been talking because he wasn't saying a word. After a few minutes he was finally able to get a word in.

"Mia. Yes, I'm listening. Let me call you back. Yes. Yes, I'll call you back. No. No, Mia, I need to talk to my sister. Okay. I'll call you back." He rolled his eyes.

"Issues?"

"Nah, Mia's just complaining about her stepdad like she always does. What's up?"

"I think Brevin and I just had our first official fight."

"Ah. Word? Ha ha."

"Yeah, and I'm not sure whether or not it's my fault." I relayed the story to KJ who really listened, made eye contact and everything, no distractions.

"He's just jealous, Ken."

"Of what? For what?"

"I mean Brevin's cool and all for girls *like you*. But he's got no

129

swag. Drew has swag, and Brevin knows it. He probably thinks you like him or something or that you will. I don't think he was ever okay with you guys being lab partners or science fair partners, and now he's calling you? Yep. B's jealous."

I sat on the bed and thought for a second. It wasn't until we became partners that Brevin would meet me at class and walk me to PE. His class is on the other end of the building. He swears that he is never late and even if he was, his teacher didn't care. She loved him. I didn't put two and two together until now. I'd just thought he was being his normal sweet and caring self, and that he wanted to see me more and that is why he did it. Now I was seeing it in a different light, and the color of that light was red.

"If he needs time to cool off, let him. When he's ready, he'll let you know."

KJ's phone rang and scared the crap out of both us. He answered which let me know that he was done with our conversation, so I silently slid out his room. KJ had given me good advice, but I didn't take all of it; I was too angry. The moment I stepped into my room my fingers went flying on my cell phone.

Kennedy:
Why did you start coming to Biology to walk me to P.E.?

It didn't take him long to answer. I knew he wasn't asleep.

Brevin:
What? Why are you asking me that?

Kennedy:
Because I want to know. Y?

Brevin:
The same reason I walk you to your other classes.

Kennedy:
But those classes are actually close, and you have done that since the beginning of the year. Y now?

Brevin:
This is stupid.

Kennedy:
I want the truth.

He didn't answer this one for a long time. But I waited, and waited, and waited until finally...

Kennedy:
Well...

Still nothing. Gotta love smart phones. I knew he received it because next to the text it said delivered and read. So I decided to help him.

Kennedy:
Does it have anything to do with Drew?

Brevin:
Look Kennedy, I'm really tired. I told you I was going to sleep. We can talk about this tomorrow.

Kennedy:
No. (I felt the Roxie in me coming out) I want to talk about this now.

This new firm attitude of mine must have taken him by surprise because he called almost immediately.

After our conversation, I still wasn't satisfied. So I texted Brees to see if he was still up. He was. I only gave him the highlights and he said something that I hadn't expected.

"Brevin is a bit possessive, isn't he?"

No. Not him... wait, but, well, was he? Brees stopped me in mid-thought.

"I mean for him to tell you who you can and can't talk to. That's a bit much. You guys aren't married." No, wait. What was Brees talking about? He doesn't... "The way he always has to know where you are and who you are with. And now he tells you that it's not you that he doesn't trust, it's Drew, and after the science fair he would appreciate it if you guys no longer stayed in touch. It's just too much."

I talked to Julia later, and she said nearly the same thing. I began to wonder.

Our conversation wasn't too eventful. Brevin just expressed his concern about my "budding" friendship with Drew. He wanted to make sure that it was just a "friendship." I didn't really understand why he was so concerned with Drew but never showed that concern with Brees.

"Because he is Brees," he said. I wasn't quite sure what he meant by that, but I didn't ask.

In order to ensure that my "relationship" with Drew didn't change, Brevin asked that I minimize my involvement with him. Only talk to him when I had to and only about school. I felt a little weird about it but reluctantly agreed. I loved Brevin. Why didn't he know that? Why didn't he trust me enough to know that I would ensure my relationship with Drew wouldn't change?

When I asked him those questions Brevin assured me that he trusted me and knew how I felt about him. It was Drew he didn't trust and he just needed me to trust him. So I did. That's what girlfriends do, right? But I wasn't sure, and my friends confirmed my uncertainty. They wanted to know why he always had to know where I was and what I was doing. I didn't mind telling him. He told me even when I didn't ask, so what was the big deal? Who knew that being in a relationship could be so confusing? It's not that I no longer wanted to be in the relationship, it just wasn't easy any more, and I already had too much uneasiness in my life and didn't need any more to add to the chaos. Maybe Mr. Perfect wasn't so perfect after all. This was something we would have to work out. After all, I couldn't choose my friends based on my boyfriend's insecurities. I wouldn't. This issue was far from over.

I continued to talk to Drew about school stuff and Brevin didn't say anything else about it, so neither did I. I had to focus on the upcoming show. We were going against nine other local high schools for districts and only the top two got to move on the regionals. Mrs. Joyner said we were a shoe in and she was right.

The first weekend in February we walked away with first place. We had a month to prepare for regionals and she determined that we would win that too. Things were going along pretty smoothly in my life until Valentine's Day. Brevin sent me a dozen roses at school which was kind of cool because I got to walk around with them all day and everyone knew who they were from. In the study hall, FBLA (Future Business Leaders of America) were delivering flowergrams which they were selling the previous week for a fundraiser. When they stopped by our room and handed them out I was surprised to hear my name. That Brevin, I thought. Always super sweet.

Brees and Julia gathered around me when I opened the card. Brees let out a shriek while my heart dropped. The card read:

Kennedy-
It's been real cool hanging out with you and getting to know you. Thank you for all of your help in science. My grades have never been so good. I would love to hang out with you some time for real. Away from this place...like dinner and a movie? Let me know what's up.
-Drew

"Ooh Girl, he likes you," Brees said in a mocking voice.

"Wait, wait," Julia said. "Let me see that again." She looked at it closely and, upon closer inspection, agreed with Brees.

"OMG," I said much calmer than I felt. "What do I do?"

"You have to tell Brevin," Julia said.

"Oh no she won't," Brees said. "Brevin doesn't have to know everything."

I didn't know what to do. Brevin was right not to trust Drew, but that still did not make up for his lack of trust in me. And why would Drew send this to me? He knew I had a boyfriend. Plus he was always hanging out with Devlyn, another bi-racial girl at our school. I thought he liked her. When I expressed that sentiment to my friends, Brees said they were not together, but it did show what type of girls Drew liked.

I wanted to talk to Drew first before I started speculating anything, and then I would tell Brevin. I didn't want to start anything if there was nothing there to begin with. Maybe he just wanted to hang out. Both Brees and Julia informed me that I was being naïve, but I'd better figure something out quickly because Brevin was just outside of the door. I stood up and, sure enough, that's where he was. He was talking to Q and then he made his way in. Brees grabbed the flowergram and placed it out of sight as I walked over to meet him.

"I see you got the roses."

"Yes, I love them. Thank you so much."

He smiled and then nodded and waved at Brees and Julia. They waved back and went on talking quietly to themselves.

"What's up with them?" he asked.

"We'll talk about it later."

That didn't seem to bother him. He sat down and we proceeded to talk about life. We laughed a lot and things were so uncomplicated - just the way I liked them. I didn't want to mess that up. I hoped and prayed that the note from Drew was misconstrued. I'd get to the bottom of it in biology, and then decide what to tell Brevin.

Brevin had been walking me to class for a few months now and Drew never paid any attention before, but today, for some reason, he did. He shoulder-bumped Brevin on his way in and said nothing, carrying on talking with his friends. Brevin didn't really react but gave me a look that said, "Did you see that, right?" I saw it alright and it kind of pissed me off.

When it was time for lab I just did my work and only spoke to Drew when I needed to. I no longer cared about what he'd written on the card. He was a jerk and I just wanted to get my work done. We had a bit of free time at the end and that's when he asked me if I was mad. When I didn't answer, he proceeded to ask me what I saw in that punk Brevin anyway. I just rolled my eyes. He asked me if I at least got the flowergram, which I promptly took out of my backpack and threw in the trash. He retorted that I didn't have to throw the flower away...what did the flower do to me? He had paid his hard earned money for that flower and a simple no to his proposition would have sufficed. Although I tried to be angry and pursed my lips together, a little laugh still managed to push its way through.

"There's my girl," he said.

"I'm not your girl," I retorted.

"You are right about that," he said. "Not yet." Then the bell rang.

When I recalled the story that night to Brevin on our nightly telephone conversation he didn't seem angry, he didn't seem much of anything. I thought for sure that he would have at least said he told me so, but he didn't. Instead he apologized.

"Look," he said. "I'm sorry for not trusting you. I know I said I didn't trust Drew, but what I didn't say was that I didn't trust you with him. And I'm sorry. I asked you to do something that I shouldn't have. I should have allowed you to make that decision on your own. I don't have that bad boy image that Drew has going on that so many girls are attracted to. That's just not me, but I do love you. And I just hope that's enough." It was. He continued. "I can't promise you that I won't get jealous if you decide to hang out with him. But I will try to be civil about it."

"You don't have to worry about that." I said as I had no intention of hanging out with Drew. Yes he was cute and funny, but he was not for me. The sooner he knew that, the better.

CHAPTER 9

"Second place is too close for comfort," said Mrs. Joyner the Monday after regionals. "An eighth of a point separated first and second place. The good news is that we beat third place by a considerable amount. After looking at the judges' comments and their scoring, it was our timing that was off a bit in 'Call Me Maybe.' We need to fix that and we have two weeks to do so."

States was in Virginia Beach. We were going against twenty-five teams in our division. Only the winners got to go to New York to represent Virginia. And Mrs. Joyner wanted that chance and that trophy. We'd already gotten her two, our first place in districts and our second place in regionals. But that wasn't enough for her, and frankly, it wasn't enough for us either.

Basketball season was over for Brevin, and he was awaiting acceptance letters for college. He applied to four schools in Virginia: George Mason, which was only twenty-five minutes away; James Madison, which was an hour and a half away; The University of Virginia, which was two hours away; and his number one pick, Virginia Tech, which was four hours away.

I'd be lying if I didn't say I wanted him to be close. Dad had told me this would happen, but I couldn't be selfish. I wanted Brevin to be happy and I knew that Tech would make him happy. We hadn't discussed what would happen to us when he went away. I chose not to think about it. I didn't understand his fascination with Tech, though. He didn't even know what he wanted to major in. Didn't that mean he could presumably go anywhere? His only reason for going there was because his dad went there and as a kid they used to go to all of the basketball games together, and Brevin had sworn he would play there someday. It was division one, and Brevin recognized that his dream would probably not come true. I didn't even know if he would try out, but he wanted to be a Hokie, and that was it.

Since changing lab partners, I hadn't really spoken to Drew. I had no need to. He would wink at me every now and again and say, "What's up?" from time to time, but besides that he didn't say anything. I didn't understand what was going on with him and Devlyn. They were constantly together, but he still claimed they were "just friends." I didn't even know why I cared. But secretly, I did.

We arrived at Virginia Beach the third week in March. We had an excused absence from school on Friday to travel and get settled in our hotel. It was on the beach and reminded me of home… California home. It was made of light blue stucco and had a Native American California vibe. It was crawling with the competition participants. Breese and I couldn't help but try to size up our competitions although we had no clue what division they were in.

There were three divisions depending upon school size. There was A, AA, and AAA. Our school was in the middle category. It was very exciting though. Seventy-five teams all with the same goal… to get a first place win to compete in New York. Only three overall would be successful. We would *have* to be perfect if we were going to be the AA winner. Mrs. Joyner believed in us, and I did too.

The atmosphere in the morning was magnetic. There were groups practicing dance moves and harmonizing in every crevice of space available. These groups were serious. Their intensity caused a feeling of intimidation in the air. That is when the nerves started to kick in. We had never seen anything like this. I started to question whether or not we could actually win this thing. There were male groups do whopping in the corner and acapella groups who sang the words and their own music! Even though I was nervous, I felt a sense of peace there, like I belonged in this environment.

Mrs. Joyner pulled us in and explained how it would work. She preferred that we not watch other groups perform before we did so we would not be nervous. She reminded us to hit our queues and to relax and have fun. We needed to be natural and energetic. There was no room for error. Nervousness would cause us to mess up and our voices to be shaky. We were to relax and be confident. As long as we did the best we could, she would be proud of us and we should be proud of ourselves too. "No tears!" she commanded, unless they were tears of joy.

The school performed in alphabetical order, which landed us right smack in the middle of the competition. We were number thirteen. Mrs. Joyner told us to get any superstitions about our number out of our heads. We didn't believe in superstitions in her group. We believed in the effort put forth in the performance, and that was all. Not watching the groups before us proved to be a good thing. We used our time wisely and went over steps and harmonies that seemed a little shaky in our last performance. We wanted to win our division, and we believed we would, but we wanted to at least beat the team that beat us by an eighth of a point in regionals…and we wanted to crush them. Time went by rather slowly and we found ourselves in a waiting game. We tried to stay loose, and kept our voices fresh but not overworked. It was a challenge, but it mostly challenged our patience. We were set to go at 2 p.m., but got called at 2:25, but we were ready. Mrs. Joyner gave us her last minute pep talk, a repeat of her instruction for us to stay focused, perform relaxed, and have fun. We listened intently like our lives depended on it, and then finally, it was time.

Getting on that stage for the first time in front of hundreds of people might have been frightening to some. But I loved it. I was in the place where I was most comfortable, doing what I loved most, and all eyes were on us. When the spotlight fell, I knew I was at home…it was time to perform! Every song went off without a hitch; each melody flowed in sync and each dance move followed. We transitioned from scene to scene with ease, and as we finished the closing act everyone knew that we had killed it. It was even ten seconds after we'd sung the last note that everyone starting jumping and cheering! As we ran off stage we hugged each other and wiped away "good" tears. Mrs. Joyner couldn't contain herself. She had never been so proud.

Watching the other teams perform after us proved to be entertaining and nerve racking. We saw some who were just as good as us, some who didn't even compare, and some that blew our minds. It was anybody's game, but we still felt good.

They were only going to announce the top ten. We all sat in ours seats patiently waiting for our school's name to be called. After they announced number ten, nine, and eight, we started holding hands. It was going to go one of two ways: either we were going to be called in a higher place, or not called at all. Number seven, then six, and then five… it felt as though our hearts beat in unison with anticipation. Could we have actually won this thing? Surely we had placed in the top ten…or had we? Number four…still nothing. Mrs. Joyner started looking differently at this point…her eyes were bigger and her breathing was heavier.

When they called our name for third place, there was a delayed reaction. We were so used to not hearing it, we were almost stunned. When we finally caught our breath, Brees screamed and ran up on stage. Mrs. Joyner encouraged me to go, so I went and got up on stage just after he had already gotten the trophy. Despite the fact that it was third place, the trophy was huge! Brees' Cameroonian muscles were struggling to hold it up. Mrs. Joyner kept on reiterating that we were the third best in the state.

"In the state," she said as though she was in a daze. The second place announcement broke our celebration, and we cheered for that team and the one that ultimately won first place. Second and first place were well deserved. We were not even a little bit surprised. After all of the confusion of the moment, we recognized that the team that beat us by an eighth of a point in regionals didn't even make it in the top ten. That made the win even sweeter! Nothing could bring us down.

We went back to hotel on cloud nine. Some kids were still crying and telling their parents about the experience, but we got dressed and ran down to the beach. Despite the semi warm March weather, we played in the water and ran up and down the beach until we couldn't take it any longer. Then we went back to our rooms and stayed up watching movies, talking, and laughing.

We arrived home Sunday evening after eating breakfast and an eventful bus ride home which included more singing, laughing, and talking. The excitement didn't leave us until our parents picked us up and we hugged each other goodbye. It was one of the greatest times of my life.

The next day at school, our administration made a big deal about our third place win. They allowed the students to stand in the hall at the end of first block while the drum line led us through the school with Brees and I at the helm holding up the trophy. The school cheered as we walked by and that same excitement returned. It was exhilarating, followed by all of the congratulations from the student body and the teachers.

Third block was chorus, and we spent most of the time planning our cast party. After that, Mrs. Joyner opened the official envelope that had our scores in it. She promised that she wouldn't open it until we were there. She'd kept her word despite how hard it was. First and second place were separated by 1.4 points. We were behind second place by five points. Fourth place came in two points behind us.

We'd beaten the team that beat us at regionals by 15 points, which was a huge accomplishment. Now onto the bad news. Why we lost. Dancer 3 broke formation. We all knew it was Cole. He had a voice like a song bird but danced like a drunken monkey. We couldn't even be mad at him; he tried. The story line needed more substance. They had seen that story before with different songs. They wanted to be wowed. They liked our performance and called it entertaining. But if we wanted to win, we needed an added twist, more pizzazz and more va va voom. They commended our effort and could not wait to see us again next year. "Good job" was their closing remark.

"These are really good remarks," Mrs. Joyner said. All of these are changes that I need to make, not you guys. Do you know how awesome this is? With a better script we will win this thing next year. And New York here we come!" She hadn't stated the obvious, but everyone knew that Cole would no longer be a problem...he was a senior, which was probably the only reason he made it to begin with. Ending the show was bittersweet. I was going to miss it, but I also was looking forward to my freedom. It would be nice to be able to go home after school and have nothing to do. I also wanted to spend as much time with Brevin as I could. He would be leaving me soon, so I wanted to savor each and every day with him. We still hadn't discussed what would happen next, and hanging out with him made me happy so I might as well enjoy it while it lasted. "God," I prayed, "Please make it last."

It was April when Brevin decided where he would go to school. It was an exciting time for him...for me too. With each letter that came, the anticipation hung heavy in the air, and he promised that he would not open an envelope without me. I was a part of this too. I knew I wouldn't be a part of decision making process, so I felt honored that he included me at all. His first approval letter came from James Madison; he was excited to have gotten in. He said it was a definite contender. They had a lot of the features he was looking for: a five year Master's program, a nice rural town, a division I sports program and some possible majors that he could see himself choosing.

While Brevin looked at all of the practical things, I looked at distance. An hour and a half away, I thought to myself. This is a possible winner. The next letter came from George Mason. Accepted. He wasn't surprised. This was his "fallback" school. I didn't know that. This one was my number one. Twenty-five minutes away. Sounded like a winner to me, but neither him nor his parents seemed too impressed. Not even his mother, and she was excited about everything! JMU right now was his first choice and I was fine with that.

UVA came a week later with his first and only rejection.

"Not a rejection," his mother said, "Just a delay."

He was put on the waiting list. So he wasn't selected, but if enough people decided that they weren't going to go there, he could possibly get in. He wasn't buying it and didn't seem to care. His sights were set on Tech, and if he didn't get in, JMU was great too.

The Tech letter came two days letter. It was a Saturday. Brevin called me when I was in the middle of lunch with Dad. He'd come pick me up in an hour. It was his main event. I'd be lying if I said I didn't put on airs and act like I was happy for him because I did, and I wasn't.

Dad saw right through my act and called me on it. He wanted to know how I really felt about all of this and what the plan was after he left. I told him that I wasn't looking forward to it and that I was afraid that once he left, that would be the end of us. It was something that I couldn't bear to think about. Dad reminded me that the scenario that I did not want to think about was one the he had warned me about, and was likely to happen. He didn't help. He also asked me if I had expressed my concerns to Brevin.

When I told him no, he said almost belligerently, "Well don't you think you should?" Instead of wishing ill will on the boy, I needed to tell him how I felt. That way I would know what to expect.

I breathed hard. I knew Dad was right. I really wanted to be happy for Brevin, but my selfish nature got in the way. What if it was me, and I gained early entry into Julliard or something of the like and Brevin didn't want me to go. It wouldn't be fair and I certainly wouldn't listen to him, but it would make it more difficult for me than it already would be. I didn't want to do that to him. But in reality I was just being fake by pretending like I was actually happy. I knew what to do. My conscience was burning a hole in me. I needed to come clean.

The conversation was very one sided as we drove. He did all of it and I kind of chimed in with a giggle or a mandated smile. And every once in a while I would give an appropriate "uh- huh," but he could tell I was distracted. I knew that he knew it, but I didn't have enough energy to care that he knew or to try to hide it so that he didn't know. I was just trying to concentrate on what I was going to say. I didn't want to come across as being selfish although that was exactly how I was feeling, and I didn't want to come across as too controlling, even though I wanted to be in control of the whole situation. I also didn't want to come off as too emotional, although the very thought of him leaving me brought tears to my eyes. I had to find a way to get my point across without being everything that I knew I was.

It was difficult to put into words, and I wasn't sure I could pull it off. As we pulled up to the house, right after he turned off the car, he turned to me and I knew what was coming next. I could have written this next part as I played the scene as though it was in a movie inside of my head.

"Kennedy, what's wrong?"

Here was the opening—do I take the bait and gush about how much I loved him and I knew that this was coming. That I didn't want to be selfish but I couldn't help myself. That I knew how badly he wanted to go to Tech and I want him to be happy but what about us and what about me. He would be surrounded by all of those college girls ready and willing to offer him something that I was not prepared to nor willing to offer and how could he turn that down. Or maybe he would meet a "good" Christian girl who could give him everything that he needed spiritually and emotionally, things that I just wasn't mature enough to understand yet. And he would be having all of these new experiences without me and there would be long stretches in between us seeing each other; that time plus distance equal failure. It wouldn't work, couldn't work, if he went to Tech or maybe he had no intentions of it working and was just dealing with me until he left and then would leave me there broken-hearted. If he loved me like he claimed why couldn't he stay close and go somewhere like JMU or even better GMU. Why would he want to leave?

Or do I play it coy, keep my big mouth shut and lie, blink my mascaraed eyelashes and in a sweet, innocent, yet deceitful voice say, "Nothing."

I chose the latter. Now was not the time, nor the place.

But he called me out on that.

"That's BS," he said. "Stop playing around and tell me what's going on."

That line shocked me. My gentle Brevin, throughout the course of our relationship, had proved to have somewhat of a backbone, and I liked it.

Okay, Brevin you want it. You got it.

I let loose. Speaking a mile a minute didn't compare to the flood of words and the emotions that followed. By the time I was finished, the mascara on my eyelashes were now gone, as tears ran down my face.

Unable to get a word in edgewise, Brevin's facial expressions were right on cue. He had expressions of initial shock as if to say, "I didn't know you felt this way." To expressions of frustrations as if to say, "I wish I could speak." To the shaking of his head saying "that's not true." To the frown that covered his normally peaceful face as if to say, "I'm sorry you feel this way." To the expression of confusion like he was really "trying" to understand what I was saying, but that I'd lost him here. Then his face would go back to that tranquil expression which said, "We will work this out."

He handed me a tissue and grabbed my hand. I couldn't bear to look at him. I felt awful, relieved, and satisfied at the same time. Awful about asking him to choose, relieved about finally getting all of this out, and satisfied that I didn't hold back and had kept it 100 percent real. No matter how selfish or controlling or emotional I got, I really let him see me. Whether I was right or wrong, that was truly how I felt, and he could accept it or not, but at least I had put it out there.

After I fixed my face, Brevin took a breath to form his words. I had a feeling that he was about to keep as real as I did. Whether I liked it or not was irrelevant, I needed to hear the truth so that, in my father's words, I'd know what to expect. So I braced myself. I braced myself for the good, the bad and the ugly. What happened next was so unexpected for the both of us that we both jumped.

Tap, tap tap.

I turned around to see Brevin's mom and sister standing at the window.

He rolled it down.

"Come on! You guys can talk later! The suspense is killing me!"

"We will be right in."

With that, without a word, he rolled his window back up, got out of the car, came to my side of the car and opened the car door, took my hand, and led me into the house.

My eyes followed along every carefully typed word as Brevin read the last of his college letters aloud. His parents waited with bated breath. Even little Samantha seemed genuinely interested. I'd known this would be his choice if he got accepted. It was everyone's dream for him before they even knew that I existed.

I regretted my selfishness. I knew I couldn't take it back but I could make up for it by jumping on the bandwagon now. I saw the words as he read them with excitement. Accepted.

His parents began to cheer and slap hands and then he told them that was not all. He would be offered some sort of a scholarship if he majored in a political or social science since his grades where outstanding in history, government, and the like.

He made the rounds. Kissing me on the cheek, hugging Sam and his mom, high fiving and chest-bumping his dad, and then handing his parents the letter and embracing his dad. His dad lifted up his glasses to wipe his face. He was so proud...even before he said so, we could see and feel it. It was a great moment.

As Brevin led me to his room, his mom yelled for us to keep the door open.

"Yes, Mom," was his annoyed reply.

He knew that we had to keep the door open. There was the same rule in my house. She sensed his annoyance and replied that she didn't want him to think that now that he was a college man all that the rules had changed.

"Got it," he said in a tamer voice.

"That's still open, right?"

I smiled. It was. But my mind kept racing to what he was going to say next. I had prepared myself no matter what the outcome. It was the anticipation of it that was getting to me.

As I sat on Brevin's bed and he sat on a chair, he put his hands on

144

his face, moved them up to cover his eyes, and brought them back down. I became uneasy. He'd gone from being overjoyed to looking stressed all in a moment. Then he spoke.

"I'm going to Tech."

I started to say, "I know," but he cut me off before I had a chance to finish. He said it was his turn. I had to respect that. He cleared his throat and began again with the words that I thought would sting my heart and crush my hopes. But they didn't. I guess it was because I already knew.

"I'm going to Tech."

I sat in silence, waiting patiently for him to continue. He paused; I guess to see if I was really going to let him have the floor and keep it. I did. I pursed my lips together to prove it.

He gave me a slight smile to acknowledge and then continued.

"Kennedy, you never cease to keep me guessing. That's one of the things that I love about you and that frustrates me about you at the same time. Just when I think I've got you all figured out, you blow my mind again. I had no clue. Call me slow, call me stupid, or maybe you are just a really good actress, but I had no clue that all of that that you laid on me in the car had been going through your brain. I don't see how you kept all that inside without exploding. That's something that we have to change. If something is bothering you, just tell me and we can work it out right then and there. Don't let it fester until it's too much to handle at once. It will save you and me a lot of time, and save you a lot of stress." He paused and moved his hand in a circular fashion around his face again.

I started to realize that this is what he did when he was stressed or had to say something that required a lot of thought and delicacy.

"Time plus distance does not equal failure. Where did you get that from?"

I wasn't sure if it was a rhetorical question or if he really wanted a response. He continued.

"I don't even know how to begin to propose to answer all of the questions that you asked. And I don't have the answers to anything. I can't tell the future. I wish I could tell you that everything is going to be great and that this will not under any circumstances affect our relationship. I know that it will. But it is up to us to determine if it is going to impact it negatively or positively. I want to be with you. I have no plans of us breaking up once I go to college. I have no plans of us breaking up while I am there. Will it be hard? Perhaps. But we have to make a commitment to make it work. Nothing worth having in life is ever easy…except for accepting Christ. After that, the battle begins. You have to determine whether or not you are willing to fight for us. I know I am."

As soon as he finished, I leaped out of my chair and planted a big one right on his lips! I swung my arms around his neck and imagined hearts floating up toward the ceiling like they do on cartoons and video games when a couple is lip-locked. I wanted to make sure he knew my answer was yes.

CHAPTER 10

After doing much hardcore researching, soul searching, listening to advice, and praying, Brevin decided to major in political science and take the scholarship. It would pay for his books for the next four years, which I heard would be at least $500 per semester, as well as pay for his housing. His parents had saved for his schooling, but the scholarship came as a big relief. Since his parents would foot the bill for tuition, he had to get a job to pay for his everyday expenses. As a freshman, he could not bring his car, so he decided to apply for jobs on campus called work-study. He applied to work in the athletics department. Since he wasn't division I material, he decided that he would get as close to his dream as possible.

Listening to him go through the whole college process made me think about where I would go and even if I would go. Mom and I used to discuss this all the time, but it hadn't been mentioned since the *Event*. I didn't even know if there was money left in savings for either one of us to go. I knew Dad had to use it all once Mom lost her job due to her depression, but I wasn't sure if he had to use our college fund as well, and if so, I didn't know if he had started to build it back up.

I asked him one day after school and he gave me the answer that I had feared. He had used it. All of it. And there was none left. He hadn't built any of it up. He was working to take care of us and pay debts that had accumulated once we lost Mom's income. He told me not to worry about it now. He had two years to get it right. Plus there was financial aid and loans. I'd be alright.

I didn't like his answer.

"Mom said that she didn't want us to get loans," I said.

"Well Mom's not available right now to make that decision, is she?" He replied.

I didn't like that either. I sighed. Dad got up from the table and left me there to ponder on my own. I wanted to go to college. Education was always important to Mom. She was a college professor after all. She understood the value in it, yet recognized that not everyone was cut out for the same type of degree.

She had already recognized the fact that KJ would probably end up at a community college or a school of technology where the focus was on doing, not so much on academics. He was a kinesthetic learner, according to her. I, on the other hand, was an audio learner, which is why my musicality was so strong. I could hear something and report it right back to you word for word. Dad was a visual learner which was why his pre-law major didn't work out so well for him. He graduated with a paralegal degree, but quickly became bored with it and ventured out into the realty world which he loved. Mom was a combination of all of them. She loved learning. She had a sense of adventure and confidence in her that was not found in most people. She would try anything at least once. And she wasn't afraid to make a fool out of herself to do so.

As I basked in the nostalgic stroll down memory lane, my phone rang and brought me back to my reality. It was Brevin. He was sure to make me feel better.

"Want to go up to my aunt and uncle's for the Apple Blossom Festival next weekend? There will be a carnival, two parades, vendors, a circus, and not to mention their annual party."

"Sounds awesome," I replied. "I'm in."

"Do you think your dad will be okay with us spending the weekend together? I mean my aunt and uncle will be there, my cousins and of course my parents will be there as well. What do you think? I would love for everyone to meet you."

It really didn't matter what I thought. It was more about what Dad would think. His 15-year-old daughter spending the weekend with her seventeen-year-old boyfriend didn't look good on paper no matter how you wrote it. But I really wanted to go and his parents would be there, and Dad trusted me, right?

"I think he'll be fine with it. If he has any questions, I'll have him call your parents. Is that cool?"

"Yep," he responded. "They are expecting it."

~

"KJ has to go too."

"Umm, excuse me?" I replied, more shocked than anything else.

"You heard me. If you want to go, you must be accompanied by your brother, or else the answer is no."

"But Dad," I pleaded, "You know he is not going to go. Especially if it doesn't involve Mia. I can't just invite her to go."

"Not my problem," he responded as he walked out of the room.

"But why?" I asked. "Why does he have to go?"

"Because I said so."

Which is my favorite response - said no kid ever.

"Do you not trust me?"

"Kennedy," he said in a warning tone. "I've made my decision."

But I couldn't stop.

"What do you think we are going to do? Have sex? If we wanted to do that, we could have been done it by now, any time of the day."

He turned and gave me a death stare.

"His parents will be there," I pleaded.

But he wouldn't budge.

"KJ goes or no one in this house goes," he said as he slammed the door on his way out.

~

"Nope," KJ said as he threw his football up in the air, over and over again during the course of our conversation.

He was lying on his back in his room and I was standing over him. I pleaded with him, but he only repeated the sentiment.

Then he added, "What's in it for me?"

As I thought of a way to bribe him, he caught his ball and sat up. He turned to me and gave me a sinister look. I knew that the wheels in that big head of his were turning. I couldn't determine if it was for a good purpose or not, but I really wanted to go on this trip.

"I'll go," he said. "But I'll find a ride myself."

That was good enough for me. I didn't know what his plan was, but at this point I didn't care. I informed Dad, which seemed to confuse him, or maybe he didn't believe me. I couldn't tell which. In either case, he called KJ down to double-check, and KJ repeated what I had already told him. Of course he would need money. Brevin would pay for Kennedy, but who would pay for him? He didn't want to go down and be bored. He wanted to have a good time too.

On the evening that we were preparing to leave, Dad kept pacing. I didn't understand why until Brevin came in with an umbrella. He pulled Brevin aside, and I could only hear part of the conversation. In a nutshell, he was telling him to be careful. He had Dad's whole world in his car, and if something happened, he didn't know what he would do. Dad then told KJ and me that he almost didn't let us go, allowing fear to get the best of him with the rain and all. Even though he knew that we would only be an hour way, he was still nervous, but he couldn't put that on us. He didn't want us to live our lives in fear, so how could he. He kissed us, cautioned us to be good, put a wad of cash in KJ's hands that he directed him to share with me, and told us to call when we got there.

When the house was out of sight, KJ told Brevin to take him to Mia's.

"What?" Brevin and I said in unison.

"Me-Ah's," he sounded it out for us. "Remember when I said I would find my own ride? That's where Mia's dad lives. I'm catching a ride with them."

I wasn't sure if I should believe him or not.

"What about my half of the money?" I asked.

"I'll give it to you when I see you," he said. "Plus Brevin's got you till I get there...ain't that right B?"

"Yes," Brevin said stiffly, "I've always got her."

"See," KJ said as he put his hand on Brevin's shoulders. "That's why I like this guy. Always looking out for my sister."

As KJ disappeared into Mia's house, I could have sworn that somewhere in conversation with someone I'd heard that Mia's dad lived in PA. But I could have been wrong. And if he was coming, how come he didn't just give me my half? Things weren't adding up, but I was not going to let it ruin my good time. Brevin shared my suspicions, so we agreed that if KJ didn't show up by tomorrow, we would tell Dad. I didn't want to get in trouble because of his antics or lose Dad's trust. Plus, it was the right thing to do whether I wanted to do it or not.

As we drove down the highway Brevin told me about his Aunt Geneva and Uncle Patrick, the relatives we would be staying with.

Geneva was his mom's half-sister and Patrick was her husband. They had four daughters: Patrecia who was twenty-four, Penelope who was twenty-two, Paris who was nineteen, and Paola who was eighteen.

Before his grandfather Vincent Brevin Stewart the III met his Grandma Georgia, he was in the military. He was stationed at Santa Cruz Air Force Base in Rio de Janeiro, Brazil and that is where he met Ana—Geneva's mother. She was a Brazilian native who worked on the base as a nurse. He was stationed there for four years, and they hit it off almost instantly. He said that he was all set to propose to her, but she had something to tell him. She was pregnant. He got down on one knee and proposed right after that, ring and all. That's how she knew his love was real and that he wasn't just proposing because of the baby. But she had a rough pregnancy and died shortly after Geneva was born. They weren't married yet because she didn't want to be pregnant in a wedding dress.

After Ana died, he didn't want to live anymore, but it was the baby that kept him alive. The air force took pity on him and sent him back to America so that his mother could help him raise the child. He took a job on the Air Force base in Hampton, Virginia. He met Brevin's Grandma Georgia when Geneva was five. She treated Geneva as if she was her own. He knew she was the one because she wasn't just trying to please him like the others. She did the right things: disciplined her when needed and looked out for her best interest. They married a year later and had Cynthia (Cindy)—Brevin's mom, and then and a year and a half later his Uncle Gregory was born.

"You'll meet him at graduation," he said.

When we pulled up to the house there were two gorgeous, tanned women standing there. One was on a cell phone, and other was looking to see who was in the car that just pulled up. They both had very dark brown hair and could have passed for twins, except one of them was shorter than the other and had highlights in her hair. The taller one looked like a model.

"Brevin," she yelled as she ran to the car.

He stepped out of the car and gave her a huge hug. I got out of the car, and they walked around to meet me.

"Paris, this is Kennedy," he said with pride.

She hugged me as well which took me by surprise.

"It's nice to finally meet you."

151

I heard a scream as the equally beautiful, shorter version of Paris with highlights saw us and came running as well. She hugged both of us.

"Aunt Cindy told us you would be bringing someone very special this year. It's about time. Hi, I'm Paola. Brevin's favorite cousin."

"Hi," I said. "Kennedy."

"Ooh cute girl to match her cute name. Brevin, get the bags."

She put her arm around me and led me into the house leaving Brevin to follow behind.

The house was huge and very colorful. We walked right into the living room which was filled with laughter and excitement. Brevin's parents were there and two other young ladies, who I assumed were Paola and Paris' older sisters. They were tall and thin like the other two with dark hair, but their facial features were a little different. They introduced themselves, and I was correct. Next I met Geneva who was shorter than her daughters with lighter hair and lighter skin and then I met Patrick, their father. That's where they got their hair, height and their tanned color.

"Where are you from, Kennedy?" He asked with a Spanish accent.

"California," I answered.

He laughed.

"No, he said. "I meant, what's your ethnic background?"

"Oh," I said nervously and slightly embarrassed. "My mom is African American and my father is white."

"Beautiful," he said excitedly. "We have a lot of girls that look like you at home in Brazil. That's why I asked. Ain't that right babe?"

"Yep," said Geneva. "It's really the reason we are together today. I looked different than what he was used to seeing, and that's what attracted him to me."

Patrick double raised his eyebrows and said, "I did good, huh? Here I am working at a construction site, and this college girl walks by. Well I whistle and she picks up a rock and throws it at me. Hit me square in the middle of my forehead. I fell off of the awning I was working on and when I woke up she was standing over me, panicking. I took one look at her, and I was hooked. I promised not to press charges if she would go out on a date with me. I followed her back to America after she graduated, and the rest is history."

"I love that story," Brevin's mom said. "It never gets old, no matter how many times I hear it."

Brevin came back from putting away the luggage and sat down next to me.

"How cute are they?" said Geneva, looking at us.

"She is so good for him. They are good for each other." Brevin's mom said.

"Congratulations on your scholarship, Brevin. We were hoping you would join Paris and Paola at JMU, but we knew if you got into Tech, that would be it."

"You're going to be our rival," said Penelope. "Go UVA!"

They laughed.

"Are you guys still there?" Brevin inquired.

"This is my last year," Penelope said, "Patrecia works there in admissions."

The rest of the night was filled with laughter, games, and just getting to know everyone. I was put in the guest room. Paris and Paola slept in Paris' room. Penelope and Patrecia slept in Patrecia's room, and Brevin and Samantha slept in Paola's room while his parents slept in Penelope's room.

With all of the excitement I had forgotten to call Dad, and I knew he was going to be pissed. I was surprised when I opened my phone and didn't see a million missed calls from Dad.

I checked my text messages. There was one. It was from KJ.

KJ:
Missed my ride. Won't be making it down. Already talked to Dad.

I didn't believe a word of it and forwarded the message to Brevin. We had all just called it a wrap, so I knew he was still awake.

Brevin:
Wow. Do you believe him?

Kennedy:
Not at all. I'll talk to Dad in the morning since it's so late. Do you?

Brevin:
LOL. Do you really have to ask me that?

Kennedy:

I guess not. I had a great time getting to know your family tonight. They are awesome. I did have one question though: Where did Geneva and Patrick meet exactly? He said he followed her back to America, and Patrick isn't really a Brazilian name.

Brevin:

Geneva went to college in Brazil. She wanted to get to know her mother's family better and learn more about that part of her culture. That's where they met and Patrick's real name is Patricio. It's called assimilation. LOL. I guess it was easier for his workers to call him that. He owns his own construction company.

Kennedy:

I got that from the conversation, and Geneva is a nurse practitioner for OBGYN's. Make's sense.

Brevin:

Yep.

Kennedy:

Well Mr. Johnson, I guess I will see you in the morning.

Brevin:

Good night, Miss Morgan. <3

Kennedy:

<3

I woke up to the smell of eggs, bacon, sausage, and cinnamon. I checked the time. It was after nine. The perfect time to call Dad.

"Hey Dad," I responded to a sleepy hello. "Did I wake you?"

"Yeah, but it's okay. Mom had a bad night last night. You guys alright?"

"I'm great. It smells like I'm about to eat a spread. Did KJ call you?"

"Yup."

"So you know he's not here."

Silence.

"What do you mean he's not there? Like he and Brevin went to the store or something?" It was in that moment that I knew that my suspicions were true. That's why Dad hadn't called last night. Even in my anger, I had to admit that KJ was clever. Stupid, but clever.

"No, like he didn't come at all. He said he was riding up with Mia because her dad was here. Then he texted me saying he wasn't going to make it and that he contacted you."

"Is that so? Kennedy, have a good time sweetheart. Call me if you need anything."

And with that, he hung up. It was scary.

I felt bad for KJ, but it was his fault and I was glad that I wasn't home for that.

~

The old adage that time flies when you are having fun is true, especially in this case. We did everything. After a fantastic breakfast, we went shopping at the vendors, then the parade, next the carnival. We were all exhausted when we got back to the house. We went to an awesome church service at Aunt Geneva and uncle Patricio's church called Impact. Afterwards we went to an animal free circus which was both interesting and entertaining. We hugged everyone and said our goodbyes after dinner. It was a great weekend.

When I got home that evening, the house was quiet. Grandma and Grandpa were nowhere to be found. I went upstairs and knocked on Mom and Dad's door. Dad answered.

"Hey sweetheart," he said and gave me a huge hug. "Did you have a good time?"

"I had a great time," I responded. "How is Mom?"

"Better," he said. "Strangely enough, she settled once KJ was back in the house. It's like she knew that you guys were away."

"Huh, that's kind of how she was on the anniversary. She just knew."

"Do you know what that tells me? That she is still in there. It gives me hope," he said. I smiled.

"So, KJ is back?" I questioned.

"Yep. Not that he can ever leave the house again," he chuckled. "I went and got him." "Go dad." I said. I was proud of him.

"Well that's another story for another time. I'd better get back to your mom."

"Ok," I said. "Tell her that I love her, and that I'll see her

155

tomorrow."

"Sure thing," he said.

I went into my room, laid on my bed and turned on the TV. As soon as I settled into bed my phone went off.

Brees:
Talent Show in June!!! You wanna do a song together? First prize is $100!

Kennedy:
Where?

Brees:
Youth Development Center. It's a fundraiser.

I sat up on my bed and thought about it for a second. That last performance was tough. For the first time, I really started to think about *why* I needed Mom there so badly. What was it that made me feel so empty without her presence? Even just thinking about it released the butterflies in my stomach. I loved to perform, but I wasn't sure if or when I would be able to do it again - at least without her.

As I sat on the end of my bed, hunched over, looking for hope and strength. What I found were memories of the last time I really felt this uneasy, this afraid. I was ten years old. My fifth grade music teacher had been looking for a soloist to sing a few lines in a song for our elementary graduation. There were no try outs. She just went down the line and asked us to sing our ABC's. She stopped each person when she'd heard enough.

Of course you had a few knuckleheads, mainly boys, who sang silly or just flat out refused to sing. Most of the girls tried really hard, and since Mom had recently discovered my talent while standing next to me at church during praise and worship, I really wanted to do well.

"Kennedy," Mom said on the drive home that day. "Do you like to sing?"

My twin answered for me and made my parents well aware that he, in fact, had a hard time getting me to shut up. "When is she not singing? Are you finally staging an intervention to get her to stop?"

They all laughed except for me. I was still thinking about her question.

She then turned to Dad and told him what she'd heard at church. "I'd always known that that girl could keep a tune but she can *sang*!"

Dad agreed that he'd heard me sing around the house and thought that I had a nice voice. "Maybe she can..." Dad started.

"I love it," I blurted out losing control of my lips. "I love it."

That was all Mom needed to hear. She was super excited about this opportunity. She had already warned me that she wanted me to take classes during the summer and had signed me up for the kids' choir at church. She had this sparkle in her eye and explained to me that she always wanted to be a singer but she learned very early in life that she did not have it. But I had it and she wanted me to use my gift.

"Using it is going to take confidence. It is going to take strength, and I know that you have it in you. Let it come out."

I hung onto every word she said. She was my biggest cheerleader, my biggest fan. She was like that with all of us. I always wanted to make her proud, but there was something about singing that made me want to make myself proud as well.

It's not often that a ten year old forgets their ABC's. But the pressure of having to sing them in front of a company of peers who have not been very nice to you while wanting to do really well because you know it will please your mother and ultimately please yourself can make you forget your first name. Not to mention the distractions of the boys and the constant comparison of my voice to that of the girls – all that is enough to make you freeze.

"Kennedy."

It was my turn. I looked up into the face of my tall, thin, gray-haired teacher Mrs. Hansen. All I could focus on was how she had gotten so tall in the last few minutes and why she had gray hair on her chin.

"Kennedy!" she said sharply, which restored me to what I was supposed to do.

I cleared my throat and determined to do the best rendition of the ABC's that anyone had ever heard...expect that no one heard. I didn't say a peep. I couldn't remember the letters, so Mrs. Hansen moved on. Having your last name begin with the letter "M" has its privileges. It is the very center of the alphabet so when you are placed in alphabetical order you do not have to go first, but you also do not have to go last after everyone else. So when Mrs. Hansen expressed her disgust of some of the students and reminded us that participation was a grade and that she would be giving those of us who did not take it seriously another chance - I was elated. I had time to repeat my mother's words in my head: "I have confidence and strength inside of me, I have a gift and I need to use it, I can *sang*, and right before my name was called, I heard myself say "I love this."

Telling Mom that I had received the solo was not the best part, but it was a great one. We screamed together, interlocked arms and started jumping up and down! She embraced me and kissed me all over my face. It wasn't just that I got the part, but that I had earned it. I was strong and I was confident and that was hard for me but I pushed through.

"My little fighter," she said. This called for ice cream.

The best part was knowing that everything she'd said was right. I had all of that inside of me and no one else saw it, not even me - but she did. She believed in me more than I believed in myself, which empowered me.

Nevertheless, it was also the time that I discovered that you can be as strong and as confident as you want to accomplish your goals; however that does not mean everyone is going to be happy for you. In fact, some people will make it their mission to bring you down.

"You are not all that," Missy yelled at me while I was swinging on the swing set.

I looked up and saw her and her three flunkies looking at me and snickering.

"Yes, I'm talking to you zebra, oreo, mutt."

"She thinks she's cute" Flunky #1 said.

"And you can't even sing" Flunky #2 added.

"Missy should have gotten the solo."

"I heard…" Missy continued, "that your mother called the school and begged them to let you have the part."

"That's not true!!" I yelled back.

"Are you calling me a liar?" Missy questioned.

I sat there as usual, tears filling up in my eyes, looking for my savior who was off tossing a football somewhere.

Flunky #3 picked up a few pebbles and threw them at me and the others followed suit.

"Half-breed, ugly…"

The words hurt more than the pebbles did and I cried.

When the teacher blew the whistle, the girls ran. It took all that I could muster to walk back in the building. I was the last one in. When KJ got on the bus, my head was down. He knew what that meant. He sat with me instead of his friends and demanded to know what was wrong. I couldn't even bring myself to say it. So he put his arm around me and allowed the tears to flow.

He was the first to tell Mom that something was wrong with me when we walked through the door. She sat me down with KJ hovering close by and allowed me to cry. I told her that I didn't want to sing the stupid solo and that I wanted to be left alone, but she wouldn't leave me alone. She knew I didn't mean it, and she was right. I *really wanted* to sing that solo.

"Did you call the school and tell them to give me the solo?" I blurted out through snot and tears.

She reared back with a confused yet shocked look on her face.

"Of course not," she said. "You earned that solo. Where did you get that idea from? Kennedy what is wrong?"

Then it all came pouring out of my mind through my lips like water flowing from the mouth of a waterfall.

I didn't notice that KJ had sat down until he jumped up demanding to know the names of the girls who had scared his little sister.

Mom said nothing. She sat there. Her face went from perplexed to anguish to fury, but still she said not one word. Finally, after I waited to hear how she was going to call the school about the girls throwing rocks at me and saying mean things to me and that they would get in trouble and if I didn't want to sing the solo, I didn't have to and how she still loved me; instead she turned to me and asked me one simple question.

"Kennedy," she said "How badly do you want this?"

"Want what?" I asked naively.

"How badly do you want to sing?"

In my ten year old mind, I didn't understand what she was doing - but I understand it now. Singing made me feel like I could do anything. It gave me such peace and joy. Even if I was having difficulty trying to get a note right or remembering the words to a song, I enjoyed that difficulty. It was the only thing that made me feel free.

"I want it badly," I responded.

"Then you fight for it," she said. "You fight with your song."

When dad got home from work, KJ told him everything before he could even set down his briefcase. He came to my room and asked me if what KJ said was true. I confirmed that it was.

He hugged me and said that he was sorry that had happened to me and that the school would be notified and that those girls would be punished - he said everything that Mom did not say but was expected to. He hugged me again and left. Fifteen minutes later, I heard a sound that was familiar to me, yet foreign. Dad's voice was raised, then Mom's voice was raised, and then both of them were talking in loud, yet controlled voices at the same time. They were arguing, and then I heard my name.

"I will not stand for it!" Dad said. "I am putting my foot down! Renee, you have got to be kidding me? And you still want her to do the solo? Is this about Kennedy or is this about you? How could you want her to continue with these kids torturing her? I will not have it!"

"What's that supposed to mean?" Mom said. "Of course it's about her! Look Mark, I am just as angry and upset as you are. These girls will not get away with this, but we can't keep running in and saving her. The world is a cruel place, as we both know. KJ is strong - a little too strong at times, but he can take it. I worry about Kennedy, and us protecting her all the time. It's not going to do her any good. Look, she loves to sing. You heard her say it herself. She told me tonight that she wanted to do the solo badly. How can we help her grow if we just let her give up every time someone calls her a name or tells her she can't sing? From the moment that we laid eyes on one another we have had to fight for our love. It was not easy. We both have suffered losses along the way, but it was worth it. Why wouldn't we allow her to fight for hers?"

Then there was silence.

The fear that I had was nothing like I'd felt before standing out on the stage. The lights were bright, and the auditorium was dark so I couldn't really see anyone's face. I had all of the textbook symptoms of being nervous: sweaty palms, shaking hands, and a dry throat.

When it was time for me to walk out to the microphone I felt like I was going to faint. As I concentrated on each step to get there, I scanned the crowd. I told them to sit on the right side facing the stage, and there they were. First KJ, then Rylie, Dad and Mom. Her smile gave me peace. I have confidence; I have strength; I can *sang*, and I love this. It took me to my rightful place on the stage where I displayed my gift for the first time and wowed the crowd.

~

That was the fear that I felt in my first concert after the Incident. Mom's smile would not be there to give me peace. Her words of encouragement wouldn't be written all over her face. Dad and KJ would not be there to give me support. Dad had to stay with Mom, and KJ always had football. My little Rylie had gone home to be with God. Not only was there this fear, but a fresh kind of pain that I'd never known. With each passing concert the pain would become familiar, but this night was new. My cheerleader was gone. She had been preparing me for this moment, preparing me to stand on my own. As much as I resented her for leaving us, I applauded her for allowing me to fight all by myself. I think that's part of being a great mother, making sure that your children are prepared when the time comes. Even though it was hard, I made it, and I know that it was because of Mom.

~

Kennedy:
Cool. But I think there is a song that I would like to do for my Mom, by myself.

Brees:
Alrighty then. TTYL

Kennedy:
:) Good night.

CHAPTER 11

Guys asking girls to prom was a big deal at this school. They would write it on their cars, have their friends sing the girl a song, and then appear with flowers. Some boys even did it over the morning announcements. It was like there was a competition to see who could ask the most creatively.

Prom was in a month and Brevin hadn't even mentioned it. I wasn't sure if he didn't feel like he needed to ask or if he just didn't want to go. Julia and Brees wanted to go prom dress shopping with me, but I refused to go until I was asked.

"He's going to ask you," Brees said confidently. "You want to get your dress before all of the good ones are gone."

"We need to go out of town to get your dress," Julia chimed in. "That way no one else will have it. My sister is going to Maryland to get hers this weekend. We should go with her!"

"I'm in," said Brees.

"Well, I'm not," I said sternly. I stood my ground. I wasn't going if I wasn't asked. "Come on," pleaded Julia. "None of us get to go. We are living vicariously through you." "Nope, not until I get asked."

As I walked into history class Mr. Piven walked up to me and said, "Miss Morgan, I believe these belong to you." He handed me three white roses with a card that had the letter "P" on it. Second Block was the same. Mrs. Boyd gave me three more and the card said "R." I knew where this was going but played along with the suspense of it. When Mrs. Joyner gave me the third card with the "O" and a set of three roses, Brees asked me again about us going shopping for the dress.

"Let me talk to Dad," I relented. He celebrated. We both knew I wanted to go, and I looked forward to receiving the final letter.

When I got to Spanish there were no flowers. I didn't say anything to Brevin and he said nothing to me about any of this. I thought that maybe at the end of class I would receive them, but when the bell rang and I got nothing, I was a bit confused. Brevin had to leave early so I was taking the bus home. Maybe he'd put them there. When I got on the bus, I kept expecting the last bit of roses with the M. I got nothing. As I walked to the house in disappointment, I thought that maybe the roses and letters weren't from Brevin, but were instead a joke.

I walked into the house and put the roses in a container with water before going upstairs to talk to Mom and tell her about my day. Once I finished, I threw my backpack in my room and came back downstairs for a snack. There on the table was the last card. It had an "M" and a question mark on it. When I looked up, there was Brevin with Brees, Julia, Dad, Grandpa and Grandma. He had the last three roses in his hands. I screamed and then put my hand over my mouth.

"Of course!" I yelled before giving him a big hug. Dad already knew about the dress shopping. Evidently Brees and Julia had already gotten to him.

"This weekend is a go," he said as he shook Brevin's hand in approval.

Before I went, I asked Brevin if there was any particular color he wanted to wear. He would match me with his tie and vest, and it was his senior prom after all. Brevin doesn't have a favorite color as odd it would seem. We have had this conversation several times over. He just doesn't. So him choosing a color was just as difficult as I supposed it would be.

"Just don't pick anything girly." He knew my favorite color was pink. "No pink, purple, or yellow. And I don't want to look like a pumpkin, so no orange. Besides that, you have carte blanche."

That only left me with a few choices. I didn't want to wear blue again, and I hated how the color green looked on me. Black and brown were too basic and boring, and for some reason, all of the white dresses looked like wedding dresses. All I had left were gold or silver. Being so limited color-wise was a blessing and a curse. I didn't have a lot to try on. Brees told me not to be so basic. I should do something colorful and then Brevin could choose whatever color he wanted that would match. It was ingenious, and that is when it started to become fun!

I finally settled on a dress that was a one-shouldered floor-length flowing gown with a 3D flower on the shoulder and the belt. The background was egg-shell with a myriad of all the colors he'd told me not to get. There were peaches, oranges, pinks, and lilacs beautifully patterned throughout the gown, but there was also black. I had enough color for the two of us.

The weeks leading up to prom I spent most of my time preparing my song for the talent show. Efforts to get Dad to let Mom go had yielded nothing. I hadn't stopped praying for her, and I hadn't stopped believing. I was dedicating this song to her, singing it for her. I felt that if I could penetrate the depth of her being, if she could truly hear me and listen to the words of my song, then she would have the strength to come back.

I explained all this to Dad and he wondered why, if I felt it was so powerful, I couldn't just sing the song to her at home while she was in bed where she felt safe. The song wasn't loud enough here, I explained. It wasn't bold enough. It just wasn't enough. I needed the stage, the lights, and the energy from the crowd to sing with all my being so she could really hear me. He still wasn't sold but I refused to give up. I needed her there.

It was a busy time for Brevin as well. Prom, Senior Trip, Awards Ceremony, paperwork for Tech, graduation practice, graduation, and graduation party were all on the agenda. He wasn't excited about the graduation party.

"I told mom I didn't want one but she says they all have one, it's a family tradition and a big deal. I think it's a waste of money, really. Let's just go to dinner to celebrate and call it a night." I laughed. He sounded so cute when he vented. "Well, at least you know the P's and aunt Geneva and Uncle Patrick will be there. And you'll get to meet Grandpa." I couldn't wait to meet Grandpa. He sounded like a handful. "My Uncle Edward's wife Brenda is a bit stuck up, though. Don't mind her. No one else does."

"I'll keep that in mind," I said. I went on to tell him how I'd been pestering Dad about bringing Mom to the talent show and how Dad had gotten to the point that he was ignoring me. Just a little bit longer and I knew he would break.

Then Brevin told me something I already knew but didn't want to hear. Q and his girl would be going with us to prom.

"I don't know why you don't like him. That's my friend. Been since —"

"Yes, yes, I know. Since elementary school. It's not that I don't like him. He's just weird and acts creepy. Why can't we go with one of your sane friends like Evan or anybody not named Q?"

Brevin laughed.

"You just have to get to know him. After all, he'll be looking after you while I'm away."

"Oh really?" I said. "I didn't know I needed to be looked after." I was expecting a reply but I got none. It kind of bothered me a little but not enough for me to say something. I could take care of myself, and what I couldn't handle, God would.

Then my mind started working a mile a minute. Was he implying that Q was going to be spying on me when Brevin left for college? Did he not trust me... again? I started to say something but convinced myself that I was taking it too far. It was just a comment, right?

"So tell me about your dress?" Nice save.

I used the same accessories that I had for homecoming. Same gold shoes, earrings, and a bracelet. It only made sense - that coupled with the fact that my dress took up my whole spending budget. I didn't even have money for food after shopping. But once I put it on again, I realized it was all worth it. My hair was different this time too. It was straightened and put in a high ponytail with a ringlet twist for my hair that cascaded out of the back. I also had a sweet bump in the front which set the hairstyle off! Makeup done, accessories on, and I looked amazing, if I might say so myself.

Getting ready by myself wasn't as fun as getting ready with Julia. Not having her and Brees there would surely make the night different. But I'd have Brevin. It was his night, not mine, so I had to concentrate on making it fun for him, even if it meant enduring Q.

Dad, KJ, and Grandpa were all speechless as I walked down the steps. KJ being there had become commonplace since he was grounded for the whole Apple Blossom stunt, without an ending in sight. He had to go to work with Dad right after school, as well as on the weekends. I don't know when he had last seen his cellphone, and if he wasn't at work or school, he was in his room. I saw a difference in his and Dad's relationship, though. They got along better, enjoyed each other's company more, and there was this newly found respect between the two of them. I even thought, although I could have been dreaming, that I heard KJ say "Yes sir" a time or two. Neither one of them ever spoke in detail about what happened that day when Dad went to Mia's to bring KJ home. Although I was curious, I was more excited about the results and chose not to ask any questions.

When Brevin arrived he was more expressive about how I looked than ever. His jaw literally dropped and I knew that I had made the right choice.

"You're breathtaking," he said. Before I could enjoy the moment, KJ snickered, followed by Grandma slapping him in the back of the head.

"She sure is," she said in between snapping pictures. "Go ahead, put on her corsage." We went through all of the pictures, and then repeated the corsage pinning again at Brevin's house, and then again at Emma's, Q's date's house. This time we went to a fancy restaurant that I had never heard of called Sweetwater and then on to the prom.

Prom was held at a convention center in a ritzy part of town that I hadn't even known existed. There were two DJ's. One spun the records and the other was the hype man. A smoke machine, flashing lights, teachers surrounding the perimeter, and a bunch of rowdy, sweaty, yet nicely dressed teenagers tore up the dance floor. It was a great time. I got a lot of complements from people I barely knew who must have recognized me from the show or knew me as KJ's twin or Brevin's girlfriend.

There was one "You look nice" that I didn't expect to hear. It was after about an hour and a half of dancing. My feet hurt, I was tired, and Brevin asked me if I wanted something to drink. He waded through the crowd to get it and I sat at one of the empty tables on the perimeter. When I heard the complement my head was down looking at my cell. As I looked up, I was shocked and unpleasantly surprised.

"Well," Drew said. "Let me see all of you." I looked at him suspiciously and slowly arose. "Very Nice. What about me?" He did a turn in his fresh black tux with a hot pink vest and tie.

"You're alright," I lied. Truth be told, he looked good - so good that my heart started beating more quickly and my mind immediately searched for Brevin. Drew laughed.

"What are you..." and before I finished my sentence, I remembered that Devlyn was a junior. He was here with her, so I redirected.

"Where's your date?" I asked haughtily.

"Where's yours?" He returned the sentiment. I rolled my eyes. "Well I just wanted to come over and tell you how beautiful you looked." With that he took my hand and gave it a kiss. I blushed. And then like that, he was gone.

It wasn't but five seconds later a sweaty Emma and an even sweatier Q sat down with me. Q just kept staring at me. I knew he'd seen. I'd have to tell Brevin before he got a chance to. I would have told him anyway but the unpredictability of Q was a chance that I could not take.

"So," I said. "I'm going to find Brevin."

"I think you should," Q said in a monotone, eerie, serial killer voice. It gave me the chills. I walked around the perimeter in time to catch Brevin before he tried to make his way through the crowd again. I motioned for him to come outside of the ballroom. He followed. We found some comfy couches and he watched me as I drained my drink and then proceeded to fan myself with an invisible fan.

"It's hot in there," I said.

"It's hot out here," Brevin said slyly. I smiled coyly.

"You know," I said. "Now would be a great time for us to sneak out and leave Q and Emma. We could go to the creek and run through it with our clothes on."

"Sounds fun. But I have to return the tux." I smirked.

"I need to tell you something, but I need to know if you want to know it now or later. I don't want to mess up your good time."

"Is it about Drew?" he asked. I looked perplexed. "Q already texted me." I shook my head.

"I was gonna…"

"I know," he said. "And I'm not worried about it, not anymore." I smiled but couldn't help thinking that Q had already started his spying duties and wondering whether or not Brevin had instructed him to do so. Just then Emma walked out.

"Brevin," she said. "They are looking for you."

"Who is they?" I asked out loud, but Brevin left as though he already knew. As I followed him into the ballroom, I heard them announce his name. Brevin had won Prom King! He was already up there, with the queen, a girl I had seen before but didn't really know.

The DJs made them dance which Brevin seemed uncomfortable with and she seemed a little too comfortable with. I wasn't jealous, though. We locked eyes. As she was staring at him, he was staring at me. I gave him a light smile and a head nod to let him know I was okay. He smiled back and then relaxed as he went through the motions for the rest of the song.

I got home at around 12:30 a.m. My feet ached, and I was tired, but satisfied. Prom was a success.

Life at school was a little different now without seeing Brevin. He was there but he didn't have any classes. Seniors didn't have to take finals. Instead they were practicing for graduation, going on trips, and doing senior stuff. His busyness began preparing me for the next school year without him. I missed him, but I had made a lot of friends this year that kept me busy, especially Julia and Brees.

My only issue was Q. He kept showing up at random places. When he started sitting closer to me at lunch, I started getting suspicious. When he showed up at our table I drew the line.

"What do you want?" I asked sharply. He didn't miss a beat. He didn't look up from his food.

"Eating."

"I can see that," I said irritably. "Why here?"

"Why not here?"

I'd had it. I laid into him about how he'd better leave me alone and I didn't appreciate his antics and how Brevin and I would have a very serious conversation about this later and that I wanted him to leave.

Q cocked his eyes to the side while still eating his food and asked me why I so angry. Couldn't a nice young man sit at whatever table he wanted to in his school's cafeteria and enjoy his lunch? I slammed my tray on the table to the dismay of everyone surrounding me.

"No!" I said.

By then my friends were starting to arrive and my frustration level had risen to anger. "Okay, okay," Q said in his own monotone way. "Calm down." He took his time getting everything together and looked at me as he arose. He took his food and stared me down as he moved to the next table. I stared right back at him until he sat down and faced the other direction. As Brees sat down, he inquired about Q, why he was there, and what he was doing. I didn't answer. I think Brees got the hint because he just started eating. I whipped out my

168

phone.

Kennedy:
GET YOUR FRIEND

Brevin:
What did he do now?

Kennedy:
He is stalking me!

Brevin:
I'll take care of it.

A couple of minutes later as I attempted to enjoy the school's semi-decent chicken nuggets I felt Q's eyes on me. Brevin must of texted him because he gave the "aye aye" captain sign. In my mind I was giving him the finger, but instead I pretended like he didn't exist. He'd better leave me alone or else I would get KJ on him, and no one wanted that.

Brevin must have kept his word or Q became a better spy. I started to notice him less and less and finally it was like he didn't exist until I saw him at Brevin's graduation party. I'd decided that avoidance was the best policy.

Brevin seemed to have invited everyone to his party. The whole church, his whole family, the whole school, and my whole family. I know they didn't all show up, but it seemed like it. There was a DJ and lots of food. KJ was grounded, Dad worked, and Grandma and Grandpa had to stay with Mom, so I ended up going alone.

Brevin received tons of gifts. It felt more like a bar mitzvah than a graduation party.

"Those envelopes," Paola motioned to the letters on the gift table, "are filled with tons of cash." Paola told me that when the Stewarts did it, they did it big! Brevin's grandfather asked him where all of the honeys were and Brevin told him that there was only one honey, me, and that I was taken.

"Well, let's take a gander at her," Brevin's grandpa said. He lifted my arm, twirled me around, called me a keeper, and winked. He said he liked ethnic women and laughed to himself...he knew that his wife was white but the first one wasn't; and laughed to himself.

After awhile, all of the faces and names of Brevin's family started to run together. When Brenda introduced herself as the wife of his mother's only brother Edward, I remembered our phone conversation about how I shouldn't pay any attention to her. She seemed nice enough to me. She was tall, thin, with brown hair. There was nothing special about her, she was very plain.

While Brenda was talking I couldn't help but wonder if Brevin hadn't introduced her on purpose. She shook my hand and seemed to size me up which isn't unusual when you are meeting someone for the first time. I did the same thing to her. And after the initial meet and greet conversation, she was on her way, as was I. It wasn't until the party was over and I was helping with clean up that I understood what Brevin meant.

I was in the kitchen when I heard my name in the hallway. Naturally I started to listen intently and moved closer so I could hear. Peeking around the corner, I saw her and her husband Edward in an intense conversation. She was doing most of the talking. Brenda said she felt that Brevin was holding himself back by being with the likes of me. I was a half-breed. Why would he do that to himself or to his family? He was too smart to get caught in that trap.

I froze. I couldn't believe what I was hearing. Edward tried to console her by saying that we were young and that Brevin was going to college. Our relationship wouldn't last, he said. There was nothing to be concerned about. Brenda said that even though Geneva (Brevin's aunt) was a half breed, at least she got with someone who was a part of her own race. What was Brevin thinking? Better yet, what were his parents thinking?

I had never experienced such blatant racism in all of my life. Never. What if I got pregnant, she asked, going on to say that this was probably my intent. A girl from my meager beginnings had lucked into a family like theirs - a home that was well above the poverty line. Brevin seemed awful serious about *that* girl and frankly, it disgusted her. She felt like it was her duty to warn Brevin's parents about letting him date a girl like me. If it hadn't been for her mother-in-law, she didn't know what shape this family would be in being that her father-in-law chose Geneva's mother first. It was up to her - up to them - to break the cycle.

My head started to hurt, and the kitchen seemed to get smaller and smaller. Tears started to streak down my face. I couldn't tell if I was crying out of anger or sadness or both. I had felt all kinds of hurt but never anything like this. I didn't know what to do.

Brevin's father scared me when he came in through the backdoor to put the trash in the dumpster. By then, my tears had fully manifested and there was no hiding them. He asked me if I was ok and when I tried to speak, I only cried harder, embarrassing us both. He didn't know what to do. He told me to stay right there and rushed out to get Brevin.

I guess his dad made it seem like an emergency because when I wiped my eyes Brevin was there with his mom, dad, grandfather, Geneva, Edward, and Brenda - all looking in. Brenda had a look of shock on her face. She hadn't known I was in there and Edward's face was red. Brevin asked them all to leave and I could hear the voices in the hallway surmising what they thought was wrong with me.

"Maybe it just hit her that he is leaving," they said. "Maybe she hurt herself."

I could hear Brevin's father saying that he'd walked in the kitchen and found me that way and that Brevin would get to the bottom of it. I could hear his mom saying that I would be okay, and I heard the P's asking what happened.

It was not a good moment for me. I told Brevin that I needed to get out of there and he happily obliged. I pointed toward the backdoor. There was no way I was walking past all of them to get to the front. He took me around back and led me to his car. He called his mom to tell her that he was taking me home, he didn't know what was wrong yet, he would make sure that I was okay, he would call if he needed help, he appreciated their prayers, and that he loved her too and would see her soon.

He got off of the phone and placed his hand on my knee. As soon as his lips formed the word "wrong" with the obvious question, I unloaded. I told him everything I'd heard and everything I'd felt. I was looking straight ahead when I heard his fist hit the steering wheel. I turned and saw that his face was beet red. His lips were pursed so hard that they were white. He stared straight ahead at the road and made a U-turn. I immediately knew what he was doing. I asked him where he was going but he gave me no response. I begged him not to do it and that I didn't want to cause any problems in his family. He said that I wasn't the problem; she was. Even though I cried and complained he wouldn't stop. He sped up to the clubhouse and told me to wait in the car. I tried to get out but he told me to wait there in a voice I had never heard before. He walked in and slammed the door.

He wasn't in there long. When he came out his mother came running after him with a look of shock on her face. His Uncle Edward wasn't far behind. He told Brevin not to ever talk to his wife like that again. Brevin's mother said, "Shut up Edward...go back inside!" She turned to Brevin and asked him a question that I could not hear. He started saying something and was throwing up his hands. I saw the look on his mom's face go from shock to horror. She covered her mouth and peeped over Brevin's shoulder and looked at me.

When he was done, he got in the car and slammed the door. His mom came to the window and tapped on it so that I would roll it down. I did. She apologized profusely. I saw tears in her eyes which made them come to mine as well. She assured me that nothing was my fault and I was welcome in their family and that Brenda was not a reflection of any of their beliefs. She said they loved me like their own and asked that I didn't take Brenda's words to heart. She was so horrified and so sorry that she didn't know what to say or even what to do.

Then she looked at Brevin. He was still angry. She begged him to calm down before he left. She didn't want him driving angry. The intensity in his eyes and the tight white knuckled grip he had on the steering wheel prompted me to ask him to calm down too. I didn't want to ride anywhere with him like that. It was a scary scene.

Brevin's mom gradually made her way around to his side of the car. She bent down and looked at him patiently. He didn't blink. He just stared ahead and held onto the steering wheel. Eventually his dad came out and she got up gradually like she was afraid to move because he would leave. He didn't. She went to talk to his dad. Five minutes later his dad motioned for me to get out of the car. I did and he sat down in the passenger's seat. Brevin's mom put her arm around me and apologized again before giving me a hug. She continued repeating how much they loved me, but I was too busy paying attention to Brevin to hear what she was saying. I'd never seen him like this before. His dad was speaking to him. Slowly but surely

Brevin let go of the wheel and then gave his dad a hug. I saw him mouth that he was sorry and I saw his dad mouth that he understood, and it was ok.

Brevin's dad motioned for me to come back and I took his place. His parents walked hand in hand into the clubhouse, and peace seemed to be restored.

When Dad found out, he shook his head. He had hoped I would never have to go through anything like that. He was sorry I did. He and mom had been through a lot because of their race differences, but it was worth it. And he would go through it all again to have the life he does now.

After Dad mentioned it, I got to thinking. I had heard stories here and there of Dad's family not accepting Mom, but when we asked where his side of the family was he would just say things like, "it's better this way," or, "it's not something that I like to talk about." A part of me believed that Dad had thought we were too young or that he was protecting us from something. It wasn't until now that I considered that maybe he had been protecting himself. I didn't want to bring up anything that would hurt him, but I wanted to know. Especially after today.

"Dad," I began in my sweet little girl voice. "What do you mean when you said that you and Mom had been through a lot because of your race? What happened?"

Dad turned and looked at me. He cocked his head to one side and just stared. Then he moved uncomfortably in his seat and shifted his lips form side to side. He was thinking.

Dad took two deep breaths and at that point I wasn't sure of what he was going to say, or if he would say anything at all. I waited.

"It was a different time then than it is now. I grew up in a place where there was no diversity. None. Believe it or not the first time that I had ever seen, in person, a person of another race was in college. I knew they existed. I'd read about them and seen them on TV but that was it. Race was never even a topic in my household. It was just me, my mother and my father. I was their miracle baby. When they were told that they couldn't have children, they were devastated. Adoption was too expensive but giving up was out of the question. They were Christians, so they did what Christians did: they prayed. They had almost given up two years later when mom found out that she was pregnant with me. She said it was a joy that neither one of them could explain. God had answered their prayers. It was always impressed on me to find a good wife and have children to carry on the family name. I'd had girlfriends but none of them lasted too long. I never knew why until I met Renee. She was everything that I was looking for. I had never seen anyone so beautiful, so confident, and so passionate about life. I was inspired by her. It didn't take me long to ask her out on a date, and it didn't take her long to say yes. At college it wasn't so bad. I mean we would get the occasional stares and comments but nothing that we could not handle together. We were a team. But the real test was when we decided that it was time for us to meet the parents. I would meet hers first."

"Hold on," I told Dad as I got up and brought back two glasses of sweet tea. I watched him as he took a drink, waiting for it to be swallowed so I could continue to listen to his story. I'd never heard this before. It was getting good.

"When she told her parents she had met someone and that he was white, they weren't too happy about it."

"Wait," I interrupted. "Grandma and Grandpa?"

"Yes." He cleared his throat and took another drink. "Grandpa and Grandma. I remember her telling me that her parents wanted to meet me but they had warned her that she was not making the right decision. They didn't mind me being her friend but dating me was going to make her life difficult and they preferred her to date a black guy."

I couldn't believe it. Not Grandma and Grandpa! They loved Dad. I just couldn't see it. I didn't understand.

"Go on," I said impatiently.

"Their intentions were good," he said. "They said that life was difficult enough for a young black woman, so why would she want to make it more difficult on herself? They didn't want her to be ridiculed because of me and they didn't think that I could relate to her. But she told them that she loved me, and that they had raised her to be strong. She didn't care what other people thought - only what they thought. After that, they welcomed me with open arms.

"When it was my turn to have her meet my parents, I wasn't nervous at all. I mean they were great, supportive, and Christians. I didn't even tell them that she was black. When I told them that I was bringing a girl home, they were excited. It wasn't until after the visit that I knew something was wrong. When they met your mother, they were as loving and kind as they had always been. They were attentive and gave no indication that something was wrong. But when we got back to school, there was a voice message awaiting me. It was my dad. He told me that if I continued to date that girl they were going to cut me off financially. He said I had embarrassed them and shamed our family name. Mom chimed in to say that they hadn't raised me like that but that I still had time to redeem myself. I needed to break up with her. That would be for the best. I can still hear that message plain as day.

"Well, naturally, I was shocked, furious, and confused. So I called them and they pretty much repeated their message. There was no question in my mind about what I was going to do. She was the only woman I had ever loved. So I got a job to support myself. I never breathed a word of it your mother. I made every excuse I could think of to protect her from it. And my parents treated me as they always had as long as I didn't mention Renee, until I told them that I intended to marry her. They accused me of destroying my family and told me that they refused to see me if I married her. My dad forbade me to give someone like that his family name, saying I would tarnish it."

"But why?" I asked intently. "Why did they feel that way?"

"When I asked them why, the only answer they could give me was that our people don't belong with those people and that's just the way it is. That's just the way it had always been. I didn't know how I was going to break the news to Renee that my parents did not approve, but she already knew. It had been three years and your mother was not stupid. I think I fell even deeper in love with her during this time because she would not give up. That woman would encourage me to continue to reach out to my parents. She believed that our love would truly win them over. She wasn't giving up on them as much as she wasn't giving up on us, even when they gave me the ultimatum. And as much as I loved my mom, and as much I loved my dad - I couldn't imagine my life without Renee.

"The way I saw it was that I was not choosing her over them; they chose their racist beliefs over me. It messed me up with God for a little while. These were Christian people! They had raised me to love everyone and to pray for everyone that we knew. But if this is was the type of people who served God, then I wanted no parts of it. But it didn't take me long to see that it wasn't every Christian who felt that way. They were just lost and I needed to pray for them.

"After we were married, my mom would send me letters every once in a while to see how I was doing and I would write her back. But when I wrote her to tell her that we were pregnant with you and KJ, the correspondence stopped. She was ashamed of me and of what I had done. She wanted me to feel shame as well. But I wasn't ashamed. I was proud. You know, I could have fought for them, my parents. I could have called and reasoned with them and done everything in my power to make things right. But instead, I decided to fight for you. And yes, I was hurt that they rejected me and my family. It took me a long time to forgive them, but I did. And every once in a while I think about them. I wonder what they are doing, or even if they are still alive, but I have my family now. If it hadn't been for God, your grandmother and grandfather treating me like I was their very own, and you guys, I would have been in much worse shape. But I have truly forgiven them and I hope that you can forgive those that hurt you today too.

I jumped out of my seat and gave my dad a hug. He was so strong.

"Brevin is a good kid. The ignorance of a family member doesn't change that." It was the first time that he'd said something nice about Brevin. Normally he was indifferent. But things were changing. I could feel it.

~

KJ stood in the doorway of my room. I was finishing up some last minute homework assignments to wrap up the school year when he cleared his throat to let me know that he was there. I motioned for him to come in. I was almost finished and didn't want to lose my momentum.

"Dad told me what happened. You alright?"

"Yup," I said, keeping my eyes on the paper.

"That sucks," he continued. "I've been there."

The statement stopped me in mid-writing.

"You've been where?" I asked curiously.

"There," he repeated as though using the same word with more force would get me to understand. It didn't. "You know, with parents and family members who didn't want me dating their daughters."

He had my full attention now.

176

"For real?" I asked dumbfounded. I had never heard this before.

"Yes, really. Not all parents are as bubbly and accepting as Brevin's parents. It's better you know that now." He stopped and I waited. Wasn't he going to tell me what happened? But he said nothing. I breathed.

"Mia?" I asked.

"No. They are great. But you know me. I've dated quite a few girls and I'm an equal opportunity employer. I love women of all races," he said with a laugh. "There were a few girls in Cali. They couldn't date me because their parents didn't approve. One was Hispanic and the other one was black. I'll never forget how that made me feel. I was pissed. I couldn't understand how the color of my skin made me unworthy to date them. Like I was beneath them. I got over the Hispanic girl but the black one messed me up for a minute. I couldn't understand how the people that I considered my people could reject me because I had too much Dad in me. It was the first time that I resented being who I was until I realized something that I heard Mom tell you. She said that you were who God made you to be and that you should embrace it. So I embraced it and recognized that there was nothing wrong with me. It was them. That was their hang up. Not mine. They were trying to put that on me, but I decided that I was not going to accept it. We are the epitome of what happens when races come together in love. And I've decided that *that* is a beautiful thing."

That KJ. He never ceases to amaze me. He was right.

~

Brevin's graduation was the Monday after his party. I was nervous for several reasons. Edward and Brenda. Apparently Brevin had uninvited them in his rant. No one knew if they would show up. I didn't let him know how I felt. It was his day. I was excited for him and his accomplishments, and I felt privileged to be his girl.

Graduation was long, hot, and boring. The most exciting part was at the end, when they handed out the diplomas. If Edward and Brenda were there, I didn't see them, which was fine by me. I just wanted Brevin to be happy and to get out of the hot sun. After Brevin took what seemed to be a million pictures and said his goodbyes, it was time to go. He was excited about opening up his gazillion cards to see how he'd made out.

"That's $1,498," I said as he handed me another fifty. It was his last card. He had cleaned up.

"How about some Sweet Frog Frozen Yogurt?" he said. "It's on me."

School was finally out for the summer. I decided to get a job so I could start saving for college myself. Between practicing for the talent show, hanging out with Brevin and my friends, going to church, and job hunting, I kept pretty busy.

I found favor at a local school of the performing arts for kids. The lady who owned and ran the place was looking for camp counselors. Every week there was a new camp and the pay was $8 an hour. I was hired to help with the acting and singing camps. There were also various art camps based on age and style, and dance classes based on age and style as well. The classes I would be assisting with were based on age only.

There was a lot of concern about me taking this job. First it was Dad, then it was Brevin, next it was Grandma, and even KJ managed to get in on the action. Was I sure this was a good choice for me to work with kids? How would I do working with nine-year-olds? Maybe I should consider a different route. My response to all of them was that I would be fine. This was a great opportunity for me and I couldn't run every time something reminded me of the *Event*. I couldn't live my life in fear; my dad had taught me that. I would choose to live; my brother had taught me that. And no matter what I faced or how badly it might suck, God was on my side; my boyfriend had taught me that. I would be okay. Change was in the air.

~

The conversation with Dad resonated with me for several days. I couldn't get it out of my head how strong Mom had been. In his story she was exactly how I had always seen her: determined and persistent - a warrior. Every battle she faced, we faced, she used her shield of faith and fought the battle on her knees first and then put her prayers into action. But this, the fight of her life, had proven to be too much for her. She didn't need our sympathy or my resentment. She needed our help. She needed us to take out shields and to fight for her. She was wounded. She didn't need our tears, she needed us to rescue her like she had rescued us so many times throughout our lives with her words of wisdom, her patience, and her love. She needed us to be strong for her. We had her back.

The song I would sing for Mom was called "Just Cry" by Mandisa. The first time I heard the song, it reminded me of her. Each verse spoke to a different place of where she was, where she is now, and where she could be. I believed that it could speak to her soul and break whatever chain held her captive. All she needed was hope.

The night of the performance I was very nervous. Through my badgering, I'd gotten Dad to at least consider bringing Mom. I explained to him why it was so important to me for her to be there just one last time. This time I reminded him of how it all started, me singing, and that Mom was the reason that I had found my passion. This song was for her, and I believed in every word.

"Please Dad," I said one last time. "Just give me a chance to share with her how I truly feel in the best way that I know how." He half-smiled and said he would think about it. I was just glad it wasn't a flat out no. Grandma, Grandpa, and KJ even got on the bandwagon. They said they would help. He said he would decide the evening of the talent show based on the kind of day she'd had. I had the youth group, Brevin's and my families, my friends, and everybody else who knew about our situation praying. I put my faith out there again… the size of a mustard seed.

I had to. I wouldn't know if Mom was there until afterwards, unless I saw my family somewhere in the crowd, which I doubted. How would I know where they were sitting? My cell phone would be turned off. I didn't need any distractions. Ten minutes before I was set to go on, I felt the urge to pray. I went outside in the back parking lot so I could be alone and feel God's peace and his presence. He was there. I sighed and released the tension I felt and then I prayed this prayer:

Father God, I thank you for this opportunity to pray to you. Today, I really don't know what to say that I haven't already. I miss my mom and I want her back. I know that you can reach her and that you can heal her. I ask that you tell her how much we love her and how much we need her. Let her know that she doesn't have to do this on her own and that she is stronger than she thinks. She has to be because she instilled it in me. I ask that your will be done in her life and in our lives. Thank you for my family. Give my dad the strength and the wisdom that he needs to make decisions…especially the one about bringing Mom tonight. I thank you God that if he does not, it's because it was your will, not mine, and

179

your will is better. Help me to accept that and to be grateful with whatever decision you make. In Jesus' Holy Name I pray. Amen.

I thought about what Mom told me about my gift.

"Using it is going to take confidence. It is going to take strength, and I know that you have it in you. Let it come out."

I determined in that moment that I didn't care what happened after this. It wasn't about winning or losing. I no longer cared if my mom was there to hear it. I would sing it for her whether she physically heard it or not. It was my gift, and I was going to use it.

Why you gotta act so strong
Go ahead and take off your brave face
Why you telling me nothing's wrong
It's obvious you're not in a good place

Who's telling you to keep it all inside
And never let those feelings get past
The corner of your eye

You don't need to run
You don't to need to speak
Baby, take some time
Let those prayers roll down your cheek

It may be tomorrow
You'll be past the sorrow
But tonight, it's alright
Just cry

I know you know your Sunday songs
A dozen verses by memory, yeah, they're good
But life is hard, and days get long
You gotta know God can handle your honesty

So feel the things you're feeling
Name your fears and doubts
Don't stuff your shame and sadness
Loneliness and anger, let it out, let it out

You don't need to run
You don't to need to speak
Mommy, take some time
Let those prayers roll down your cheek

It may be tomorrow
You'll be past the sorrow
But tonight, it's alright
Just cry, just cry

It doesn't mean you don't trust Him
It doesn't mean you don't believe
It doesn't mean you don't know
He's redeeming everything

You don't need to run
You don't to need to speak
Mommy, take some time
Let those prayers roll down your cheek

It may be tomorrow
You'll be past the sorrow
But tonight, it's alright
But tonight, it's alright
Just cry, ooh, just cry

Why you gotta act so strong
Go ahead and take off your brave face...

I sang the whole song with my eyes closed. It was like I was in a different world, just her and me, and I was singing it alone. All of that changed when I heard the roar of the crowd. I opened my eyes to bright lights and a standing ovation. I was in awe. I said thank you as the coordinator ushered me off the stage. Brees would be performing soon so he was still backstage. He grabbed and hugged me tightly. He told me that I'd killed it and had given him chills. He said everyone had stopped what they were doing to listen to me and that half of the acts didn't want to go on after me. He was sure I had won. But I didn't care about any of that. I had sung for Mom.

I won second place which was $75. I couldn't see my family in the crowd so I decided to wait outside for them to come out. First I saw KJ and Mia, then Grandpa and Grandma, and eventually Dad. He was pushing a wheelchair. It was Mom! I immediately made a b-line to the wheelchair ramp and waited for him to push her down. He gave me a great big hug and told me Mom loved my performance.

"How could you tell?" I asked.

"She said your name."

~

Mom's recovery slowly progressed over the summer. I would come to her room every day after work looking for another sign of continued healing. One day, after I told her a story about a little girl who was so nervous when asked to sing that she would pee on herself, she reached out and touched my face. She started at my forehead and felt my eyes, my nose, my lips, and my hair. This one I wouldn't keep for myself. I was so excited that I couldn't wait to tell Dad. I ran down the stairs and told Dad that he had to see this. He came up and I sat down and began to talk to her again. She took her hand and ran it down my face again. Dad stepped back. He almost looked scared. I told him to take my place. I actually had to get up and lead him to her. He just sat there at first, staring. I encouraged him to speak. He turned and looked at me.

"Go on Dad. Speak to her." He cleared his throat.

"Hey Renee. It's me, Mark. I miss you babe. Every day I pray that you will come back to us." He paused. "Do you remember when we were dating and I used to take you on long walks and we would pretend that there was music playing and we would dance under the moonlight? Or when we went out on our first date and I was so nervous that every time I tried to talk my voice cracked? Boy you got a kick out of that. Or when…" Dad stopped and watched her hand move. She put it on his face and felt all of his features. When he began to cry she wiped his tears. Then she did the same thing she had done the night of the concert. She said his name.

"She said his name?" Brevin asked as I told him the story.

"Yes. And not only that, she said my name, and when we told KJ and he came in to speak to her she said his name, and when Grandma and Grandpa came in and followed suit, she said 'Mom' and 'Dad' as well. She hadn't spoken since the night of the talent show. Dad had even begun to question whether or not he really heard her that night. Now he doesn't question anything. He knows that he did."

"Wow," Brevin said. "What else?"

"Nothing else. If you go in and talk to her, she rubs your face and says your name."

That was just the beginning. After a few days, Mom started sitting up on her own and then there was the smiling every time one of us walked into the room. None of was prepared for the time she took the spoon out of Grandma's hand and started feeding herself.

Once she starting feeding herself that's was it. No one had to feed her again. It was KJ who discovered she was going to the bathroom by herself. He walked in to talk to her and heard the toilet flush. I can imagine the look on his face when he saw her walk out. He ran to get Grandma and when they got back she was back in bed. So everyone was on bathroom watch throughout the day. And about an hour and a half after feeding herself dinner, she got up and went to the bathroom again. We all witnessed it. It was true.

The underlying fear was that she would regress just as quickly as she was progressing. Some days she wouldn't do anything but revert to her old self. Lying in bed, lost in the battleground of emotions. But when she did make strides, she made big ones. That's just like Mom and that is where KJ gets it from. If they were going to go for it, they were going for it big. I was starting to see a little bit of that in me, too.

Even though she was making strides, expectations became an increasingly dangerous game to play. We decided as a group that we would continue to have faith and expect a full recovery, but we wouldn't put a timeline on it. We couldn't, and we would keep each other accountable to that promise.

Some days were easier than others to hold up our end of the bargain, but Grandpa made us aware that fighting alone is what had made us weary, but fighting together in prayer would pack a punch. We were already relying on God, but we decided to rely more on one another, too, so we could encourage one another to praise our way through Mom's illness rather than suffer our way through the journey as we had done for almost two years.

We started rejoicing in the smiles and the touches and chose to be content with those until God gave us something bigger.

One day we were all sitting at the table talking and laughing when we heard footsteps.

"What's that?" I asked while shoveling a spoon full of mashed potatoes into my mouth. Dad got up but didn't move. We all looked in the direction of the stairs and there she was, walking down the steps. We all watched intently to see what her next move would be. She came in and sat down. Dad jumped up and got her a plate of food. We all watched her as she ate. Grandma whistled through pursed lips for us to act normal, so KJ started talking about this coming football year and we all chimed in and continued to have a group discussion. She smiled when things were funny and continued to look around. She didn't speak, but she was present. She was there.

After Grandma cleared the plates, Mom got up and went into the family room and looked at all of the pictures. We watched her intently and were amazed by what she did next. She started naming people in the pictures and smiled while tracing their faces with her fingers. She'd missed us too.

The thing that scared everyone was what was going to happen when she got to Rylie's picture. I tried to go get it but Dad held me back. I guess he wanted to see if this was for real, if she could actually handle it. I just wanted to make sure that all progress was not lost. Grandma gasped when Mom picked up the picture. Grandma grabbed my hand and began to pray. Mom's smile slowly faded; she cupped her face in her hands and let the tears flows. She must have looked at the picture for at least fifteen minutes while the rest of us looked on in silence. Finally she looked up with a half-smile and said, for the first time in almost two years, "Rylie."

CHAPTER 12

Life seems very busy during a time of year when you are supposed to relax. You don't have school, you go on summer vacations, hang out with your friends, take day trips to the beach, hike, or do anything really to pass the time that you are supposed to be trying to savor. Kids go to camps, get summer jobs, and prepare to leave for college. Statistics show that summer is the time of year when people are depressed the least. But summer was the time of year when my mother's depression began and, subsequently, when it ended.

Mom started talking more and more after that fateful room in the dining room. Pretty soon she started laughing and then eventually began speaking in complete sentences. She showers, dresses herself, sits alone on the porch, and takes long walks with Dad. She started taking pleasure in the little things and talked about us slowing down so that we could enjoy every moment. Time was short, she said, and she wanted us all to stop and smell the roses.

Mom began answering the door and found herself playing catch up trying to get to know Brevin and Mia. She also found herself trying to get to know us… again. Two years is a long time, and we had all grown and changed - mostly for the better. Tragedy will do that to you sometimes.

Mom was determined to make up for lost time though. She started by teaching KJ and me to drive. It was a fun experience filled with laughter and mistakes. It took her a while, but she eventually started going back to church.

"I was mad at God for a long time for taking my baby," she said. "But now I am just grateful for the time I had with her and for the time I have with you guys now."

She loved the church I attended. The next thing I knew, we were all going as a family. The support she received there was unreal. She still had bad days, of course, when she wouldn't come out of the room and spent all day crying, but those days were getter few and far between. We went out to dinner to celebrate our 16th birthdays. She told us to invite everyone that was important to us because if they were important to us, they were important to her. I invited Brevin, his parents, and his sister Samantha (which Mom was fine with to my surprise), as well as Brees and Julia. KJ invited Mia, Isaiah, and Trey. And of course Dad, Grandma, and Grandpa came. We had a fantastic time.

Then there was she and Dad. It was as though they'd started dating again, going out to dinner and dancing. Gazing into each other's eyes. Fooling around in a corner, and just genuinely being in love. And while their love was rekindling, mine was changing. As much I loved to spend time with Mom and see her gradually regain her joy, I selfishly wanted time to slow down before I lost a part of mine. Brevin would move into Tech on August 18th, and time after our birthday seemed to move really fast. I don't know if it was because I anticipated him leaving, or if I was bracing myself for the anniversary of the *Event*, but both dates were creeping up and my anxiety worsened.

When August 8th arrived Mom didn't come out of her room for a long time. But there was no screaming, no wanting to die, just an occasional sniffle. She was hurting, we all were, but it seemed to be a little better the second go round. That evening, Mom came out and invited us all to meet her in the garden. We watched her dig a hole and when it was deep enough, she said, "The protea is a rare flower that means valiant and courage. It is rare in North America. Ninety-two percent of them are found in a region in Africa. Today we will plant this rare flower here. Rylie was a rare flower whose name meant 'valiant' and 'courage.' She was one courageous little girl. KJ, remember the time she rode every single ride in the park when we went to Six Flags with you? Rides that the rest of us would have never thought of? And Mark, do you remember how she used to jump off of everything? She really had a sense of adventure. And Kennedy, she wanted to be just like you. Remember the time she sang at church and she was terrified! Her voice shook so badly

186

because she was so nervous but she fought through her tears to accomplish her goal. She was courageous and she was valiant. A couple of weeks ago I sent for a protea to plant in remembrance of our little girl."

With that she took out a pink plant that was so unique in its form that you couldn't help but to stare at it. It looked like it had several layers, one to represent each person in our family. She put it in the hole and we all helped her cover it up with dirt. We all sighed deep sigh of relief. It was a sign that she could really move on, that we all could, together.

~

"I found out what happened to KJ that weekend we went to Apple Blossom," I told Brevin as he loaded his luggage in the car.

"Oh yeah?" he said. "What was that?"

"Well, I overheard Dad telling this story to Mom. He said he was so angry with KJ that he asked Grandpa to go with him because he was afraid that he might hurt him. On his way over to Mia's he called Hargrave Military School to set up an appointment. In his mind KJ was done. When he knocked on the door, Mia answered and lied and she didn't know where he was, but Grandpa spotted him climbing out of a window and chased him with his cane."

Brevin laughed.

"Oh wait," I said. "It gets better. So Grandpa falls, and KJ saw it and came running back to make sure he was ok. Grandpa swings his cane and knocks KJ off of his feet and rolls on top of him trapping him beneath him, and then Dad comes and they wrangle him into the car. About halfway to the academy KJ started questioning about where they were going. No one said anything. When they pulled up an officer met them and pulled him out of the car... and Dad drove off."

"Wow."

"Well the next day, KJ called Dad crying."

"Crying?"

"Yes, boohooing. Promising that he would behave if Dad came to pick him up. Dad told him that he was grounded until next school year. That he had to work with Dad until football started and then Dad would decide if he could play based on his behavior. That KJ had run out of chances. And if he slipped once, he was going back, and this time to stay."

"So that's why he's been so… good lately."

"It's a part of it. But there's something different about him. He's become…nicer."

Brevin smiled, but it wasn't his normal smile. This one was forced.

"I'm gonna miss you Ken."

"I'm going to miss you too," I said, holding back tears. "I'll see you in three months, though," I said, trying to lighten the mood.

"Yep. Three months," he said while looking at the ground. Finally he looked up and grabbed me and we hugged and gave each other a nice kiss. We had been saying goodbye to each other for weeks now, in our own way. It was just that today was for real.

His parents came out of the door. They were ready to go.

"Do you need a ride home?" his mom asked. "Your house is on the way."

"No," I said as I pulled my keys out of my pocket. "I drive now, my mom taught me."

I waited for them to drive out of sight before I left. As I got into the car, I thought about all that had transpired since moving to Virginia: meeting and falling in love with Brevin, making the show choir, becoming best friends with Brees and Julia, building better relationships with KJ and Dad, going to my first homecoming and prom, joining an awesome youth group, watching Mom recover, and becoming stronger and developing a real relationship with God. As I turned the car key, with put my foot to the gas pedal, I realized that I was pulling off into a brand new adventure.

ABOUT THE AUTHOR

Clarissa Lee-Kennerly knew at an early age that God called her to write. Compelled to write more personal non-fiction novels like "My Husband's Not Saved" which was published in 2008, and having worked with teenagers all of her career, she was inspired to write a contemporary novel that teens today can relate to and still experience God's love. She resides in Virginia with her husband and two children.

If you have enjoyed reading this novel, consider telling others about it, and leaving a constructive review to help others discover her works. You may also follow Clarissa Lee-Kennerly through Facebook, Twitter @AuthorClarissaK, or online at: www.kharispublishing.com, for details about release of her upcoming titles.

A sneak preview…

KENNEDY CHRONICLES Part II
LOSING TOUCH

I'm trapped. I already know what this is. I know where I am and I know what happens next and I am afraid. Rylie's favorite song is playing on the radio. Mom keeps looking back and smiling while singing along. "I'm not Rylie!" I try to open the car door. It's locked. I try to unbuckle my seatbelt but to no avail. "Let me out of here!" I scream but she doesn't hear me. She just keeps singing "*Starships were meant to fly, hands up and touch the sky!*" She keeps looking back as though she expects me to sing it too. The rain increases and I know the time is near. "Mom!" I scream. "Turn around! Pull over! Turn around! Pull over!" And then I saw it…the lights from the other car coming full speed ahead on my side of the car. I closed my eyes and brace myself for impact. And as I hear the glass break and the look of terror in my mom's eyes as she turns around one last time. I scream. I scream.

"Kennedy! Kennedy! Wake up! First day of school! First day of school! First day of…" "Okay," I murmured as I opened my weary eyes. This was their mantra from *Finding Nemo*. I'm sure it was theirs and every other parent of a little kid who loved that movie. Problem is, I was a sixteen year old junior. They have done it every year since we were five and went to see it. It was our first movie at the movie theater. It was right after Rylie was born. Mom thought it would be nice to do something just for us since everyone was making a lot of fuss over the new baby. One of mom's really good friends watched the baby while the four of us went out. She was right. It was a memory that I will never forget, and even if I tried, they wouldn't let us off from the first day of school shenanigans. Only one more year I told myself as I focused on their smiling faces. And then it dawned on me. Mom was there. I smiled. Maybe this tradition wasn't so bad.

As quickly as they came, they were gone. And then I heard the mantra again. KJ's room. My twin had grown a lot over the summer in statue and in maturity. He started the summer working with dad in real estate, and ended it working in construction. $15 dollars an hour. He bragged every time he received his paycheck. It was a win-win for him. The physical labor made him stronger which anyone who knew him before could physically see. The football coaches loved it, not to mention the fact that he probably grew 3 inches which they seemed to love as well. Their starting quarterback had changed the face of the game for them. They were determined to win at least regionals this year, and with the new and improved KJ, they believed they could. Him working construction certainly didn't hurt him with the ladies. His butterscotch skin was now caramel from him working in the sun which really made his green eyes pop and he grew his hair to a small curly fro. I guess he needed to add a finishing touch by getting his ears pierced... both of them. I actually liked it on him but I was the only one in the house that did. That didn't matter to him, he didn't care that grandma said she was disappointed and grandpa turned up his nose. Dad shook his head and mom just stared. I think that sometimes it is hard for her to find her voice since she had lost it for so long-especially when it came to us. But the girls, they liked it... maybe a little too much; probably what caused him and Mia to break up. He said he didn't want to talk about it. But whatever it was... his grieving period didn't last long. It seemed like every other day he was on a date with a different girl. It was hard to keep up, so I didn't try. But his attitude, the dissension with Dad was pretty much gone. When Dad talked, he listened. No back talk. And it seemed that dad had to talk to him about his behavior less and less. Things were good.

As for me...I hadn't changed. I didn't look any different, I didn't feel any different, everything was pretty much the same. I was getting used to not seeing Breven. We talked every day. Sometimes two or three times and we texted each other all of the time. He loved Tech. He loved his classes, he loved his roommates, he loved college life. He said that the only thing he hated was not seeing me. I missed him too. Now that summer was over, I was hoping that school would help me get my mind off of how much I really did. I would see him in October. I could do this. The only thing that was new was the dream. It had been two years. Where did this come from? I hadn't told anyone about it, not even Breven, although I'd had it several times. A part of me thought that if I said it out loud, it may become a reality and that is why I was afraid to say it. Another part of me was just trying to forget it, and pretend like it didn't exist. But every night, before I went to bed, a chill ran through my body right before I fell asleep. "Please God, don't let it come tonight" seemed to be my last request before the heaviness fell on my eyes. Sometimes it worked, sometimes it didn't, but every morning I woke up, I was grateful to survive.

"I want to get a car." KJ said as he shoved a forkful of Grandma's eggs in his mouth. "That's great." Mom said. Everything we said to her was great. She was still trying to fit in, still trying to find her place, her voice. Although she never said it, I think she felt guilty for leaving us. This was her way of making it up. It was cool at first, but even though she was back, she wasn't quite the same. I was thankful, don't get me wrong. This mom was better than no mom, but sometimes I missed my real Mom. The one I knew before the *Event*. "Give her time" Breven said. "She'll come back." "I want a car too!" I blurted out. I was tired of driving Grandpa's "boat". It was a 1994 Chevrolet Caprice Station Wagon. It was white with wood paneling on the side. KJ and I shared it during the summer but neither one of us wanted to drive it to school. We were juniors and as far as we were concerned, riding the bus wasn't an option. Mom agreed to take us which wasn't a surprise, and since KJ was no longer dating Mia and Breven was gone, what choice did we have but to have our own cars? Dad couldn't afford to get us both cars and I was saving my money for college. There was no way that I was getting a car. "I have $2,500. I saved it from working this summer. I figured if you and mom matched it, I could get something decent." Dad stopped eating. He was almost as shocked as I was. "$2,500?" Dad asked. "Yup." KJ continued. "What do you think?" Dad must have really been stunned because he didn't resume eating which was one of his favorite pastimes. "Let me think about it. We'll talk this evening. Let your mother take you today. She's looking forward to it."

The ride to school was nothing short of what I imagined it. Mom said less than words. She kept smiling nervously as though she had never done this before. KJ was more receptive than I was. She had always been the parent that he could turn to; he had always taken her side. It was this incredible arrangement that in his mind she was always right unless she was against him, well then of course, it was a different story. But since her recovery he had been her biggest advocate when I thought I would have been. He had more patience, more understanding, and he just tried harder. I couldn't understand where that was in me. Where was my resolve? Where was my 'sticktoitness'? All I could manage to give her was a few words of encouragement from time to time and a falsified jaded smile. I was the one who fought for her, on my knees and otherwise. I assumed that her coming back would be the answers to all of our problems... and maybe it was, to everyone else. I just couldn't figure out what was wrong with me.

As we got out of the car, Mom gave her own fake and tired smile and forced out the same sentiments as every other parent on the first day of school. And as we did the routine wave I couldn't help feeling relieved as the car pulled away...

ACKNOWLEDGMENTS

Thank you for reading Losing Rylie. Hope you are able to leave a comment or review to help others find encouragement through this story. And thank you!

God the Father, the Son, & the Holy Spirit: Thank you for your love, your grace, your mercy, and for choosing me to bring this message through. I am forever grateful.

My Husband Mark: Thank you for tough love, your patience, an unrelenting listening ear (I know it was hard...lol but you were awesome), your advice, and for being my biggest supporter and best friend. I love you!

My Mother Julia: Your strength inspires me, your love humbles me, your faith reminds me of who I am in Christ and who you have raised me to be! Thank you for always being there for me in prayer, in word, and in deed. You are phenomenal.

My Grandmother Gertrude: You saw this coming and believed in me way before other people believed in me. I miss your words of wisdom, your encouragement, the way you said my name, your laugh, and your soft cheeks! I hope I have made you proud!

To my daughter Kylee: Thank you for being my cheerleader and my critic. Thank you for telling me the truth, even when I didn't want to hear it, and encouraging me when I didn't think I could do it. I love you so much! Thank you for making me better!

To my son Sai: Thank you for sharing mom with this process and for always being so positive. You inspire me more than you'll ever know.

To Madison: Thank you for all of your help and support! It is because of you that I felt like I could do this! You have been my biggest fan from day one! Your ability to make people feel good about themselves is such a blessing and I hope you know what a blessing you are. I love you so much! You are an amazing young lady! I look forward to seeing how God is going to use you!! It's going to be awesome!

My students: Jackie, Dejuan, Desmin, Matt, Dominique, Xavier, Dennis and Daniela - Your support in the beginning stages was amazing. Thanks for encouraging me!

Kenglish: Addison, Chris, Jack, Jacob and Sean - You guys are awesome! I don't think I have laughed so much in all of my life! Thanks for your support and just for always brightening up my day!

To my girls: Dariona, Savannah, Maegan, Taylor L., Kayla, Taylor W., Alexa, Kaelyn, Zaira, Tanisha, Dyani, Quira, Quinn, Quimera, Shayla, Chyna, Yenelle, Denise, Tiana, Alana, Avery, Reagan, A'lahya, Selena, Katrina, Olivia, Sophia, Alexandria, Juliet, Lauren, Jamira, Janessa, Annabelle, Anaiah, Marisol, Zaniiah, Abbi, Ava, Cameryn, Leah, and Daelyn. This is for you!

And to all of my family and friends, thank you guys so much for your love and support!! I am truly blessed!!

ABOUT
KHARIS PUBLISHING

KHARIS PUBLISHING is an independent, traditional publishing house with a core mission to publish impactful books, and channel proceeds into establishing mini-libraries or resource centers for orphanages in developing countries, so these kids will learn to read, dream, and grow. Every time you purchase a book from Kharis Publishing or partner as an author, you are helping give these kids an amazing opportunity to read, dream, and grow. Kharis Publishing is an imprint of Kharis Media LLC. Learn more at https://www.kharispublishing.com.

www.ingramcontent.com/pod-product-compliance
Lightning Source LLC
Chambersburg PA
CBHW060643260626
47161CB00008B/2972